Wedding Days at Halesmere House

Suzanne Snow writes contemporary an̶d̶ ̶w̶o̶m̶e̶n̶'s̶ ̶f̶i̶c̶t̶i̶o̶n̶ with a vibrant sense of setting and ̶e̶m̶o̶t̶i̶o̶n̶ ̶connecting the lives of her characters. A ̶f̶o̶r̶m̶e̶r̶ ̶l̶i̶b̶r̶a̶r̶i̶a̶n̶ ̶w̶ho lives with her family in Lancashire, her ̶s̶t̶o̶r̶i̶e̶s̶ ̶a̶r̶e̶ ̶inspired by a love of landscape, romance and rura̶l̶ ̶l̶ife.

Her first novel in the Thorndale series, *The Cottage of New Beginnings*, was a contender for the 2021 RNA Joan Hessayon Award. Suzanne is a member of the Romantic Novelists Association and the Society of Authors.

Also by Suzanne Snow

Welcome to Thorndale

The Cottage of New Beginnings
The Garden of Little Rose
A Summer of Second Chances
A Country Village Christmas

Love in the Lakes

Snowfall Over Halesmere House
Wedding Days at Halesmere House

SUZANNE SNOW

Wedding Days at Halesmere House

CANELO

First published in the United Kingdom in 2023 by

Canelo
Unit 9, 5th Floor
Cargo Works, 1-2 Hatfields
London SE1 9PG
United Kingdom

A CIP catalogue record for this book is available from the British Library.

Print ISBN 978 1 80032 876 1
Ebook ISBN 978 1 80032 875 4

Cover design by Cherie Chapman

Look for more great books at www.canelo.co

Printed and bound in Great Britain by Clays Ltd, Elcograf S.p.A.

1

To Deb, with lots of love, for everything

Chapter 1

Lizzie Martin's hand crashed onto her desk, nearly dislodging the phone tucked between her neck and her ear. 'Halesmere? You're not serious?'

As an events planner, nothing thrilled Lizzie more than securing happy endings for her clients, but this particular event might just mean the unhappiest ending for herself.

'Of course I'm serious,' her best friend Gemma responded, the tone of her voice suggesting she wasn't unsympathetic to Lizzie's shock. 'I'm all out of jokes right now. I think it could be perfect and we're getting pretty desperate.'

'We're not, not really.' Lizzie bit her lip at the white lie, time was tight to secure a venue for Gemma's wedding in a couple of months. Lizzie knew she would probably be having sleepless nights were it for anyone other than the practical and resourceful woman she'd known since their first faltering days in primary school.

Gemma had met her fiancé Simon in the final months of secondary school when he'd moved nearby for college. They'd been together ever since; through university and into careers as solicitors until Simon retrained as a paramedic. After getting engaged in Barcelona, their first wedding had gone the way of everyone else's in lockdown and Plan B was in serious doubt thanks to a fire in the hotel booked for their second date.

I

'I'm on it right now, Gem. I've actually found a place I think we should check out. I was about to message you. It's a barn, just converted this year for events; intimate, great views, straightforward to find.'

'Come on, Lizzie. Even you, with all your superpower planning skills and the most optimistic person I know, have got to admit we're in trouble. We couldn't possibly have foreseen the fire but quite frankly Simon and I will be counting ourselves lucky if we're not eating fish and chips out of trays in the street, given this will be our third attempt to get married. Halesmere was Mum's idea, she's already been in touch with the new owners and the date's free. You know how she feels about the place.'

Lizzie did, and she understood. They'd all loved Halesmere once, a gorgeously remote Georgian house in the Lake District, even though life had inevitably moved on and she had absolutely no desire to return. But Gemma hadn't finished her pitch yet, her voice becoming more excited with every word.

'We'd have the house and garden to ourselves, we could throw a marquee up on the lawn and find a hotel nearby to recommend for everyone else to stay over. It's not as though we're having a huge wedding, there's only sixty people in total. What's another twenty miles west from the original venue between friends? Or guests?'

'Er, Scafell Pike. And a single-track road with hedges wide enough to walk on. It's probably more like a thirty-mile detour than twenty.'

'Mere details,' Gemma replied airily, and Lizzie was picturing her waving a dismissive hand. 'We can include directions with the invites seeing as we've only sent save the dates so far and tell everyone to ignore their satnav. It could just work, Lizzie.'

'It could, I suppose.' Lizzie was still trying to get her pulse under control at the mention of Halesmere coming at her without warning. They both knew she was fighting a losing battle given the time between now and the wedding, but Lizzie attempted a mild protest anyway. 'Have you even seen the state of the place? It was a mess the last time I looked. And what about the actual service? Are they licensed for weddings?'

'No, but I don't think that'll be a problem. Mum knows the new rector and she's happy to meet and see what she can do if we get a move on. The church is only a mile away. Wait until you see the house now, Lizzie. It's stunning. And I haven't even told you the best bit yet.'

'There's a best bit?' Lizzie abandoned her laptop to scribble nervously on a notepad. Writing lists always helped her focus. What now?

'Ha ha.' Gemma was triumphant. 'Mum said they've just had a last-minute cancellation for a weekend retreat, so why don't we go while we have the chance? Bride and bridesmaids for some much-needed R&R and time out together.'

'What, you, me, and Bea, staying in the house? When?' Lizzie was hoping for some time to prepare for that little adventure, but she always knew when her friend couldn't be dissuaded. Fingers hovering over the laptop again, she typed 'Hales' into a browser, bringing up all sorts of nonsense she had no interest in.

'Friday.'

'This Friday? Seriously?' Lizzie's hand skidded across the keyboard. 'But it's already Wednesday and we're supposed to be spending Saturday seeing venues.'

'Well, technically, this *is* seeing a venue. I know it's last minute, but you've got the weekend off and Simon's on shift. We could do with a bit of fun, don't you think, after all the misery of the last couple of years? Once I know you're up for it then I'll message Bea.'

Gemma was more cajoling now and Lizzie knew she had no choice. As chief bridesmaid and unpaid wedding planner she had to roll with the bride's wishes. There was that patter of her pulse again, thoughts of the past running through her mind like autumn leaves blowing from branches to fall at her feet.

'Lizzie?' Gemma put aside her enthusiasm and her voice became gentler. 'I know you haven't been back in forever, and how you felt about him and what happened. We didn't intend on never going back, it just kind of turned out that way. I wouldn't ask if I thought you'd truly be upset, but it was so long ago, and it might be our only chance at a proper wedding without having to change the date again.'

'I'm fine, Gem, I promise.' Lizzie dredged up a smile and straightened her shoulders. Gemma was right. The past was ancient history, and she wasn't going to be standing in the way of her best friend's special day because she'd had her heart broken twelve years ago in the very place Gemma was proposing to hold her wedding reception. 'You're absolutely right, we should definitely see the house if it's available. After all those lockdowns you don't need to be looking at a third date if this could work out.'

'That's wonderful, hon, I'm so pleased. And we'd be mad to pass up a weekend away with all the delights on offer at Halesmere, I've already checked out the retreat. So Friday afternoon to Monday lunchtime then? You can get away?'

'Should be fine.' Lizzie brought up her calendar. 'I'm meeting a new couple on Monday evening, but I'll be back in plenty of time for that as I'm seeing them at The Courthouse and it's not too far away.'

'Nice. We'd have loved it there if it wasn't booked up years in advance, even before lockdown.' Gemma paused. 'What about Jack? Where's he going to be over the weekend?'

Lizzie pulled a face as she tapped the pencil on her desk. 'No idea, and it doesn't matter anyway.'

'How are things with you guys?' There was concern in Gemma's voice this time, the frivolity and relief from before temporarily banished.

'We're muddling along. I keep catching him giving me apologetic looks and we're being very nice to one another.'

'Ah.'

'Exactly. Bit late for all that.' Lizzie scowled. 'He knows cheating is definitely a deal-breaker for me.'

'Have you found anywhere else yet? What was that house share like the other day?'

'Grim. Made me feel eighteen again and not in a good way.'

'Something will come up, don't worry.'

'I know, Gem, thanks. Jack did offer to take the spare room, but it is his house after all. I'm the one who's going to be moving, just as soon as I can find somewhere decent. I'll catch you up over the weekend.'

'So it's a yes to the retreat then? You're in?'

'I'm in.' Lizzie knew it was a rhetorical question and she huffed out a laugh. If Halesmere House really was much improved in the care of new owners, then maybe it would be the solution Gemma and Simon desperately needed. Lizzie was prepared to do everything she could to help create a wonderful wedding for them, and if that meant returning to the scene and the summer of her first love, then she'd do it and with a smile plastered on her face as well.

Of course there would be reminders of that special time in her life, but she'd come such a long way since then. She'd laugh about it when they arrived, would shrug off the sorrow and leave her sadness in the past where it belonged. It might even help, stop the thoughts that still occasionally crept into her mind and made her smile or sometimes cry.

'Perfect, make sure you pack some wet weather gear. We're not going to be lounging around inside all weekend.'

'Have you forgotten we're Cumbrian born and bred, Gem? I keep a coat and boots permanently in my car.'

'Are you bringing your camera?' The quiet understanding was back in Gemma's voice.

'Maybe.' That was something Lizzie no longer kept close at hand. It represented so much of her past and she used her phone for the everyday images she took now. 'I'll dig it out, see if it still works.'

'Of course it will. Please bring it, I know how much you miss it.' A beat of silence lengthened before Gemma returned to practicalities. 'So, I'll be getting the train. Could you pick me up at Lancaster please?'

'Sure can.' Lizzie was updating her calendar, happy to be distracting herself from memories of Halesmere by making plans she could depend on. 'And then it really must be my turn to come visit you. I want to see what this new kitchen is like, I'm sure Instagram doesn't do it justice.'

'I love it almost as much as I love Simon.' Gemma was dreamy and Lizzie laughed. Baking was another of Gemma's passions, alongside her work in family law,

Simon and their dog. 'I'll rustle up something delicious to bring, we can work it off on the fells.'

'What exactly does this retreat involve?' Lizzie wrinkled her nose as she closed her laptop. 'You specifically said delights and I'm not getting any relaxing facial and indulgent massage vibes right now.'

'I'll tell you when I see you, promise me you won't look it up? It'll be a wonderful surprise. I'll message you with a list of stuff you'll need.' Gemma's voice disappeared for a second. 'Sorry, I've got a client due in two minutes and they've just arrived. Lizzie, you're a superstar and you're gonna love Halesmere again, trust me. Mum says it's fabulous now. So I'll see you at the station at three, yeah? I need to talk to Bea and see if she can make the weekend too instead of just Saturday. Can't wait, love you.'

'Love you too,' Lizzie said as she swiped the call away, thinking it was a good job she did love her best friend so much. First a weekend and then a wedding in the very last place she wanted to see again. But her memories and all she'd felt that summer twelve years ago didn't matter anymore. All she needed to focus on now was the wonderful day Gemma and Simon deserved.

—

On Friday Lizzie was still telling herself it was ridiculous to be feeling this unbalanced by thoughts of the past since Gemma's call. Halesmere had been the backdrop to so much of their teenage years, its familiar setting in the valley she adored one of the few constants then in Lizzie's life. Gemma's mum had been the housekeeper and their family lived in a cottage attached to the house. Lizzie had got off the school bus with Gemma every day and the house had felt almost like their own. Holidaymakers had come and gone, and they paid little attention to a couple of girls roaming around the grounds or sneaking into an empty flat in the courtyard.

Lizzie's parents ran a very successful software company, and with two older brothers grown and gone, it was just the three of them in their rambling country house not far from Halesmere. She was very close to her parents, to whom she was their adored little miracle after years of trying for a third child. Aware of how comfortable and charmed her life was, with parents still very much in love, she'd dreamed of a family of her own one day. Lizzie hadn't realised how much she took for granted until almost everything she knew crashed virtually overnight.

Her mum and dad had sat her down three months before her A levels, her dad crying, his despair complete, as they explained they'd lost their business and with it their home, which was to be sold immediately. Her mum hadn't been able to restrain her own tears when she confessed that the university fund Lizzie had been expecting, afforded to both of her brothers, was also gone, along with the flat they planned to buy her when she moved away to study. Within the space of twenty-four hours, Lizzie felt as though she'd become a spectator in her own life, watching it crumble as her dreams for the future fell away.

Shocked and numb, she tried to comfort her parents as she offered her own support and assured them she would make her own way. Lizzie was utterly determined not to burden them with any additional worries about how she would manage. Their beautiful home sold within days and she had never forgotten packing up the bedroom she'd slept in all her life. Posters, pictures and precious belongings stuffed into two boxes; the curtains her mum had made framing a view of the garden Lizzie knew as well as her own face left behind for the new owners.

Her parents managed to cling on to enough to afford a tiny cottage in the Scottish Highlands where her dad found work on a fish farm and her mum returned to primary school teaching. Gemma's parents had offered to let Lizzie stay with them so she could finish college and sit her exams there rather than make the move north with her family. She could still picture her dad in the car, all three of them trying not to cry, as Lizzie and her mum carried the few things she'd kept from home into Gemma's room in the cottage.

Staying with Gemma made sense, but Lizzie missed her mum and dad desperately, and they spoke every day. Her mum wished aloud she could rent something nearby so she could see Lizzie through her exams, but Lizzie was having none of it and there wasn't the money anyway. Her dad was struggling and she knew he needed her mum's support more than she did. For the first time ever she'd realised her future depended on her own efforts and she quickly abandoned her plan to spend the summer volunteering for a turtle conservation project in Costa Rica.

She found a job in a supermarket in town instead, and every hour she sat scanning shopping at the checkout brought immense satisfaction as her savings for university increased. Her brothers helped where they could, but with one just about getting by in musical theatre and the other an accountant with a growing family, Lizzie thanked them and refused what little financial help they could offer, aware they felt guilty that she had missed out on their own advantages.

As Lizzie drove to meet Gemma now, journeying ever closer to her old home and her heart, she reminded herself firmly how far she'd come since those teenage days at Halesmere: a first-class degree in social anthropology and a successful career in public relations in London with a social change communications company before she'd left to plan events for a city bank.

Eventually she'd taken the leap and moved north to Carlisle, planning weddings for couples instead of corporate clients. But within six months the pandemic had hit. Overnight everything was cancelled and her new business crashed to an immediate halt. Lizzie, who had also just moved in with her boyfriend Jack, couldn't shake off the fears of the past and swiftly found a new way to support herself.

She took a job driving supermarket deliveries and put her dreams on hold to become one of millions of crucial key workers. She and Jack barely saw one another as the stresses of his teaching career became ever more apparent and she worked every hour she could.

As life eased into a new normal, she kept her supermarket job and gradually reduced her hours after she updated her website and social media accounts. She was elated to have a leap in interest for her services as couples rushed to book the weddings they'd had to postpone. Cumbria had always been home for her, and she was growing her network of connections as she sought out more suppliers and venues with whom she could work.

Almost at the station now, there was that flicker of apprehension again, the one that popped up every time Lizzie thought of Halesmere. She couldn't seem to stop memories of her past falling into her mind, no matter how often she banished them. And he was in every single one, the boy she had loved that last, special summer before she'd left. She reached Lancaster a little early and thankfully Gemma's train was on time. She and Lizzie were hugging tightly the moment Gemma stepped onto the platform.

'You look amazing, I love your jacket.' Gemma was eyeing the black leather cafe racer around Lizzie's shoulders. 'Don't leave it lying around or it might not make it back with you.'

Lizzie, who'd come straight from a meeting with a new client planning a brand launch and so wasn't wearing her supermarket delivery uniform, laughed as she popped the car boot and Gemma dropped a case inside, followed more carefully by a cake tin. 'I consider myself warned. What time's Bea arriving? I'm so looking forward to a relaxing weekend together, it has literally been years since we did this.'

'About six, she couldn't get away from work any earlier. Then Ella, one of the partners at Halesmere, is going to take us through the retreat. We spoke yesterday and decided to scale back a couple of things as they're usually for six or eight people, and we're just three.'

After almost an hour on the road catching up on each other's news, Lizzie was driving along quiet, once-familiar lanes, past the community shop and the pub, her uncertainty flaring again as she turned into the entrance to Halesmere. The long drive was much the same, with a row of ancient lime trees shading out the sun, and she caught her first sight of the house. It did look much improved, as Gemma had promised, having explained on the way about the artists resident in the old stables which had been converted into studios.

Evergreen ivy was confined beneath the first floor instead of clambering unhindered to the roof, and every window looked new. Lizzie followed Gemma out of the car, liking the elegant borders on either side of the front door filled with textural green plants and splashes of white flowers, bright through the shade on this north facing side of the building.

'Wow.' Gemma tucked her arm through Lizzie's. 'Looks fabulous, doesn't it?'

'It does. Finally we get to experience a whole night in here.'

As soon as the words were out Lizzie realised her mistake. Twelve years ago there had been that one stolen night she had spent in the house with him, a fact still unknown to Gemma. And then there were all the others in the grounds, tucked in a tent and huddled together to ward off the cold. Lizzie felt as though she were watching a replay of her own life; her memories so vivid and real she imagined she could hear his voice, feel his touch, catch that smile. But that was ridiculous, and she swiftly blinked away the thoughts as Gemma spoke.

'The key's in there, shall we go in?' She was pointing to a small black box near the door to the porch. 'Or would you like to stretch your legs first?'

'Maybe a quick peek at the courtyard.' Lizzie leaned into Gemma, grateful her friend had realised she wanted a moment alone. 'I can't wait to explore the studios and see what's on offer.'

Lizzie's gaze went to the arch separating the cottage from the house. 'The cottage looks good too, Gem,' she remarked. 'I like all those plants outside, loads of colour. Very cheerful and welcoming.'

'Yeah, Mum always said she'd have liked a front garden as well as a back one, it was never big enough for her. But the pots do make it up for it. How about you go ahead, I'll open up and meet you back in here in ten? Then you can tell me which artists I'd be interested in; I haven't checked them out yet.'

'Perfect.'

Lizzie had a quick wander around the courtyard. Gone was the general air of abandonment she remembered, the faded paint on rotting windows filled with panes of cracked glass, weeds poking between ancient cobbles. All the woodwork, including smart new barn doors, was now a subtle sage-green, looking fresh and modern without detracting from the buildings' sense of history. She decided to check Instagram later for links to follow the artists, already thinking over the potential for new suppliers she might be able to recommend via her business.

But it was time to see the house; she could return tomorrow and explore properly when the studios were open. Lizzie was heading back towards the arch when her peripheral vision caught someone on her left crossing the courtyard. Her awareness exploded into high alert as her head snapped around and she pitched to an unsteady halt. Even in so brief a moment she had seen something familiar in the length of his stride, the way he moved, like a wolf, alert to his surroundings without seeming aware of them.

Her stare leapt to his face. She saw the curve of the jaw her fingers had so often traced, outlined by a short beard now; the messy tawny hair she remembered cropped very short. He, too, jolted to a standstill, as she registered the sudden tension in his hands, always so gentle, now tightened into fists. Her eyes fixed to his, and though she was too far away to make out whether they were hazel, she knew without taking a single step towards him that they were. Eyes she knew as intimately as her own. Once,

Lizzie had been able to judge his mood by the elements they had seemed to possess: fire, ice, fear, desire, love. He'd spoken to her in gestures at first: a lingering look, the merest touch, a trusting hand, his lips burning against hers. His eyes, when she'd come to know him completely, had finally revealed all he'd felt with the words he'd eventually been able to find.

She saw them sweep down the length of her, take in the heeled ankle boots she hadn't changed since leaving the city, the effortlessly elegant white polka dot shirt dress, makeup perfectly applied, her favourite black designer sunglasses perched on her head and nestled among long blonde hair that fell around her face.

She sensed he could even detect her perfume in those few seconds as all sound was drowned out and the world seemed to have halted on its axis. His gaze went to her hands, and she knew he was searching for something she didn't wear. The life she'd lived since him, revealed in the gloss that clung to her like a new skin, hiding what lay beneath. Her heart was pounding and movement, words, composure, confidence, all had deserted her.

'Lizzie? Are you coming?' Gemma appeared and Lizzie was still planted where she stood. Her good sense refused to catch up as she sought the right reaction and tried to make herself nod, walk away, anything that didn't reveal more of the shock and wonder flooding into her body. This silent, frantic moment made her feel eighteen again as the last twelve years seemed to dissolve in the air she was gulping into her body.

'Oh, no.' Gemma's voice was a horrified whisper and still Lizzie had nothing, her eyes frozen on the past as her present hovered beyond the arch. 'No, it can't be.'

Cal Ryan offered a tiny tilt of his chin, the merest fraction of acknowledgement, before he resumed his stride across the courtyard. Gemma grabbed Lizzie's hand and yanked her away.

Chapter 2

Twelve Years Earlier

It was midsummer, Lizzie's eighteenth birthday, and she'd never felt so free in her life. She'd made it through the loss of her home and her parents' move, hugely relieved to turn her back on A levels and the pressure they'd brought. She had taken on more hours at the supermarket to add to her savings and was trying to park the apprehension she felt over her results, knowing she'd pushed herself to the limit aiming for the grades she needed for her first choice at the University of St Andrews.

She'd discovered a passion for photography at thirteen when her dad had passed down his old Nikon and suggested Lizzie give it a try. She had quickly realised she loved to capture the world around her and make sense of its beauty through her lens. Her dad often took her out and they'd spend hours tramping the fells and comparing the images they took.

The Nikon went nearly everywhere with her and, much as she knew she was good, after her parents' move, financial independence and a practical degree that would lead her into a flourishing, sustainable career was Lizzie's only goal rather than pinning her hopes on becoming a full-time photographer.

She spent a weekend with her parents in Scotland to celebrate her birthday a little early, her mum and dad sad but understanding that she wanted to remain at Halesmere with Gemma for the summer. Lizzie liked her parents' new house, but it felt alien, perched on a windswept coast in a small fishing community. Her camera was her constant; her creativity and skill flourishing as her confidence grew. She loved the certain world she saw reflected back through her images, the solidity of an unchanging landscape weathering every storm, just like she had.

Her parents managed to fund a small party for her eighteenth celebrations and there was only one place she wanted to hold it. She and Gemma had been hanging around the White Hart, the pub down the road from Halesmere, since their exams were over and they loved the small, annual summer festival there. It wasn't the original party Lizzie's parents had suggested months ago, dinner and dancing at a country hotel, but she was more than happy with the Hart, a small buffet, and her friends.

No one cared if the decor was worn, the tables scuffed and the pub only just coming round to the idea of more than one gin behind the bar. Gemma persuaded a friend of a friend to DJ and the party was set. Lizzie couldn't shake off the excitement, as she and Gemma got ready in the cottage beforehand, that tonight was the first step on the path to what she hoped was a bright new future.

They were buzzing with anticipation when they arrived. The smallest of the pub's three rooms had been set up with the buffet and it was typically busy for a Saturday in June, its numbers swelled by holidaymakers and walkers. Most of the girls' college and school friends were there and the landlord made a point of serving Lizzie and Gemma himself, treating them to a bottle of Prosecco on the house for Lizzie's special celebration.

After an hour of dancing and greeting friends, she still hadn't managed to get to the bar to order her own drink now it was actually legal, and as the DJ moved onto another party track Gemma grabbed her arm.

'Lizzie, you've got to see this guy!' Gemma flicked long hair from her face. Lizzie knew they looked striking together: Gemma with her Titian mane and Lizzie with equally dazzling golden hair. She turned to cast her eye over Gemma's boyfriend Simon and his mates to see if they'd brought anyone new to the party.

'He's not with Simon.' Gemma was towing Lizzie through the crowd. Lizzie was laughing and managed a swift mouthful of Prosecco on the way, impatient to dance again.

'Who is it then?'

'The guy behind the bar.' Gemma had to shout over LMFAO blaring from the speakers. 'He's hot. You'll see. You should totally check him out.'

'I'm not interested, Gem. That's the last thing I want.' Lizzie's first and only boyfriend had dumped her when he learned she wasn't going to Morocco with him and planned to spend her summer on a checkout scanning shopping instead.

'So? Who said you can't have some fun just because you're working? I'm not suggesting you marry the guy next month and have his babies. Just ask him for a drink. See what happens.'

One advantage of shooting up to five feet eight in year nine meant that Lizzie could see over quite a lot of people's heads, and in heels at the crowded bar, it really helped. The DJ moved on to another track and she was laughing with Gemma at this first taste of grown-up freedom as they sang along.

'What can I get you?'

The words were shouted at Lizzie over the din and her hips, her feet, were still moving as Gemma slipped away. She turned and her drinks order fled as she met the barman's gaze. Her pulse rocketed, sending a blush racing into her cheeks.

It was his eyes she drank in first, instinctively leaning towards him. They were an unusual shade of hazel with hints of gold, framed by strikingly long lashes. She took in untidy tawny brown hair falling to his brows, around his ears and grazing his neck. A green T-shirt emblazoned with the name of a band she knew across his chest. A generous mouth, a day or two's stubble.

She saw him glance at her lips as though he might be trying to read them and they parted with a silent gasp. She'd always had that classic English rose colouring, an oval face with sky blue eyes, and a hand went to her hair to flick it from a shoulder above her strapless aqua party dress. She hadn't planned the gesture or thought it through, it was just an instinct as natural as the way in which he'd captured her attention with so little effort.

'What can I get you?' This time a smile to soften the intensity of his look as he repeated the question and Lizzie was certain she wasn't the only one who'd felt the air between them shift.

'Can I take your picture?' He was ridiculously photo-genic, and the words were out. People were crowding around the bar and she couldn't care less if she was holding up the queue.

'What?' He had to shout back.

'I want to take your picture!'

'Now?'

'Yes.' She had her phone and wished for her camera. She wanted to read his face with her lens and work him out, and she knew one image would not be enough for that. But the phone would have to do and she pulled it from her bag. His mouth quirked in a wry grin, one hand on the bar, as she snapped him before he changed his mind.

'Now do you want a drink?'

'Yes please. It's my birthday.' Lizzie was exhilarated, emboldened by what she'd done and his quiet attention. Maybe Gemma was right. Maybe this summer could include some freedom and fun, and Lizzie had started it all by taking a photo of a stranger and a gorgeous one at that. She ordered another bottle of Prosecco and appreciated the view of him in snug jeans from behind, a rip across one knee.

He was soon back with the bottle and reached for glasses, the T-shirt riding up. Her stomach flipped as she took in the expanse of tanned skin suddenly revealed and she didn't want to leave, taking her time to find the money. She looked up and he was waiting, his amusement suggesting he knew she was lingering on purpose.

'How old are you?'

She felt caught, sensing that jolt pass between them again, the din of the music almost smothering their words. He tried to return her change, tilting his head in acknowledgement when she refused it to tip him.

'Eighteen.' There was something in his voice that marked him out as different, told her he wasn't from around here.

'Hey, it's my turn! You've chatted him up long enough, I've been waiting ages to order.' A middle-aged man was scowling at Lizzie, and she glared back. Time with her stunning stranger was gone for now and she would have to find another way. She tucked the cold bottle underneath her arm and collected the glasses. He was already taking the older man's order and their eyes fastened together one last time before she turned.

She wondered if his gaze really was burning into her back as she walked away on unsteady legs. Yesterday had been one life, dominated by college, her parents' move, exams, getting through. Today, tonight, was a step into another one and a shiver stole down her spine at what this summer might now hold.

Lizzie danced the rest of the night with her friends, merry but definitely not drunk, and she knew the high had come from meeting someone she was seriously attracted to for the very first time. As the evening edged towards a new day, the crowd thinned, but she didn't go to the bar again. She didn't have to. Whenever she looked across, she found the barman's gaze with ease, and it seemed to be always waiting for hers.

It was almost eleven and there wasn't much of her birthday left. The pub would stop serving soon and Gemma's dad would be here to run them back to the cottage. Lizzie wanted some air, dancing wasn't the only thing that had heated her skin and Gemma nodded when Lizzie said she was going outside.

She leaned against a low wall, ignoring the noise and laughter of people leaving, trying to understand this new, almost overwhelming excitement and the sense of danger thudding through her veins. She didn't usually allow this to happen to her; since her parents' business collapsed, she'd quickly learned to detach herself from feelings that threatened to overwhelm her. But it was a beautiful, warm evening and barely dark. Midsummer was upon them, and it seemed magic was in the air all around her.

'Hey. Some craic tonight.'

She sprang away from the wall and saw the barman drop an empty crate outside the back door. She'd wondered if he might have noticed her leaving. She wanted to see him, to hear his voice without the din of the party drowning out everything he said, and now he was here. Her skin was hot, her breath quickening.

'Happy birthday.' The crate rattled as it levelled, and his hands were in his pockets as he walked slowly towards her.

'Thank you.' Her words were a croak, her throat dry. 'Your accent? Is it Northern Ireland?'

'Dead on.' He smiled as he halted in front of her, the earlier wariness diminished by a flash of warmth. Lizzie already loved the soft lilt and melodic note in his voice, though she had the sense he spoke more with his eyes than with words. 'Not everyone gets it right first time.'

'What are you doing here?'

He tipped his head to the building behind them. 'Working.'

Close up she realised he probably wasn't much older than her. 'Why haven't I seen you before?'

'So many questions.' His voice was low, drifting into the night and she shivered, his gaze refusing to let go of hers. 'I just got here, that's why. I'm new.'

'Are you staying?' She didn't know why she already cared, but her words were impatient as butterflies danced in her stomach.

'No. Does it matter?'

'Yes.' Lizzie could only offer the truth. She knew she'd never forget his eyes or how it felt to be held by them like this. She saw a faint scar below one brow and she reached out, touching it, fizzing with excitement and new confidence. He was utterly still, other than the pulse leaping in his throat. Her hand moved to his cheek to explore the roughness of his stubble beneath her palm.

'What's your name?' He covered her hand when she went to lower it, holding her fingers lightly against his skin. His gaze was roaming over her face, as though he were committing every detail to memory, and she couldn't prevent a gasp when it lingered on her lips.

'Lizzie. Lizzie Martin. What's yours?'

'Cal Ryan.' He took a final step to dismantle the space between them and reached for her other hand to hold it. 'So, Lizzie Martin. Can I kiss you happy birthday?'

She nodded. There was no other reply she wouldn't regret for the rest of her days. She already felt on fire as he dipped his head and she brought hers to meet him. His lips pressed briefly against hers and she was tentative, not certain he'd meant to offer anything more than this light-hearted gesture.

'Did you get everything you wanted?' His voice was a murmur, and it wasn't enough. Her fingers were trembling inside his and the hand had fallen from his face to trace the narrow shape of his shoulder.

'No. You haven't kissed me properly yet.'

She waited an agonising beat to see how he would respond, eyes hitched to his, breath trapped in her throat. Then his mouth was on hers, claiming it as though he'd been waiting all night to kiss her this way. Her lips parted beneath his and when she heard a whimper, she realised it was her who'd made it. Cal was leagues ahead of her previous boyfriend and she gave herself up to it, felt the racing of his heart beneath her palm when it reached his chest. He let go of her hand to pull her into him and she arched her back, trying to hold every part of her against him, wanting to make their kiss last forever.

'Lizzie? Oh. Sorry.'

Utterly dazed, it took her a few seconds to locate Gemma hovering behind Cal through the dusk, his arms still holding her close.

'Just checking you're okay. I'll be inside if you need me.'

Lizzie couldn't find more of a reply than a nod to let her friend know all was fine. She saw Gemma turn away and heard the door of the pub bang shut. This had never happened to her before, and she knew she would always remember it. No one had ever looked at her this way, stripping back every layer she possessed to see all that lay beneath, as though they understood her without ever knowing her until this moment. She heard the ragged breath he was still trying to find as Cal touched his forehead to hers, startled to realise he seemed as stunned as she did.

'I have to get back,' he muttered hoarsely. 'Before they miss me.'

'Can I see you again?' It was the only question in her mind.

'Sure. I'm here five days a week if I'm not already sacked.'

It wasn't the reply she wanted, and they both knew it. Frustration and disappointment followed, Lizzie desperately wanting to hold him to a more certain answer, another opportunity to do this again.

'Lizzie?' Cal straightened and placed one hand on her shoulder, running a finger down her cheek. 'I'm not looking for anything, okay?'

'Why do we have to be anything? Can't we just have some fun?' She was astonished to see the glint of something brighter in his eyes. His own regret maybe, the desire unabated as his gaze returned to her mouth and he snatched his hand from her shoulder as though she was burning him.

'I don't think so.'

'But why?' Her voice was scratched, urgent, wanting to find something, anything, to make him stay.

'Because I just had the best kiss of my life and I can't go there, Lizzie.' He was already walking away and paused to look back. 'I'm sorry. It's not why I'm here.'

–

The next morning Lizzie was perched on Gemma's bed and in a very unfamiliar agony. She'd floated back to her party after the incredible kiss with Cal, utterly crushed when he hadn't looked at her again even once, offering, it seemed, a very deliberate indifference from what they'd shared in those moments outside. She'd cared about her first boyfriend until he dumped her, but he hadn't troubled her heart, already bruised and fragile after her parents' business collapse and move.

She and Gemma analysed every word Lizzie and Cal had shared in those few minutes alone together: the way he'd looked at her, with amusement, desire and longing, before shock had followed straight after their kiss and he'd walked away. And still, the sharp realisation came that Lizzie had landed straight in one of her own romantic dreams, and fallen utterly and hopelessly in love with someone who didn't want to see her again.

'It's ridiculous, Gem. Even for me, who still thinks happy endings actually exist.'

'It is. Nuts.' Gemma was nursing a hangover and a mug of builders' tea. They'd already eaten the bacon butties her mum had brought up.

'I mean, come on! Who, ever, seriously falls in love at first sight?'

'No one?' Gemma blinked over the mug, her auburn hair making her face seem even paler.

'Well, apparently some people do, and not just in movies,' Lizzie said fiercely. She jumped from the bed to pace the small room and gave up when she had to keep ducking beneath low beams jutting from the ceiling. 'Please tell me I'm not one of them. But then maybe it was bound to happen, I've seen *Love Actually* too often. Jamie and Aurelia gets me every time. Tell me to stop watching it.'

'Stop watching *Love Actually*, Lizzie,' Gemma said mildly. She put her mug down and lay back on the bed. 'So, what are you going to do? About Cal?'

Lizzie's smile was suddenly hopeful, her decision made. 'I'll tell you tonight after we've been to the pub.'

'Is that really a good idea?'

'Same answer.'

–

Lizzie and Gemma strolled into the White Hart before the evening rush, past the few locals and usual holidaymakers. Lizzie was already checking the bar, despondent when she didn't see Cal with the other two staff members. She and Gemma found a corner table and ordered drinks, her fingers tapping the glass impatiently.

'You do know you're making a statement, turning up here like this the very next day. He's going to know why

26

and will probably turn you down again.' Gemma softened her bluntness with a smile. 'I'm sorry for being direct, I just want you to be prepared.'

Lizzie nodded. 'Better that than finding out he's gone, Gem, and I never had the chance to see him again. I know it's crazy. My heart's already halfway to being broken, I might as well see where the other half lands.' She huffed out a laugh without humour. 'I just need to understand why he doesn't want to see me, that's all. I know he liked me.' She knocked back a mouthful of wine as her gaze roved over the room yet again. 'Doesn't look like he's here.'

'Sure about that?' Gemma tipped her head towards a door on the far side of the pub and Lizzie's glance raced after it.

Cal had his back to them as he walked behind the bar and Lizzie tried really hard to be casual. Tried with everything she possessed to suggest that she sat here with her best friend every Saturday night and wasn't really waiting for a glimpse of the man she'd just fallen in love with, hoping he would notice her too. She felt like a different young woman to the one she'd been yesterday, before they'd kissed, and she'd seen her own wonder reflected in his face. The surprise at the emotion and the passion they'd found so easily and that Cal apparently didn't want to risk repeating.

'Lizzie?' Gemma reached for her hand across the table. 'Just be careful, okay? Are you really sure you want to throw yourself into something with a stranger who's not going to stay?'

Lizzie shrugged and Gemma knew as well as she did it was too late for that. She slugged back the rest of her wine and picked up the empty glass. 'Another? I'm going to the bar.'

'Fine. Good thing I'm driving.' Gemma settled back in her seat. 'Diet Coke please. And I'm not leaving until I know how and when you're getting home.'

Lizzie threw her a grateful glance and was gone, the glass unsteady between her fingers. She thanked someone who made room for her, deliberately positioning herself at Cal's end of the bar. He gave nothing away to suggest he'd noticed her, didn't rush across or help her jump the queue. With growing impatience she watched him serve everyone else with the same quiet, efficient attention and finally it was her turn.

Chapter 3

'What can I get you?' Cal tipped his head as he repeated his first question from last night. Lizzie saw the lingering tension in his stare. Crushing disappointment at his casual tone was already following and she pointed to her empty glass.

'Another Pinot Grigio and a Diet Coke, please.'

He took the glass, turned away, and she bit her lip. She didn't dare look at Gemma for fear of finding sympathy from her friend, it would be the undoing of all the emotion she was doing her best to hold steady. He was soon back with the drinks and Lizzie handed over cash as she thanked him politely. This was a mistake and she wanted to escape.

Cal shook his head. 'I'll get them.'

'There's no need.'

'Sure there is.' His hand was briefly on hers to refuse the money and the unexpected contact was a thrill. 'I think there's an unwritten rule that says when the barman behaves like a jerk, he should buy the drinks.'

'Right. Thanks.' By way of apology for his blunt attitude when he'd walked away last night it wasn't much, and Lizzie felt the moment of hope crashing inside her. 'You really don't have to.'

'Ask me again.' Cal took some cash from his pocket and put it in the till.

'Ask you what?' She already felt she'd humiliated herself enough by turning up. Her presence here made it clear she wanted to see him again. His indifference, it seemed, the same reply.

He leaned forwards to stare at her, arms on the bar, as the queue of waiting customers grew longer. 'If I want to see you again.'

'And why would I do that? I get it. I just came to see if you'd tell me why not.'

'Because this time I won't lie to you and I'm sorry I did.' His lips were offering a smile, his eyes more like surprise. 'I can't stop thinking about you, Lizzie Martin. Do I get another chance? Please?'

'Are you staying?' Lizzie's voice was a shocked whisper at his confession, joy already brightening her face.

'That wasn't the question.'

'Just tell me.' Her immediate future was going to be decided by his reply and she already knew he held her heart. Crazy, just as she'd said, and yet so very right.

'For now.' He took her hand, touched her fingers to his lips. 'I can't promise more than that, Lizzie. I'm leaving after the summer.'

'So am I, and that's ages away.' The weeks and months stretched almost endlessly in front of them, and she'd take it. Would take anything that meant they could be together and, for now, the doubts and fears were banished to the back of her mind and her heart was full.

—

It didn't take Lizzie long to learn that Cal possessed almost nothing. He'd arrived at Halesmere with his life in a rucksack, his new home a battered green tent. When she discovered he was camping in a field and would have to move on, she begged Gemma's mum to let him stay in a quiet corner of the grounds at Halesmere. She agreed, as long as he kept out of the way of guests and made himself useful by doing some basic jobs in return. By the end of the week, Lizzie had managed to switch her hours at the supermarket to align more with Cal's at the pub.

In those first days she sensed his reluctance over their relationship easing as they learned more about each other, instinctively understanding he had come here in search of something. She waited and when he told her his story, revealing the details of his life in Ireland, without family to anchor him there or any plans to return, his trust and his strength only made her love him more.

He'd grown up partly in care, sent to a foster family at ten when his mother could no longer manage a child after a serious accident left her in constant pain and subsequently with a chronic drug addiction. There was a blank space on his birth certificate where his father's name should have been and his mother had revealed, shortly before she died from a stroke two years ago when Cal was seventeen, that she'd met his father at a festival in Cumbria.

Cal had his bricklaying qualification, some savings from a job in construction and a strong desire to somehow find his father before moving on. Lizzie couldn't relate his own experience of family to hers, but she did understand what it felt like to have your world flipped upside down and be left reeling. She empathised and offered her support as they made plans to search out the other half of his family.

He didn't have a phone and he refused to pin his life to the address of foster carers in Belfast where he no longer lived. So she couldn't text kisses from her bedroom late at night or message him when she was bored in the moments between customers at the supermarket. She couldn't share the images she took of them on her phone which she knew she'd always treasure, and wished he could, too.

Lizzie had never been in love before, but everything she shared with Cal was a confession of how she felt, including her attempts to help him find his father. She caught sight of Cal's own feelings before he shared the words in the hurried glances he gave her across the pub, a quick smile, the cheeky wink meant for her alone, tightening the invisible thread binding them together. The deliberate touch of his hand when he passed her a drink or the exhilarating kisses they had to keep stopping to share when they walked back to Halesmere through golden days and warm summer evenings that she wished could last forever.

They had very little to go on in the hunt for his father. Cal's mother, Marianne, had sung with a folk group and so Lizzie researched everyone that could be of interest, trying to find a band that might have included a young Irish woman run away from home. They met with little success and gradually Cal stopped searching as the distance in his eyes receded.

The days ran into weeks that soon became a month, and Lizzie ignored thoughts of their futures to look no further than their plans for each day. Cal had a deep love of the landscape; it seemed etched into his bones, despite a life lived in a loud and busy city. From a young age he'd disappeared alone into the mountains whenever he could, and Lizzie understood he craved the open sky to help him breathe more easily.

She captured everything on her camera, always with her, as they explored isolated bothies, ruined farmhouses, secret tarns and tracks worn into the ground from the days when coffins had been hauled to their final places of rest before roads made the journey easier. They bought cheap mountain bikes to cycle old trails and a second tent so they could camp out under the stars and watch the sun rise, as though each day and this private world they inhabited belonged only to them.

They swam in freezing tarns and waterfalls, daring each other and testing their own limits as their confidence and fitness increased. As she'd missed his nineteenth birthday in April, she dipped into her precious savings to give him the gift of walking with wolves, loving him all the more as she watched his awe and wonder in the company of such primal and exceptional animals.

Cal spoke of little else for days and showed her without words what the experience and her gift had meant to him. He loved to sketch, so she bought him a book which he added to every day, tiny details of animals so lifelike she almost expected them to blink, or quick drawings of her he would laughingly refuse to let her see before giving in.

He soon became used to Lizzie's camera and his earlier self-consciousness disappeared as she recorded their summer through the images she took. The camera loved him, and her favourite shots were the ones when he would turn to show her something, and she'd catch his unfettered excitement and the wide grin he seemed to reserve just for her.

Occasionally she would wonder how they felt so complete together when their lives until this summer had been so very different. Every day he revealed more of himself in tiny gestures she wasn't expecting: a sketch he'd tuck in her pocket for her to find when she was at work, the wildflowers he picked and threaded in her blonde hair, the poem he wrote and she'd forever treasure, as precious as the heart he promised was hers.

The only times they ever fought were about her family. Lizzie saw her parents every couple of weeks when she took the train up, and she spoke to her mum most days. Her parents knew about Cal and wanted to meet the young man who had so captivated their daughter. He flatly refused to travel north with her and one trip, when her mum and dad came south, Lizzie booked a table for four at the pub and was humiliated and steaming with rage when Cal didn't show up. His reason, he reminded her curtly, was that family wasn't for him and he didn't see the point in getting involved when he wouldn't be staying in Cumbria. He was a lone wolf, something she'd sensed from the start, and only Lizzie was allowed near the centre of his soul.

The day Lizzie got her A level results was the day her parents finally met Cal. And the day everything fell apart. They'd barely ever spoken about the future, but she'd assumed he would come with her to St Andrews as he'd shared no other plans. At dinner that night, celebrating her results with her parents and Cal, she chatted excitedly about flat-hunting for the two of them, but Lizzie froze as she saw the old wariness return to his face.

He did have his own plan, he informed her, and it included asking Lizzie to travel to New Zealand with him. He had a visa and a temporary job as a lifeguard lined up, and he intended to find work on a construction site putting his bricklaying skills to good use while he decided what to do next. As he hadn't found his father, he'd decided he'd spent enough time in Cumbria and was ready to move on.

A lingering silence crashed over the table as three heads swivelled to gawp at him. He was perfectly still, and Lizzie was mute with disbelief as she saw the sudden plea in his gaze on hers. She was grasping for a coherent reply to replace the shock thudding through her mind, leaving her quivering with adrenaline.

'I'm sorry for not telling you before. I was going to ask you tonight to come with me anyway.' Cal gripped her hand, his eyes alight with hope. 'Once you had your results so you could decide what's next.'

'You know what's next! I'm going to university.'

'You don't have to.' His voice fell and Lizzie's relief over her results was slipping away as he presented the impossible choice. 'We can travel round the islands, you can be anything you want, Lizzie. Bring your camera and come with me.'

'But my life is here,' she rushed out in a panic, still trying to process his invitation, and hardly daring to give it air. Would she really move halfway across the world and give up her plans for him? For love? For a new dream, or was it merely a mirage? 'I need a career, it's what I've worked for. And my family is here. It's different for you.'

'Different for me why, Lizzie?' Cal dropped her hand, and she felt the chill of his gesture on more than just her body as his eyes bored into hers. 'Because I don't have a family or anyone who cares about me?'

'That's not true! You know how I feel about you, and you have friends here, Cal. A life. A reason to stay, even if you don't come to St Andrews with me. I could come back once I've got my degree.' Lizzie faltered. She hadn't really given moving back to Cumbria afterwards much thought. She couldn't stay in Gemma's cottage forever and she'd never be able to afford anything of her own without a brilliant job.

'Lizzie, you'd be a fool to go with him to New Zealand after everything you've worked for. He's got nothing. Where do you think that's going to get him? Or you? If anyone knows what use nothing is, it's me and your mother. You're too clever to live that sort of a life with someone like him.' Her dad finally gave angry voice to his thoughts and her mum's hand went to his arm, trying to still any other harsh words he might have to offer. Lizzie felt the pressure of their pride in her achievement pressing in, all the greater because she'd come through the dismantling of the only life she'd known right before her exams.

She reached for Cal's hand, trying to find peace, but he snatched it away. A tear slid from her eye at the flash of pain she read in his.

'Ach and what would I do in St Andrews, Lizzie, while you're busy living your student life,' Cal said bitterly. 'Sit around in some wee bedsit again, working some crappy job I don't want, waiting for you? Or have you tell me you've met someone who isn't a bricklayer with nothing to his name, like your dad said.'

A waiter came to check on their food and he shot away when Cal glared at him. 'I haven't found what I was looking for here and I'm not going to stay. Sure, you knew that from the start. This was always going to happen.'

'But I love you,' she whispered brokenly, swiping at another tear. 'I thought you loved me, too. Why do we have to choose?'

'I do love you. But I'm not going to hang around four more years to find out you've stopped, Lizzie. You assumed you could fit me into your family because I haven't got one of my own. I don't need a family, I just wanted you. My father's a ghost and there's no one else out there for me.'

Cal shoved his chair back, standing to face her parents. 'Thank you for the invitation tonight,' he said flatly. 'I understand why you don't want someone like me in Lizzie's life. You think I'm a drifter, a nobody who'll persuade her to throw away her big chance.' She flinched at the sudden steel in his gaze. 'I just want her to be happy with someone she can lean on when she needs to. I thought that might've been me, but I was wrong.' He bent down, cupping Lizzie's face between gentle hands. She saw the finality written in his eyes as he dropped a kiss on her mouth. 'I'm sorry. I stayed too long.'

She was too stunned to do more than track his swift progress across the room, oblivious to the stares coming their way. The restaurant door clattered and the realisation that he had gone had her pushing her own chair back until her mum gripped her arm.

'Don't, Lizzie, please. He's already hurt you and he's right about one thing. Your lives are just too different and it's better you see that now. What if you go to New Zealand with him and he ends it? What then, if St Andrews is gone and you've got nothing to show for all your hard work? Don't upend your life for him, you're much too clever for that. There's so much more out there for you.'

Tears tracking down her face, Lizzie slumped back in her seat. Her world had flipped again in a second and she felt derailed by the impact of Cal's refusal to join her in St Andrews. A glance at her dad was enough to see the fury in his red face. The food she'd eaten was churning, threatening to come back up. Had she and Cal really been fools to fall in love and spend a perfect summer together? Where was the way forward for them now, after those last few horrible moments?

'He doesn't understand who he is, Lizzie, and I don't see the point in him dragging you along to find out. I know that's hard to hear, my darling girl, and I'm sorry.' Her mum placed a hand on her cheek, nodding at a worried-looking waiter for the bill. 'Come home and let us look after you. One day you'll be glad you didn't go to New Zealand and throw everything away on a whim, I promise. You know you can't build a life on dreams and wishes. We all have our mad moments when we're young and you'll get over it.'

Lizzie felt the fight draining away, the desire to go after Cal fading as the hopelessness of her love and their situation fell in on her. He needed time to cool down, they both did. He'd always been a dangerous choice and she'd known it from the beginning. She'd risked her heart for a summer of love and the awful realisation came that maybe she hadn't fought hard enough for him. That she'd been wrong to assume he'd simply tag along with her because he had no one else. As though he needed nothing more than the landscape and Lizzie to love him, which she knew deep inside her wasn't true.

She'd seen the hurt he tried to hide when he'd spoken of his family. She'd felt the distance he tried to maintain from anything that threatened to come close and unbalance him. He'd let her in, briefly, and now he was shutting her out again. He had a life of his own to make and she was aching as she finally understood he wasn't going to attach his to hers and hope it would last.

When her parents reluctantly dropped her off at Gemma's cottage, her mum made her promise to call tomorrow. Lizzie crawled into bed, thankful not to have to face Gemma, who was off camping somewhere with Simon. Sleep didn't find her until late and Lizzie was wide awake again at dawn, restless and unsettled. She leaped out of bed and threw on shorts and a T-shirt. Cal's tent had been pitched near the tarn beyond the gardens of the house, and she sprinted through the meadow to find him.

They'd first swum here together, and it was one of their special places. One memorable day she'd photographed him walking out of the water, laughing because she'd deliberately thrown his clothes out of reach. The image was one of her favourites because he was so relaxed and at peace in his surroundings, and with her.

Surely they'd find a way forward if they loved each other? Goodbye wasn't for a day like this, with the sun already high and warm, hours to be filled with a new promise for the future. She wanted to bask in his smile and kiss him hello, put everything between them to rights once again. Tell him she was sorry for her assumptions and find out how he felt.

Lizzie skittered to a halt on the narrow scrap of shingle which passed for a beach at the tarn, searching for signs of Cal. Her heart began to slam with fear as she read his absence in the space where his green tent had been, the shrivelled patch of grass scuffed to nothing, his mountain bike gone. Her gaze picked out an envelope pinned to the trunk of a nearby birch and her throat was dry as she snatched at it with clammy hands. The envelope tore and something fell to the stones around her feet. She ignored it as she hurriedly unfolded the plain white scrap of paper ripped from his sketch pad.

I'm sorry, Lizzie. I can't go to St Andrews and wait for you to tell me it's over. I never planned to stay, you were the reason I did. This is all I have and it's yours now. Cal x

Lizzie fell to her knees, her search made nearly impossible by the tears pouring down her face, the rough stones scraping against legs bared by shorts. Her fingers found a tiny object and she picked it up, brushing off a bit of soil. Dirt smeared across her face as she swiped at her eyes to stare in shock. She was holding Cal's silver Claddagh ring, given to him by his mother and the only thing of her few belongings Lizzie knew he had kept. She slumped to the ground and sobbed, his note and the precious keepsake clutched in her hand.

Chapter 4

Present Day

'Lizzie, I swear I had no idea he was here. You have to believe me. I don't even want to say his name. Desperate as I am to sort out the wedding, I'd rather be having fish and chips in the street than putting you through this.' One of Gemma's hands was in Lizzie's and with her other she thrust out a glass. 'Get this down, it'll help with the shock.'

Lizzie hadn't uttered a single word since Gemma had quickly steered her back to the house and onto a comfortable sofa in the drawing room. She'd barely glanced at the changes since she'd last been in here, the renovated fireplace or the long floral curtains covering the expanse of curving bay window either side of the French doors. Cosy sofas and armchairs were in differing colours, decorated with pretty cushions, with occasional tables for serving drinks close at hand, and antique cabinets filled with porcelain stood against walls.

Bea was due to arrive soon, and Lizzie knew she had to get a grip. Moisture was a sheen on her palms, heartbeat still a roar in her ears. Three nights on retreat at Halesmere House suddenly felt as long as three weeks and she gulped a mouthful of the whisky, coughing violently as the alcohol burned down her throat.

'Better?' Gemma was hovering worriedly with the bottle.

Lizzie shook her head.

'Have some more.' Gemma splashed another measure into her glass, and Lizzie knocked it back, spluttering, her eyes watering as she raised them to stare at Gemma.

Lizzie's voice was a croak, her throat on fire. 'You're sure you didn't know? He isn't the reason you didn't want me going online to find out more about the weekend?'

'What?' Gemma nearly dropped the bottle. 'Of course not, we haven't spoken about what happened between you guys in forever. I'd never have come near the place if I'd thought crashing into him like that was even a remote possibility.' Her eyes narrowed suspiciously. 'Wasn't he in New Zealand? What do you think he's doing here?'

Lizzie opened her mouth, and it was a few seconds before words could make sense of her thoughts. 'How would I know? It's been years, Gem. He could have been anywhere.' She sank back onto the sofa. 'Why does he have to be here, now? It makes no sense. He literally could be anywhere else in the world.'

'I could ask around?' Gemma clattered the whisky back onto a drinks tray. 'If you think that's a good idea?'

Lizzie knew it wasn't on every level. Cal Ryan belonged firmly in her past and he had left her behind twelve years ago. She didn't need to know what those months and years had brought for him since they'd separated. She wasn't interested in whether he was single, divorced, married, a dad, successful, happy or not. He was nothing to do with her.

And yet. 'Maybe you could google him, Gem,' she said casually. The whisky burn was easing and she felt more alert, as though the shock of seeing Cal out of the blue had freed her brain from the fog and enabled her to focus again.

'Or you could…?' Gemma's reply was hesitant.

'No thanks, not going there again. I've resisted that temptation for a long time, I'm not giving in now.' Lizzie cleared her throat, put the glass on a small table beside the sofa and found a weak smile. 'We're here for a fabulous weekend and to sort out your wedding, Gem. I'm not letting anyone, least of all him, get in the way of that.'

'Right. That's exactly right.' Gemma's voice softened. 'It's just…'

'What?' Lizzie was picturing Cal in her mind again. That look, his stillness, eyes fixed on hers.

'You've had a shock, that's all. He didn't just break your heart, Lizzie, he smashed it, leaving the way he did and you never being able to find him afterwards.' Gemma took her hand again. 'Whatever you think of him, you need some time to process what you're feeling.'

'I'm fine.' Lizzie was impatient, unsettled, wary. 'Absolutely fine.'

'You're a terrible liar.' Gemma squeezed her fingers. 'He must be here for a reason. I hope we're not going to be bumping into him.'

'I'm sure we won't.' Lizzie bit back the anxiety that hadn't yet abated as Gemma voiced her other worry. 'Like you said, it was a shock and I'm over it now. Thank you for getting me out of there so quickly.' The sound of a doorbell had her leaping up from the sofa, relieved to have something else other than her history with Cal to think about.

'That'll be Ella,' Gemma said, checking her phone. 'She's going to welcome us and run through the plans for our weekend. Bea's messaged to say she's about twenty minutes away.'

'Perfect. It's going to be wonderful, Gem.' Lizzie was alongside her as they left the drawing room. The stunning, glossy black piano in the hall was new. She'd got to grade six as a teenager before her lessons went the way of everything else then in her life. Bea played too, maybe they'd have a go later.

'So shall I ask around, find out what Cal's doing here?'

'It wouldn't hurt to know why he's at Halesmere, I suppose. Just so I can be sure to avoid him. And that's it. Whatever else he's been up to, I don't want to know. Let's not mention it to Bea yet, I don't want to spend the weekend talking about him and you know what she's like, she'll want to know everything.' Lizzie plastered a smile on her face as Gemma opened the front door to a woman of similar age to them.

'Hello, welcome to Halesmere, or should I say welcome back. I'm Ella Grant, it's so lovely to meet you both.'

Lizzie liked Ella's open and friendly manner at once. A blonde pixie crop suited her delicate, heart-shaped face and an athletic figure clad in a pink and green running kit.

'Hi Ella, I'm Gemma. We've spoken a couple of times. This is my best friend Lizzie, chief bridesmaid, and wedding planner extraordinaire.'

'Not extraordinaire at all, Gem,' Lizzie protested with a smile. 'I'm just happy to be helping you.'

'Well, you do love your job and I'm very lucky to have you. Simon's wonderful but he's not much use when it comes to flowers, favours and who's going to sit next to Uncle George.'

'You're a wedding planner, Lizzie?' Ella looked at her inquiringly. 'Where are you based? Gemma mentioned the three of you are all in the North.'

'I plan other events too, but weddings take up most of my time. I live in Carlisle at the moment.' Another unwelcome reminder of her love life, this time Jack and sharing a house with her ex.

'Haven't you got something coming up on Windermere soon, Lizzie?' Gemma was smiling.

'Yes, an American couple who love the Lake District and Doug wants to propose to his partner there. They knew each other years ago and got back together last Christmas.'

'That sounds gorgeous,' Ella said. 'I do some volunteering with an outdoor centre on Windermere, it's beautiful. It'll be a wonderful place to propose.'

'Lizzie's brilliant, I'm so lucky to have her help and expertise,' Gemma said loyally, linking arms with her. 'Bea's my other bridesmaid, Ella, and she's on her way, she shouldn't be long.'

'Perfect. I'm sorry I wasn't here when you arrived, I'm just back from collecting the kids and we're running a bit late.' Ella pointed to a pair of gorgeous redheaded children, a girl and younger boy, playing with a big, mostly white dog outside the cottage across the drive.

'That's Lily and Arlo, and Prim our dog.' Ella's smile was lit by love and she turned back to Gemma and Lizzie. 'Max, my partner, would love to meet you and find out more about the house. He bought it last year and I moved up in November. Your mum mentioned she'd been the housekeeper here and you'd lived in the cottage, Gemma, when I spoke with her.'

'I did, we both kind of grew up here really. Lizzie's parents moved away in her last year of college and she stayed with us to finish her A levels.'

Gemma was still talking but for Lizzie the mention of A levels was another sharp reminder of Cal. She'd noticed the new maturity he possessed in just those few moments in the courtyard earlier; the boy become a man. Her gaze flickered to the arch. He had been here not twenty minutes ago. Was he still? After twelve years of silence, was he so easily within reach once again?

'Sorry, what?' A flush crept over Lizzie's cheeks as she tried to focus on the conversation taking place around her.

'I was telling Ella how much freedom and fun we had here. We used to pretend the house belonged to us and that we were very generously allowing strangers to visit when of course it was the other way around.'

'We did.' Lizzie offered a wide smile, trying to make up for her distraction. Concentration was one of her best skills and already it was threatening to desert her after one glimpse of Cal and her past. 'Do you remember those awful old sofas in the drawing room, Gem? The red draylon things with the pink cushions?'

'Vividly.' Gemma shuddered. 'I'm glad you've got rid of those, Ella.'

'So am I, they sound grim.' The lovely white dog trotted over and plonked itself at Ella's feet, staring up at her with a happy face. Ella stroked her head, and Lizzie saw the cottage door open and the children wave before they ran inside. Lizzie waved back with a grin as Ella continued. 'The house had already been refurbished when I arrived, so I didn't see it at its worst. We usually give guests a quick tour but I'm sure you already know your way around. Maybe we could get together over the weekend, if you have time, for a few stories?'

'We'd love that,' Lizzie said firmly, mentally shoving away more memories. She was going to do whatever it took to make this weekend special for Gemma and plan a wonderful wedding as well. 'I'm sure we'll have time.'

Ella was still stroking Prim, who was nudging her leg gently, as though asking why they weren't going inside the cottage in search of family or food. 'I was so sorry to hear about your wedding being cancelled after the hotel closed, Gemma. Such awful timing.'

'Thanks, Ella, it really was. The first cancellation with Covid was one thing, but two is starting to look suspicious.' Gemma's smile was rueful. 'I'm hoping you're going to come to our rescue. Mum said she'd spoken with you about holding the reception here and the date's free.'

'It is, I've blocked the weekend off until you decide.' One of the children emerged shrieking from the cottage and Ella looked over her shoulder. Arlo was clutching an iPad with an irate Lily hot on his heels, and Prim shot off to join them. 'Sorry, I'd better go and sort them out. Sandy, the rector at the church, has a ceramics studio here and she mentioned you're meeting with her to see if she can take the service. Why don't we get together after that and talk through your ideas for the reception? I'm sure we can work around the plans you've already made, and we have contacts with many of the local producers and suppliers.'

'That sounds wonderful, thank you so much.' Gemma let out a breath as she grinned, and Lizzie was filled with relief. They had a venue, and it was going to be Halesmere House. She had to focus on the plans they needed to make and keep all thoughts of Cal Ryan from her mind. There was work for her to be done this weekend, however much time she, Gemma and Bea were supposed to be spending retreating from ordinary life.

'I had a quick look around the courtyard earlier,' Lizzie said causally. Her tongue felt thick as she did exactly what she'd told Gemma she wouldn't, feeling the heat of her friend's stare. 'I can't wait to explore the studios. Are they all occupied? I'm hoping to find something gorgeous to take home with me.'

'Oh, you'll definitely be able to do that. Marta's candles are so elegant and smell amazing, our cottage is full of them. If jewellery's your thing, then make sure you check out Ana's work, her bracelets are exquisite. They're a great bunch, Sandy of course being one of them. So, your weekend?'

Lizzie hoped she had disguised her disappointment at learning nothing more about Cal. Ella glanced at the children running down the drive and pulled out a phone, unlocking the screen. 'You've got the itinerary for the weekend, Gemma, and if there's anything you want to change just let me know. I'll meet you down at the tarn in an hour. Everything you ordered is ready for you in the house and supper tonight is a smorgasbord platter, it's perfect with a gin and tonic to start. You just need to toast the baguette and there's chocolate ginger cookies for after, nice and light.'

'Wow, that sounds amazing!' Gemma's face lit up. 'I can't wait to try everything.'

Lizzie hadn't got beyond the mention of the tarn. She'd never forgotten finding Cal's note pinned to the birch, the memory of the morning he'd left running on a loop through her mind. 'The tarn? What are we doing there?'

Gemma squeezed her hand. 'Ella's taking us kayaking. She thought it would be a lovely way to start the weekend.'

'Just a gentle paddle to appreciate the view and ease you into the retreat.' Ella grinned. 'I used to row competitively before university took over and I like the practice. I was also a chef before I came to Halesmere and it's good to keep my hand in cooking for the retreats.'

'Now I'm looking forward to dinner even more.' Lizzie nudged Gemma, doing her very best to convey total enthusiasm. 'I hope my wetsuit still fits, Gem. That water doesn't warm up very often.'

'You'll be fine,' Gemma assured her and Lizzie nodded firmly.

'We're just across the drive if you need anything, and you can message me if that's easier.' Ella glanced at the children running back towards the cottage. 'The studios will be open in the morning so there'll be visitors wandering around the courtyard. Obviously, the house and gardens are private and there's a separate entrance and car park so they shouldn't get in your way. Occasionally somebody takes a wrong turn, and we point them in the right direction again. Or Prim does.'

'Thanks, Ella.' Gemma's arm was still through Lizzie's. 'See you in a bit.'

–

'A wetsuit? Why would I need one of those before we eat? I thought you were joking.' Gemma's second bridesmaid Bea had just arrived, hugged her and Lizzie hello, exclaimed over the beauty of the house and wondered loudly how they'd managed to grow up here so far from town. Now Bea's hands were planted on her hips, a large tote over one arm and huge sunglasses hiding her eyes. 'Have you any idea how long it's taken me to get here and now you're telling me the first thing we're doing is going in the water? What happened to our cocktails?'

'Not actually in the water, Bea, unless you capsize. The idea isn't to get wet. What's the worst that can happen?' Lizzie laughed as Bea pushed the sunglasses up and raised her eyebrows with a knowing look.

'Yeah, well, you just said it. Get wet before we have a drink.' Bea grinned as she pointed keys at her car to pop the boot.

Gemma and Bea had met in halls at university in Leeds when they were both studying law. They'd become close friends, seeing one another through the highs and occasional lows of moving away from home and learning how to adult.

Short and curvy with long dark hair, Bea had inherited her love of good craic from her Irish mum, and her confidence and warm nature from her Barbadian dad. Bea was also fiercely loyal, a master of debate and utterly passionate about family law, in which she now practised as a barrister. Her absolute favourite thing was being underestimated in court and she used her beauty and razor-sharp intellect to great effect.

Lizzie, Gemma and Bea had had many a fun night out over the years, with flourishing careers no hindrance to them continuing whenever they could. It was three weeks since they'd last been together, though crisis wedding calls were a constant right now.

Lizzie was at the car before Gemma and she reached inside. 'Bea, seriously, how many coats? The weather's meant to be glorious this weekend.'

'Ha! I'm not falling for that one. You both messaged to remind me the weather here can turn in an instant and to bring plenty of layers. I'm not planning to get soaked halfway up a hill just because the sun's shining when we set out. And what's with all the secrecy, Gem? What else have you got planned for us this weekend that you didn't want to share?'

'You'll see,' Gemma said airily. She'd followed Lizzie to help, and her arms were full of the coats as she led the way back to the house. 'And you'll love it, I promise.'

'You promised me a great meal with cocktails and right now that's all I can think about.' Bea collected another bag and set off after them. 'Come on then, let's get this weekend started, Bridezilla.'

'Don't call me that.' Gemma flashed Bea a mock glare. 'I'll only be invoking Bridezilla if I come away from here on Monday without the church booked and a wedding planned.'

Lizzie laughed, beginning to feel more like herself again now they were all together. She ignored the court-yard as she crossed the drive, refusing to give in to the desire to check for another glimpse of Cal.

–

'Leave my phone in my room? No posts? All weekend? You're not serious?' Bea was glaring at Gemma, the tote at her feet and phone in hand. They hadn't got further than admiring the beautiful grand piano in the large hall and mutiny was already breaking out. Evening sunlight was pouring down from a huge atrium onto cream walls, catching the glint of glass on cabinets and the wooden floor, partly covered with a colourful rug.

'But this place is made for Instagram, Gem, I've been following the house since you called the other day.' Bea looked like she might stamp one foot still clad in high heels. 'And I've promised the whole family, including Matteo's, that I'll be posting at least twice a day to show them what we're up to.' Matteo was Bea's gorgeous husband, a successful chef who she had met at university and married soon after.

'Then message them tonight and tell them you can't.' Gemma rolled her eyes. 'This is meant to be a rewilding experience, Bea, connecting with our surroundings and each other. How are we meant to do that if we're permanently tethered to our technology?'

'iPad?' Bea was looking a shade less mutinous and she picked up her bag.

'No. There's Wi-Fi but surely we can all learn to do without it, just for a few days.'

'Oh Gem, come on! You know what my family is like. If I'm not visible on social media every few hours Mum starts to panic and pester Dad to send out a search party.'

'Tell them you're perfectly fine and not going to be in touch until Monday.' Gemma injected a sweeter tone into her voice. 'Don't make me invoke Bridezilla yet, Bea. Because I can and you won't like it.'

'You know my mum doesn't trust silence, she only likes noise and being kept in the ever-expanding loop of her children's lives.' Bea slumped into a chair with an exaggerated sigh and Lizzie laughed as Gemma headed towards the stairs.

This was fine. They were going to be fine. They had the house and garden all to themselves, and she wouldn't go looking. Wouldn't search out all the places she and Cal had explored or remember the nights they'd spent together in his tent. He was her past, and her friends were her present and her future. It was all very simple.

'Are you going to tell us what we're doing tomorrow?' Bea had a glint in her eye now. 'I take it this rewilding thing means we're going to be outside again?'

'I know as much as you, Bea, and I'm assuming so.' Lizzie linked arms with her as Bea stood up and they set off up the wide staircase behind Gemma. 'There's not much rewilding we can do in the house.'

'Oh, all right, let the fun commence. I'm up for anything, as long as I can do one tiny post a day. Just one.' Bea had caught Gemma up and gave her a pleading look between long, dark eyelashes.

'One,' Gemma warned her. 'Don't think I won't be checking. You can post as much as you like once we've left and returned to normal life.' They reached the landing and she pointed to her left. 'You're down there, Lizzie, in the East room as you love the morning sun. Bea's in the West room on the other side.' Gemma grinned. 'And I'm in the master, because, you know…'

'Bridezilla,' Lizzie and Bea chorused, and they all laughed as they disappeared to their rooms.

Chapter 5

The kayaking was a success and Bea loved it, happy to partner with Ella who took her through the basics. Gemma and Lizzie had done it before and as it was such a lovely warm evening, especially for late April, they opted to leave the wetsuits behind, wearing shorts and T-shirts instead. Bea was already defying orders and capturing everything on her phone, and Lizzie couldn't blame her for exclaiming at the views. High rocky crags and fells were achingly familiar, blunt, grey and emerging green against blue skies, and she felt a sharp jolt of longing for her camera to capture it all, left behind in her room in case it got a soaking.

They chatted about the wedding as they glided side by side on the water and Lizzie knew Gemma had set her heart on holding it at Halesmere. Ella was interested in hearing more about Lizzie's business, explaining that she used to work for a catering company who created high-end events and parties, often for corporate clients. The big event in their lives now, she said with a smile, was planning Arlo's fifth birthday party next month, and apparently sheep and dogs would be involved. Before Ella left them for the evening, they arranged to meet her back at the tarn at eight in the morning for their first wild swim.

The sun was slipping down behind the fells and the scent of honeysuckle was in the air as Lizzie, Gemma and

Bea brought dinner out onto the terrace, desperate not to miss a minute of such rare and glorious weather so early in spring. Wooden chairs snug with cosy cushions were comfortable as they shared cocktails, relaxed and energised by their first activity. Lizzie felt a little of the load she'd been carrying since Gemma had first mentioned returning to Halesmere lighten, tilting her face to enjoy the last of the sun.

'So how's things with Jack, then?' Bea put her empty cocktail glass down and uncorked a bottle of white wine Ella had included with their meal. 'You haven't found anywhere else yet?'

'No. I've looked at a couple of places, but they just didn't feel right.' Lizzie pushed a tomato around her plate, uncomfortably aware that both of her friends were settled with homes of their own and she was about to go back to living like a student again. Her thirtieth birthday was close and another house share hadn't been in the master plan for that milestone.

'What about a place of your own?' Bea got straight to the point. 'Your business is growing now, surely that's an option?'

'It is doing better, thankfully. But I'd rather share for now than spend more of my savings on a flat just for me. I don't want to get tied up in a long-term lease and I'm paying for the office space as well.'

'Better that than working from a bedroom in Jack's house. You could stay with me and Matteo, Lizzie, if it helps.' Bea was savouring that first taste of excellent wine. 'Leeds isn't a million miles away and you mentioned you're already doing some meetings online anyway.'

'Thanks Bea, that's so generous.' Lizzie gave her a grateful smile. 'It's probably a bit far with the work I have here but it's very kind of you.'

'Plus I don't think it's doing you any good, mooching around Jack's house. Unless you're planning on getting back together?'

'There's no chance of that,' Lizzie said firmly. 'It took me long enough to decide to move in with him, I don't fancy getting another WhatsApp asking if I know about him and Wendy whatshername from school.'

'Dead right.' Bea was already topping up glasses. 'You need to move on ASAP, Lizzie. The minute Jack casts his eye over some other woman he'll be shoving you out the door before you can say "cheating shit".'

'Funny, I never had him down as the cheating sort,' Gemma said thoughtfully. 'He just seemed so straightforward and quite boyish, like Harry Potter all grown up. Cute glasses, floppy hair.'

'Yeah, I thought that too,' Lizzie said dryly. She'd been desperately hurt by the knowledge that Jack had spent a night away with one of his pupil's mums, but she knew she wasn't heartbroken. For two years she'd believed she had found something with him that would see them into a future together, until he'd shattered her trust so thoughtlessly for something he'd assured her meant nothing, which seemed even worse. But then they'd both been distracted and under pressure with lockdown, distant, unseeing of one another sometimes. Their problems hadn't been all his fault, she knew that.

'Are you sure you're not being too hasty, Lizzie? There's no chance you can work things out?'

'You're not serious, Gem? What, you're suggesting I sit around and wait for him to cheat on me again?'

'No, of course not. You'd need to resolve some stuff first. It's just, I know what you're like. One strike and you're out. You've always been like that, ever since...' Gemma tailed off, her smile apologetic.

'Ever since Cal, you mean,' Lizzie said flatly.

Gemma reached for her hand. 'No one's perfect, Lizzie. I know you know that, and I also know why you do it. You're just trying to protect your heart before someone else smashes it for you. But if you love someone, you'll have to find a way of forgiving them their mistakes, just like they will you. Maybe you haven't ever forgiven Cal for what he did, and you use that as a benchmark for everyone else.'

'I haven't forgiven him, Gemma, how could I? I never had the chance because he was never sorry for what he did.'

'I know this a bit deep for a Friday night, but I think him leaving the way he did was his way of protecting himself. And I'm not for a second suggesting he was right – he hurt you too badly for that – but you do the same when you're threatened, you back off and shut down your feelings. What happened to you and your parents, and when it did, was a very big deal, Lizzie, and it's not surprising it changed you. One day I hope you'll love someone enough to let them in and please, please, don't let the fear of losing your own home stop you from ever making a proper one. I don't think it's good for you, bouncing from one place to the next the way you do.'

'I'm not doing it on purpose, Gemma,' Lizzie said heatedly at the sharp reminder of her past and her parents. She was shocked by Gemma's words and the memory of her own failings with Cal, the guilt over her assumptions towards him that had never quite abated. Lizzie's hand slid from Gemma's and she reached for her glass. 'I hadn't exactly planned that Jack and I would split. I know you're concerned about me but I'm fine, honestly. And you're right, this is definitely too deep for a Friday night. Could someone please refill my wine, I think we're going to need another bottle after that.'

The second bottle of wine was quickly opened and the three of them saw off a platter of spicy hummus, freshly made tomato jam, goat's cheese, olives, and almonds with toasted baguettes followed by the ginger cookies. They sat out until the daylight had long disappeared, making new plans for the wedding. They could do no more until Gemma had met with Sandy to arrange the service and they shared hugs when they eventually parted late.

Lizzie woke before six after a restless night, despite the benefit of a luxurious mattress and soft Egyptian cotton sheets. She jolted up in bed as she remembered the shock of seeing Cal so unexpectedly, then slipped from underneath the duvet to open the curtains. The glorious spring sunshine from yesterday had given way to a cloudy morning and still her spirits lifted at the once-familiar view.

Silvery drops of dew were glittering on the lawn, a blackbird hopping busily across the grass. Last night, kayaking around the tarn, Ella had explained that Max was a landscape architect and he'd just finished rebuilding the garden, which was stunning in its elegant simplicity. Early perennials were beginning to flower among spring bulbs, and Lizzie didn't need all her event planning experience to understand that Halesmere would be a glorious setting for Gemma and Simon's wedding reception.

She glanced at the camera beside her bed, a flicker of excitement stirring. She checked her phone and knew she had time. They weren't meeting Ella for the swim until eight and breakfast would come after. This was the golden hour and now Lizzie was away from the city she had an overwhelming urge not to miss it. She threw on her yoga kit and picked up the Nikon, feeling its familiar contours and weight, the rightness of it in her hand as she lifted it from the case and ran downstairs, the rest of the house silent.

She loved the fresh air on her face as she stepped onto the terrace and quietly closed the French doors. Back in Carlisle it was all noise, traffic and people, and this felt like coming home as she took in the fells and crags on the horizon. She set up the camera and took a few shots of plants and the blackbird now singing in a holly tree, then a stone wall bordering the garden, its pale colours a contrast to the glossy green shrubs planted in front of it. She was out of practice and she pulled a face when she checked the small screen.

But the pleasure in what she was doing, as she refocussed her lens on an elegant, handcrafted wooden gate leading to the meadow, felt utterly joyful. She laughed, hearing her own happiness floating on the morning air.

She captured everything that caught her eye: the bright green leaf unfurling on an ancient lilac tree; a sheep offering a beady stare, its dark body a sharp contrast to the white on its face. She altered the focus and caught an early morning hiker on a fell, the flash of red clothing as they strode on to the summit ahead.

She wished she'd worn her swimsuit beneath her yoga kit as she strolled along to the tarn, then she could have waited for the others here instead of having to return to the house and change. The scene was constantly shifting as glimpses of sunlight landed on the fells between the clouds, altering the view in an instant. Lizzie had to be quick to capture it, elated at being back in this special place.

Why had she stayed away so long and banished her own self from all that she loved about this valley? Cal was history, no longer part of her life and she'd moved on a long time ago. He couldn't hurt her now or jolt her off balance for a second time this weekend.

At the water's edge she lifted the camera to frame a heron across the tarn, but her hand stilled. Her lens had picked up not the large, grey bird hovering on the bank among the reeds, but someone swimming towards her, cutting through the water with a stroke that spoke of years of experience.

She froze as alarm darted through her. She didn't need the man to raise his head for her to know he had cropped hair she wasn't yet used to, or watch him walk to recognise that loping, easy stride he'd always had. Lizzie was caught, trapped between wanting to run and daring to stay as she hid her face behind the camera.

He reached the shallows and stood, running both hands over his face, and she saw his sudden indecision as he halted. He glanced to her left and her gaze followed, spying the T-shirt and shorts she hadn't noticed before sitting on the bank. So he still liked to swim naked and her body ignited into a dangerous awareness of how he looked in this moment. She refocussed the lens on him and pure instinct had her clicking the button before she lost the shot.

It wasn't difficult to identify the changes from the young man she'd once known, and Lizzie was angry with herself for so easily appreciating how he'd matured. The shoulders wider, muscles running from his neck to well-defined biceps. And when had he developed pecs quite like that, covered with golden brown hair, or the six pack being revealed with every hesitant step he took?

Her eyes snagged on his left arm and the single tattoo of a tribal wolf running from shoulder to elbow, its jaws raised in a silent howl. His right arm was inked from shoulder to wrist, but she couldn't interpret all the images from where she stood. She spotted a surfer on his board skimming the waves below a monochrome mountain range, the ridges rising to a night sky lit by a moon. Her stomach was fizzing madly, her mouth dry.

'I wondered if you'd be here. Ach, it was always your favourite time.' He lifted a hand to the view but Lizzie had eyes only for him, the first real opportunity she had to share her contempt at how he'd left her, the hurt she'd carried all this time. Anger flared again as heat rose on her cheeks and the camera fell from her face to swing on its strap. His voice, that soft lilting accent she'd always loved, seemed edged with something different now. Was it Kiwi? She had no idea and wasn't planning on hanging around to find out.

'So you thought you'd pop down for an early swim and catch me out.' She couldn't keep the sarcasm from her words as she backed away.

'I had no idea you were going to be at Halesmere, I swear.'

'Neither did I. I'd never have come if I had.'

Cal was wading from the water, and she turned before it was too late and she couldn't make herself leave. She still wanted him, and she hated that the years of separation hadn't changed even this. The love she'd once had for him, she would have to think about later, when she was very far from this place, and him.

'Lizzie, wait. You might want to know I'm—'

She wasn't going to wait, not for anything right now and certainly not for him. She wasn't interested in anything he might want to tell her. Her own thoughts were a mess again and it was going to be hard enough to sort through them and see where they landed without talking to him.

She ran back through the meadow and the gate rattled behind her as she slammed it. Little more than twelve hours at Halesmere and she'd already seen Cal twice. And there was still another two days and two nights to come before she could return to the city and what remained of her normal life. Right now Carlisle and all that waited for her there was looking like more of a retreat than Halesmere House ever would.

After a glass of water and forty unsettled minutes in her room, Lizzie was back at the tarn with Gemma and Bea. Cal was gone, having typically left no sign to suggest he'd even been there. Only her camera could provide the evidence, the vision she'd captured of him emerging from the water imprinted just as clearly in her mind.

Ella was already there with Gemma and Bea in wetsuits this time – Lizzie hadn't even thought of hers, she was so distracted. Ella talked them through what to expect from the swim, how their bodies would respond to the cold and the best way to combat the shock.

Slowly they waded in, Gemma swearing like a trooper as they went deeper. Bea wasn't easily dissuaded from any challenge unless it was avoiding social media, and Lizzie noticed her mouth was set in a grim line as she too tried to adjust to the sudden drop in temperature. The water would be warmer in the afternoon, but Ella assured them there was nothing like a quick early morning swim in the open to set them up for the day.

They didn't stay in long and they'd all brought warm robes to change into, leaving the wetsuits in the shade of a nearby tree to dry out. Ella left to return to her family and it wasn't long before the three of them followed, energised and hungry, bringing their breakfast into the garden now the sun had broken through. Gemma and Lizzie knew all too well that weather such as this in Cumbria wouldn't last forever and they wanted to make the best of every moment. They settled in a cosy gazebo on wrought iron chairs, still in their robes, the sun glinting through leaded windows to warm them.

Gemma held up two large glass storage jars. 'Cinnamon and cherry granola or apricot and ginger? Homemade of course, apparently it comes from the community shop. Cereal only ever came in boxes when we lived here, didn't it, Lizzie?' Everyone opted for ginger and Gemma shared some between three bowls before slanting a look in Lizzie's direction. 'So. Cal.'

'What about him?' Lizzie asked, watching Gemma add yoghurt so thick to her granola that the spoon stood straight up in the bowl. Lizzie helped herself to a dollop of local honey as well and offered it round. She never ate breakfast as good as this back in Carlisle.

'I saw Ana earlier, one of the artists based here, and asked her about the others as well. I thought it was the easiest way to find out without giving away our interest in him.'

'Wait, let me get this straight.' Bea's spoon clattered against her bowl. 'Cal? As in the very same Cal who broke Lizzie's heart? He's here?'

'Unfortunately.' Lizzie softened her sharp reply with a smile, stirring the honey into the yoghurt and turning it gold. She supposed they couldn't have kept it from eagle-eyed Bea for long, despite Lizzie's intention of not speaking about him. 'We sort of bumped into him last night and Gemma offered to find out why he's back at Halesmere.'

Lizzie wasn't about to mention seeing him again this morning. She'd checked the shot of him when she'd returned to her room and it was perfect. He was her foreground, the light falling onto the fell behind him, water glistening on his body. He was still as beautiful and easy in front of her lens. She'd make herself delete it later – it wasn't a memento of this weekend she ought to keep.

'I'm all ears.' Bea sat back and Lizzie knew that sharp focus in her eyes. She was an excellent listener with a prodigious memory for detail. Whatever Lizzie might miss in the fog of her current mood, she'd be able to get it later from Bea. If she actually wanted to, which seemed unlikely.

'It's quite the story.' Gemma was casually helping herself to fresh fruit and Lizzie guessed she was trying to spare her feelings if she could. 'So long to short, he moved to New Zealand, which we knew about. Job in construction for a few years, travels, then starts up a sustainable clothing business with two friends, becomes the face of the brand when the early beach shots he's in go viral. Huge success follows, and eventually he and the partners sell to an American company who take it global.'

Lizzie seemed to have lost her breath, her resolve to avoid the details of his life already crumbling. Cal was a businessman? A brand? A bricklayer? All of those things, or none? Was triumph and apparent wealth what the past twelve years had brought for him, while she'd settled down with a boyfriend she wasn't certain about and had given up on her own happy ending as she busied herself planning them for everyone else?

'Then he walks away from the brand, the business, everything. Goes to art school in New Zealand and – get this – he's a blacksmith now.' Gemma sat back with a satisfied smile, her bowl full of breakfast she hadn't yet touched. 'Gave away most of the money he made from the company, kept enough to set himself up when he moved back here and apparently invested in a business in Cornwall. He took over the old forge after the studios were relaunched and accepts commissions.'

'So he actually works here now? He has his own studio?' Lizzie felt nauseous, the few mouthfuls of granola stirring uneasily in her stomach. 'Perfect.'

'Seems so.' Gemma reached out a sympathetic hand and Bea did the same, covering both of Lizzie's. 'It's just a weekend, hon, we'll get you through it.'

'The way I see it, you have two choices.' Bea was always decisive, and she leaned closer to Lizzie. 'You can pin him down and find out what the hell he was thinking, leaving you that way, and move on. Or you can take the opportunity to tell him once and for all to fu—'

'I get it,' Lizzie said dryly. 'Thanks. Your second option's looking good right now, Bea.'

'Yeah, well, I know you, Lizzie Martin.' Gemma was blunt. 'You'll start with two and before we leave here on Monday, you'll be asking him for the first one as well.'

'I will not.' Lizzie didn't need to force the indignation out.

'I bet he's good with his hands, though. I wonder what he makes?' Gemma took a dreamy mouthful of triple berry smoothie and caught sight of Lizzie's face. 'Sorry.'

'So how's the rest of our day looking?' Bea had her phone face down on the table and Gemma glanced it with raised eyebrows. 'Just the one post, I promise.'

Gemma's hand was hovering above her own phone and Lizzie tried to relax into the excitement she heard in her friend's voice. 'I've got absolutely the best thing planned for us today. I was waiting for confirmation, and I've just had the email to say it's on.'

'Go on.' Bea leaned back. 'Please tell me I don't have to get soaked for a third time?'

'You won't get wet. Not unless you fall in the lake on the way.' Gemma was dividing her triumphant attention between Bea and Lizzie. 'We're going walking with wolves. Isn't it amazing? I literally can't wait. It's all part of our rewilding experience and connecting with nature, taking time to really be in the moment and step back. And the wolves are going to help us do that.'

'Wolves?' Bea snatched up her phone with a grin. 'That sounds incredible, I'm so up for that. I don't care what you say about technology, Gem, my phone's going with me. I'm posting about it for sure.'

'You can take it, but you probably won't be able to use it while we're with them. They're wild animals, we can't expect them not to notice if our phones are beeping every five seconds.' Gemma's grin was wide. 'We'll find out later. We're hiking to the enclosure from here with a guide and a picnic lunch, and the wolves are part of the experience. Lizzie? What do you think?'

'It sounds amazing, Gem.' She was concentrating on not letting her fingers tremble around the smoothie she was holding. Gemma must have forgotten, and Lizzie couldn't blame her. She'd already had an encounter with wolves in her past, from the belated birthday gift she'd given Cal twelve years ago. Her mind jumped back to the tarn this morning, and the tattoo of the wolf running down his arm. But she wasn't about to let her friend suspect there were more memories of that summer with him already stirring at the thought of seeing those exceptional animals again. 'Perfect for our rewilding weekend.'

'It really is.' Gemma's eyes were shining. 'After the hike we can chill in our rooms or the hammocks in the garden. Then dinner outside again and stargazing to set us up for another good night's sleep.'

'What time are we seeing Sandy tomorrow?' Lizzie put her glass down and focussed on finishing the bowl of granola. She needed to eat if they were going hiking, however much she didn't feel like it right now.

'Twelve, after she's taken the morning service. I thought I might walk down and join her for it. Simon won't mind what the church is like as long as we've got something booked.' Gemma was pouring coffee from a cafetière, and she pushed a cup towards Lizzie. 'Then Ella suggested we could have lunch with her and Max at the pub, if you fancy it.'

'Sure, sounds good.' Lizzie swallowed. Another old haunt. She was starting to feel like Ebenezer Scrooge as her past life flashed before her eyes. Maybe this weekend was supposed to be telling her something after all. Keep away from gorgeous ex-boyfriends, she thought, choking back a wild giggle. That was all she needed to do, and it would be easy enough once she had the motorway and the mountains back between them. It wasn't like she and Cal were going to be spending any time together.

Chapter 6

Lizzie had never stamped her foot in her life and right now she'd never wanted to do it more. Even Gemma paled and swore under her breath when they gathered in the courtyard and saw their guide walking to meet them. Cal slung a large rucksack over both shoulders and his gaze flickered uncertainly from Lizzie to her friends until he pulled down polarised sunglasses to shield his eyes. She wished she'd thought to do it first; hers were still holding back her blonde hair from her face.

'I know,' she murmured, squeezing Gemma's hand, her other grasping the camera hung around her neck, itching to hide herself behind its lens. 'It's not your fault.'

'It sort of is. I arranged it with Ella, but I had no idea he was involved.' Gemma tugged Lizzie closer to mutter into her ear. 'Look, we don't have to go with him, I'll tell him to sod off. We can walk on our own and there's enough food in the fridge to feed a family. It's not like we don't know our way around.'

Lizzie knew the landscape here better than she knew the city where she now lived, and for a second she was tempted by Gemma's offer. But her two friends were excited to have a guide lead them into something special and she found a quick, brittle laugh. 'Why would we do that? We're here to have a good time and it's apparently Cal's job to provide it.'

'That's Cal? Seriously? Shit, Lizzie, you never said he looked like that.' Used to being in court, Bea's voice always carried. Lizzie gave her a sharp nudge.

'Yeah, well, he was skinnier back in the day. No tattoos,' she hissed. The T-shirt he wore seemed moulded to his chest and she scowled, wondering if he bought it smaller on purpose to outline his shoulders and arms so impressively.

He'd never been vain when she'd known him, or aware of his looks and the impact they sometimes had on people around him, girls mostly. Several times Lizzie had seen them melt away when she'd turned up at the pub to wait for him. She and Cal would leave together, stopping every few yards up the lane for the kisses they'd waited all day to share.

The introductions were tricky, and Bea was cool now she'd quickly got over her first impression. She offered a hand to Cal, forcing him to take it as Gemma and Lizzie kept theirs to themselves. He settled for a polite greeting to the two women he'd known nearly half his life ago.

'Good to go?' He seemed to be directing his attention to Bea and Gemma, and that annoyed Lizzie even more. She was far from invisible in their little group and if anyone was going to be doing the ignoring around here, it would be her. 'We'll head out past the garden and make our way to the lake through the woods.'

He paused to check his comment had registered as only Bea nodded. 'Ella said you wanted fairly low-level, not too much climbing. This walk is around eight kilometres, and we'll spend an hour or so at the enclosure with the wolves. If we're lucky we might see red squirrels, maybe some roe deer, but it's not really the best time of day for that. There's quite a lot of birdlife so I'll tell you what to look out for and when, if that's your thing.'

Cal nodded over to Lizzie and she and Gemma fell into step behind him. Tomorrow morning they had a choice between yoga or a mindfulness session in the barn and right now Lizzie was opting for yoga; she didn't want any more ideas on how to be 'in the moment', unless they could teach her how to *escape* the moment and put her mind somewhere else instead. The only tiny consolation was that Cal looked as uncomfortable as she felt.

Once they'd left the courtyard the track was wide enough for two abreast and Bea slotted in beside Cal, tilting her head to look up at him.

'Have you been guiding a while, Cal?' She sounded innocent enough and Lizzie was familiar with the casual tone her friend was employing, hiding Bea's steely determination. Lizzie might have decided she'd rather not search out more information on this man, but apparently Bea wasn't going to pass up a golden opportunity when it landed in her lap.

Lizzie was staring at the back of his head, the short hair, deep suntan on his neck revealing a life still lived outdoors. Her fingers on her camera, she removed the cap from the lens, focussing it to take a quick shot of an ancient sycamore tree that looked as though it belonged in Middle Earth. She'd dared Cal to climb it once and he'd shimmied nearly to the top with effortless ease as she'd laughed in astonishment from the ground.

'I've just completed my training and set up a mountain leader business,' Cal replied casually. 'I did some guiding when I lived in New Zealand, and Ella and Max have been generous enough to give me work through the retreats.'

'So what else do you do? Navigation, that sort of thing?'

'Yes, mountaineering, trad climbing, bouldering. Anything on the fells really, small groups, one to one. I'm qualified to train as well.'

'I'm sure you're very good. And New Zealand, that sounds gorgeous.' Bea's legs were working quickly to keep pace with the stride Lizzie knew Cal had already shortened. 'I have an auntie who lives in Wellington. Is that near where you were?'

Cal took a drink from a water bottle he'd pulled from his rucksack and Lizzie noticed a tension in his shoulders, a tightness to the tone of his voice that was usually softer.

'Not really.' He replaced the bottle and glanced at Bea. 'I lived in a place north of Auckland, on the coast. Wellington's pretty far south of that.'

'I bet you surfed, didn't you?'

'Why would you say that?'

'Like, duh! You're such a surfer, I can tell.' Bea was looking pointedly at his right arm. 'And your tattoos, of course. The surfer one is pretty cool. Bet that hurt.'

'Thanks.' He ignored her quip about the pain. 'So how do you three know each other?'

Lizzie wondered if he was playing Bea at her own game and doing a little digging of his own. His question sounded innocent enough, a guide making casual conversation with his clients. Did he wonder how Lizzie had spent the last twelve years? If she ever thought of him? Would she admit that she did, especially now?

'Oh, Gemma and I have been friends since our first year at university. Then I met Lizzie through her and we're all close now. Gemma's getting married, did you know?'

'No. Congratulations.' Cal offered the word to Gemma over his shoulder and a nod was the extent of her equally cool thanks. He picked up the pace as they walked through a woodland full of conifers, some of which had been felled, and he informed them it was to make way for a mix of deciduous trees to increase biodiversity on the land.

Lizzie was trying to memorise the changes in the land-scape she'd always loved, having to catch the others up after a quick halt to snap dappled light on the vivid shade of bluebells. She hid a smile as she realised Bea hadn't yet finished with Cal, her questions like guided and fully loaded missiles.

'My husband Matteo would love your T-shirt, where did you get it? Will I find one in a local shop?'

'This?' Cal's laugh seemed self-conscious as he glanced down, as though he'd forgotten what he was wearing. 'You can get them online. I think a few shops here stock them.'

'It's a great fit on you and obviously made for wearing outdoors; it definitely looks breathable. What's the brand?' Bea was relentless when she wanted to be, never one to back down if victory was within her grasp. Lizzie was almost starting to feel sorry for Cal. Almost. She could only admire Bea in the face of his reluctance. He probably had no idea he was dealing with a tough barrister who always got her questions answered.

'Er, it's called Apera.'

'Thanks, I'll be sure to check it out. Moss green is definitely your colour, has anyone ever told you that?'

'Funnily enough, no.'

'It works really well with your hair. So why the name Apera? Do you know?'

He gave Bea a patient smile, accepting her tenacity and giving in to it. 'It means breath in Māori.'

'That's very cool. I'd love to hear more about New Zealand, it must have been amazing.'

'Not much to tell. Had a job, went to work, saw friends. Surfed, climbed a bit.' He shrugged. 'Just life. I'm sure you know how it is.'

'What made you come back to the UK? Family? My mum's from Fermanagh and there's definitely a similarity in your accents.'

Lizzie could imagine exactly the purse of his lips without needing to see his face. He used to hate being challenged, having to reveal anything of himself. She held her breath. So many of the questions she longed to ask him herself hinged on his next reply as she waited for him to brush Bea off. The path narrowed as they left the woodland and snaked along the edge of a meadow full of emerging wildflowers.

'I suppose you could say that. Ach, it was time. This place is home for me.'

Cal indicated Bea should step in front of him, and Gemma followed as Lizzie tried to process the astonishment snatching at her concentration. What did that mean? He'd left what little connection he had to Ireland years ago. Did he have a partner now, with a family of his own? Did it matter? Had he ever found his father? Was he sending her a message, speaking in some sort of code or just being polite to Bea? All these thoughts were bouncing through Lizzie's mind and she wasn't expecting the broad expanse of his back thudding against her chest when he halted, her hand automatically flying to his shoulder to steady herself.

'Sorry.' She jumped back as he spun around, her heel catching an exposed tree root, twisted and uneven beneath her boot. His own hand was swift on her upper arm as it shot out to catch her, averting her fall. Their eyes locked together, the shock of their contact reflected in his before he blanked it from her sight.

The last time they'd touched was still seared in her mind – that kiss twelve years ago in the restaurant, the night he'd run out of her life. Her body remembered too, the spike in her adrenaline alerting her to the flare of desire she couldn't prevent. He snatched his hand from her arm but it made no difference, she could still feel the heat of his fingers as though he hadn't yet let her go.

'Ach, Lizzie, you were always doing that.' A memory surfacing, a quirk to one corner of his mouth.

'Doing what?' She couldn't think, her mind slower than her body and still processing the craving for more of his touch, hearing her name again on his lips.

'Not looking where you put your feet, usually because you were staring through your camera. I'm happy to see you've still got it. You were grand.'

'It's just a hobby.' One she hadn't practised for a long time, and she'd missed it. Over Cal's shoulder Lizzie could see Gemma watching them, and she went to step around him.

'You're a photographer at heart, Lizzie, where it matters.' He paused. 'Don't you think we should talk?'

'What, now?' Her laugh was startled, defensive, as she was stilled by him once again. This weekend wasn't yet twenty-four hours old and already she'd realised a part of her heart belonged irrevocably to him. It had taken her a very long time to remove the rest from a grasp he probably didn't even know how fully he'd had.

'After twelve years you'd like a little chat? About what, exactly? Walking out on me the way you did, twice if you count the restaurant. Or how you must've known it would be impossible for me to find you when you left? I couldn't even check to see if you were okay, not that you ever thought to check on me. You had my number. You knew where I would be.'

Sorrow and hurt were framed in her face as she finally gave way to her anger, her voice a furious mutter she hoped wasn't carrying to her friends. 'I don't see the point in us having a conversation. It's too late, Cal. I'm out there, with my own business, on social media, a website, using my name. You could've found me any time you liked. Please don't pretend you were looking for an opportunity to talk for any other reason than I just happened to turn up.'

He reached out, one finger touching hers as he stopped short of taking her hand to delay her. Lizzie's gaze fell to take it in, the burn of his skin on hers, the memories of their love she'd locked away surging straight back.

'I've been sorry since the moment I walked away, Lizzie. I wish I hadn't put you through that.' Cal glanced over his shoulder. Gemma and Bea were chatting and pretending not to notice what was going on. 'We can't talk here, we're keeping them waiting. Please, Lizzie? I owe you an explanation. And an apology.'

Hopelessness was filling her soul and Lizzie tried to blink back the hurt, somehow just as sharp in this moment with him now as it had been that morning twelve years ago. 'There's no point. We both did what we did, let's just leave it. I'm here for my friends, not the past. We've got plans and you've got form, I'm not going to be waiting for you to show up.'

She stepped around him and caught up with Gemma and Bea, leaving Cal at the rear as they set off. Lizzie was trying to focus on the landscape through her lens, watching for the instant when the light changed. She framed a round, half-submerged rock in the lake, breaking clouds scudding across the sky as the sun fell through them to land on a patch of fell and a heap of old stones fallen from a wall, waiting for hands to rebuild its history.

Sometimes she caught Cal watching, and she wondered if he thought he was seeing the Lizzie she'd been before. She was a different woman now, one who had loved again, worked hard, knew professional success and appreciated the life it brought her. Cal gave nothing away to suggest he minded the short delays when she fell behind to aim for the perfect shot, he simply slowed the pace until she joined them again.

The breeze was rippling through her hair, the sun warm and she felt all sense of her city life and its problems draining away as she breathed in air so pure, it was almost as if it was cleansing her. Gemma had been right. This rewilding, in this place, was exactly what Lizzie needed and maybe she would lay a few old ghosts to rest while she was here. Seeing Cal again after all this time would surely help her move on.

They reached the lake and Bea was entranced by the view, her phone recording everything she saw. Lizzie exchanged a grin with Gemma, her social media ban safe as there was absolutely no signal even if Bea did want to upload something. They watched a few paddle boarders out on the water as Cal was telling the three women they might spot buzzards. This wild and rugged place was known for them as well as barn owls, skylarks, and green woodpeckers.

He was back in front as they headed up along a path that was becoming rough, edged with bracken clinging to the steep fell on their right, the water glistening twenty feet below. Lizzie was at the rear, alternating between glimpses of Cal, searching for a shot and making sure she didn't trip again. She hadn't been back in this place since she'd camped here with him, and despite how everything between them had ended, a part of her soul was soaring at the sight.

A rocky scramble was approaching and they paused. Hands would be needed to climb through the crag, Cal explained, advising them not to focus on the sharp drop to the water beside them. Lizzie's camera went in her bag, and she set off with him behind her; she'd done this scramble dozens of times and every ridge, every rock was familiar as she took her time to enjoy the effort it needed to climb to the plateau at the top.

She knew it wasn't for her benefit that Cal was telling them, as they reached a flatter bit of ground, that it was thought to be Bronze Age and rarely visited by anyone other than hikers. The standing stones were exactly as she remembered, eleven set into the ground. She only had half an ear on his explanation that the stones were re-laid after a nineteenth century farmer was thought to have helped himself to a couple for gateposts.

The view of the high fells and sloping green meadows, dotted with buildings leading down to the lake below, was exceptional and she was entranced. Nothing about her life in Carlisle, or London before that, could bring exhilaration to match being in this landscape again. Woodland lay to one side and sheep were grazing the grass in between huge boulders.

She was caught when her gaze landed on Cal's and found his waiting for her. They shared their first natural grin at what lay before them. Was he, too, remembering the times they'd sat up here alone following the stars through the night sky to morning? They were both at home here and that glance was enough to know he too loved this place still.

The four of them sat among the standing stones to share lunch and Lizzie fell on it, certain the pure Cumbrian air was responsible for her increasing appetite. She'd been hungry since she'd arrived and they all devoured the savoury torte layered with mushrooms, cheese, spinach and roasted red peppers served with a crunchy apple salad, breakfast bars stuffed with oats, pecans, raisins and coconut, followed by a raspberry and key lime parfait and an orange and apricot mimosa punch. Blueberry and banana bread with fresh coffee was on hand for anyone who could manage more, and Gemma eventually leaned back against a stone.

'How much further, Cal?' she asked sleepily. 'You surely don't expect us to take another step after that.'

They were all getting used to his presence among them, even Lizzie. Just two days ago she would have driven herself to the other end of the country to avoid him had she known he was going to be at Halesmere, much less their guide responsible for the day.

'Just the four kilometres.' He smiled at Gemma, and Lizzie looked away, biting her lip. He'd smiled so sparingly when she'd first met him, coming to love how it expressed his ease with her then. 'It's pretty level on the way back.'

'I heard you're a blacksmith, too.' Bea sounded relaxed but there was a sharpness to her attention on Cal and the statement, not a question. 'What do you make?'

'Stuff I see that I like.' He was packing away the remains of their lunch and seemed to realise he'd been a bit terse as he shrugged. 'Wildlife mostly.'

'Cool. I'd love to find something to take home with me. Can I come and see your studio later?'

'Sorry.' His smile was apologetic as he stood and slung the rucksack over his shoulders. 'There's somewhere I've got to be.'

'Tommorow then?' Bea wasn't giving up as she got to her feet and tied her coat around her waist. It had been cool while they ate but now the sun was high and warm. 'Will you be open then?'

'Planning to be around all day, so yeah, call in if you're interested.'

Cal caught Lizzie's eye and she grabbed her camera to fiddle with the focus. She didn't want messages like that from him.

'Great.' Bea was triumphant. 'Why don't we all go and take a look? You might even find a wedding present for Simon, Gem.'

'Hey, that's a shout. With the cancellation and all the problems we've had rearranging, I haven't even thought about a gift for him. He's a paramedic and he loves animals, it's a close thing between me and our dog as to who he loves more. Maybe you remember meeting Simon before, Cal?' She gave Lizzie a guilty look and hurried on. 'Probably not, it was ages ago.'

'Sure, I remember.' He gathered up the rubbish and stuffed it into a bag. 'I met him through Luke and Will at the farm. We hung around together at the pub sometimes.'

'That's a nice idea, Gemma.' Lizzie smiled and Gemma gave her a relieved glance. Lizzie wasn't about to spoil the potential for the perfect present just because her ex-boyfriend had made it, even if it would be a permanent reminder of Cal. 'I bet Simon would love that.'

Chapter 7

The path levelled as Cal led them across a footbridge, the lake narrowing to a river flowing into it. They walked through a meadow that meandered to a narrow lane, bordered by a stone wall and more woodland on their left. After half a mile or so he pointed to a turn off along the track.

'This is where we're going to meet Kelly and Chris, the wolf handlers. Ella said you were up for it.'

Lizzie's eyes darted to his arm and the glimpse of that tribal tattoo beneath his T-shirt. She'd never forgotten the day they'd spent here all those years ago, or how he'd loved the animals and the wildness they represented.

'Totally up for it. All part of our rewilding experience.' Gemma grinned at Lizzie and Bea.

'Gemma said we're not allowed to wear anything loose or carry food. I don't suppose we should be messing with our phones while we're with them.' Bea shot Cal a nervous smile. 'I hope they're friendly.'

'Ach, you'd be surprised. We're not very interesting to them once they realise we're not prey and accept us in the pack.' He gave her a reassuring nod. 'They're pretty chilled, not big on wasting energy.'

'Prey? Pack?' Bea's voice had risen a notch. Cal was at a high metal gate, speaking into a monitor and the gate slid slowly back. 'There's a pack?'

'Just the two.' He let them pass through first and a pickup was waiting in the car park, two women offering friendly smiles and raised hands beside it. 'The wolves are both males, Mackenzie Valley hybrids. These guys came from Montana originally and they've been here since they were sixteen weeks old.'

'Right.' Bea didn't sound terribly reassured.

Cal removed his rucksack as he made the introductions and Kelly took them through the first steps in meeting the wolves, who were waiting patiently in the back of the pickup. Lizzie had forgotten most of what she'd learned about the animals that first time here with Cal, and soon Kelly asked her and Cal to step up to the truck and place a hand against the grill.

The wolves sniffed them for a second and then ignored them. Lizzie was astonished to hear that the animals would remember their smell, their scent receptors many, many times stronger than a human's. These two wolves, introduced as Kai and Yas, already considered Lizzie and Cal as part of their own pack as they had visited before.

But Bea and Gemma were new, and the wolves spent a few more seconds sniffing their hands and offering a solitary lick before ignoring them too, accepting the women into the pack. Bea took a nervous step back when the intimidating animals jumped from the truck, slip-on leads around their necks.

With thick coats in shades of brown, black and paler biscuit, the wolves moved with lithe and confident ease as Kelly and Chris led them to an enclosure, securing the gate once everyone was inside. Bea flashed Gemma another anxious look when Kelly calmly informed them that wolves rated as highly as lions and tigers for levels of danger around people.

Kelly handed over her lead to Lizzie and explained that Yas must always go in front as he was the bodyguard of the pair, his role to protect Kai as the leader of the pack. The animals had been taught not to jump up at people as long as they held out their hands flat, and Lizzie smiled as Bea's hands shot out when a wolf came near, though he was uninterested in her behaviour and busy investigating the far more exciting scents of the other wildlife that found their way into the enclosure. Chris was beside Kai, leading him with Gemma and then Bea.

Lizzie was barely aware of anything that was said as they walked along, following the pace the wolves set and stopping whenever they did. She was acutely conscious of Cal nearby, sharing leading Yas with her, as they'd done once before. When it was time to let the wolves off and see them run free, Kai soon settled on the ground as Yas positioned himself on a higher slope, keeping careful watch. This was a good moment for photographs and Lizzie wasn't expecting Cal to make his way to her side as Gemma and Bea went first.

'What do you think?' His voice was low, preventing it from carrying to the others around them.

'About what?'

He held out an arm to their view, the formidable wild animals alert in the shot with Gemma and Bea. Lizzie didn't have long, it would be her turn for a photograph with her friends any moment.

'This. Rewilding, the wolves. You gave me one of the best days of my life here with them. I've never forgotten it.'

Her gaze flew up and she was almost winded by the sadness in his. 'They're incredible, Cal, but then you know that.' Her eyes went to his arm and the wolf tattoo. 'When did you get that?'

'Six months after you and me ended.' Her breath hitched as he slid the short sleeve up to reveal the whole powerful image. 'I needed something to hold on to.'

'And you chose a tattoo of a wolf?' Gemma was waving and Lizzie made herself inch away from him.

'I hope you know why, Lizzie. You know what they represent, and I had to be better. Learn some lessons.' His eyes were burning into hers and she swallowed. Strength, loyalty, protection. All aspects of his character he'd had when she'd known him and which he'd extended to her, making her feel so cherished and secure, even when he hadn't known what it was to grow up in a proper family of his own. Something he didn't possess and had been searching for, hoping to find out where he fitted. It had taken her a long time to accept he had not wanted a place in hers and she knew the fault was partly her own for assuming he hadn't needed more than all she could offer.

'What are you trying to say? That you've grown up?' She'd seen it for herself. His new maturity, the man revealed, more comfortable now with his own self than the young one she'd known before.

'Yes.'

'I suppose we all do eventually.' Lizzie gave Cal a bland smile as she headed off for her photo with the wolves and her friends.

The return to the house was mostly conducted in silence, with Gemma and Bea still awed by what they'd seen and experienced with the wolves. Lizzie had felt it again herself, their elemental nature, had been drawn in by the age-old wisdom in their amber eyes and the complete understanding of the world they inhabited with ease. Their howls had been spectacular and even Bea had fallen silent as she fumbled for her phone to record it.

Back in the courtyard at Halesmere there was an awkward moment after they thanked Cal for a wonderful day. Gemma caught Bea's eye and very obviously tilted her head towards the arch between the buildings.

Lizzie spotted it and she jumped in. No way were they leaving her alone with him. 'I need a nap.' She yawned on purpose, covering her mouth and feigning a tired eye roll. 'Must be all that fresh air, I'm so used to city life. I'm off to try out a hammock in the garden with a cocktail. Who's with me?'

'I am, definitely.' Bea got the message as she linked arms with Lizzie, Gemma quickly joining them. 'Who knew that rewilding yourself is so exhausting? Wake me up for dinner if I'm still asleep, I don't want to miss it.'

'You and your food.' Lizzie was happy to leave Cal behind, certain she felt his gaze boring into her back. 'It must be wonderful, being married to a chef as good as Matteo.'

'He does love to cook for me,' Bea agreed dreamily. 'Did I tell you about that time on holiday when he made me a—'

'Yes,' Lizzie and Gemma chorused. 'And how he served it naked, and you missed the boat tour you were meant to be going on. We know. Thanks for sharing. Again.'

'Sorry.' Bea's phone was pinging, and she ignored it as they reached the house. 'I love him, what can I say?'

They helped themselves to already prepared cocktails and wandered into the garden. Lizzie realised she was more tired than she'd pretended to Cal and the paperback she'd found in the house soon fell to the ground as she dozed off in her comfortable hammock. She dreamed of him, unsettling thoughts chasing through her mind that she couldn't pin down. Lizzie running after him and never being able to catch up as he disappeared from sight time and again.

She awoke with a jolt, almost rolling out of the hammock before she realised where she was. Lying still as her breathing slowed, she tried not to picture the hours they'd shared today and how much she still loved seeing him outdoors where he belonged. It was dangerous, to allow that pleasure in his company to wrestle with the heart he'd broken. *He* was dangerous, she'd always known it and polite acceptance of the past and looking ahead to separate lives was their only future. If she didn't live the life she'd refused to share with Cal in New Zealand, what was the point of the years she'd spent without him?

She caught up with Gemma and Bea in the house and they took dinner onto the terrace again. This lovely spring weather day after day was rare and they made the most of it, setting up a playlist of their favourite party tracks and dancing on the lawn until darkness fell. Eventually they remembered the app they were supposed to be consulting for the Dark Skies experience.

'It's all about the phase of the moon and nautical twilight.' Bea was leaning over Lizzie's shoulder to stare at her phone. 'When the sun is twelve degrees below the horizon and the moon is dark. I dunno, something like that.'

'Have you tried looking up?' Gemma took a few steps across the lawn and tipped her head back. 'Wow! That's incredible.'

'Woah, that's beautiful.' Bea flopped onto a nearby lounger. 'It's easier doing it this way, Gem. Anyone know what we're supposed to be looking for?'

'Just enjoying the view, I think, is the general idea. The moon in April is called a pink moon, after a wildflower in North American culture.' Lizzie joined Gemma on the lawn and lay flat out on the grass, loving the still-warm air fluttering over them as she stared at the thousands of stars glittering in the dark sky.

'And how do you know that?' Bea left the lounger and brought her phone to lie nearby.

'Just something I remember from back in the day.'

'Back in the day with Cal, you mean.' Bea had already given up stargazing and she rolled onto her stomach. Lizzie couldn't see her face clearly but felt the weight of her stare anyway. 'How was it, coming home and seeing him again like that?'

'Fine.'

'Fine? That's all you've got? Not happy or angry or sad?'

'Well, two of them anyway,' Lizzie said dryly. 'I'll let you decide which and there's a few more I could add.'

Bea's use of the word 'home' bothered Lizzie. Home had always meant Halesmere, and returning had reawakened a vital part of her she was now aware had lain dormant for a long time. And it wasn't just seeing Cal again. It was something elemental, tied up with him and her memories of their special summer, but more than that, it was to do with the life she'd imagined living, the one that always seemed to lie just out of her reach.

In her room earlier she'd gone over the shots she'd taken this weekend. Some weren't great but she'd keep them for now, a reminder of needing to improve before she replaced them with better ones. In others she could read the images as though she still stood in the landscape and saw how she'd captured the fell reflected in water, the beady orange eye of a blackbird alert on the gnarled branch of an apple tree.

She scrolled through the ripple of the river as it flowed into the lake, and moss clinging to the ancient stones where they'd eaten their picnic with Cal. She'd been careful not to take any images of him on the hike or with the wolves; she didn't want any more reminders. She still had that one perfect shot of him emerging from the water this morning, wanting to make herself delete it, hating that she hadn't.

'Are you coming with us to see Cal's studio tomorrow?' Bea had flipped onto her back again as Lizzie stared at the night sky without really seeing it this time.

'No, you two go on ahead. There won't be anything of his I'd want to take home. I might see what's on offer in the others and try the yoga as it's outdoors this time.'

Soon after, they shared hugs goodnight though Lizzie was too alert for sleep after her nap earlier. She stood at her bedroom window, staring at the darkened garden, hearing the call of an owl nearby. She thought of Carlisle, of returning to Jack's house and a place that didn't feel like home, the need to find somewhere else to live – and soon – a pressing weight on her mind. She couldn't shake the feeling that this was where she belonged, this was what she loved. With a sigh, she realised that the rewilding experience was beginning to work a little too well for her liking.

Chapter 8

On Sunday morning Lizzie couldn't quite settle into the yoga session with Ana, a jeweller with her own studio here. She hadn't seen Bea and Gemma since breakfast and assumed they were with Cal, in the old forge. Maybe it wouldn't have looked like she was avoiding him quite so obviously if she'd gone with them, but she really couldn't face it. Sandy had messaged Gemma to confirm their meeting at the church before lunch and then they were going to the pub with Ella, Max, and their children.

Lizzie fell in love on the spot with Ana's elegant and handmade jewellery crafted from recycled silver, and they chatted about her inspiration, taken from her love of the natural world. Lizzie bought a pair of white topaz and silver stud earrings for her mum's birthday and lingered on a gorgeous necklace from a collection Ana had named Pirr, after an ancient word for a breath of wind. Her own birthday was coming up and she knew her parents would be happy to gift her a piece if she found one she wanted. She loved how Ana had somehow captured the ripple of a breeze studded into the silver and she bought the necklace as well, intending to put it away for her birthday.

Lizzie wandered into the next studio and chose a tote bag woven from the wool of Herdwick sheep, naturally dyed in a berry red that instantly reminded her of fiery autumn shades. She hadn't missed the candles in every room of the house since they'd arrived, and found one to take back in a studio run by Marta, buying two more as reminder gifts for Gemma and Bea too.

As Lizzie and Marta chatted, she learned that Marta was a college lecturer and lived on the farm whose sheep supplied some of the wool for the fabrics next door. She also discovered that for every sale made in the studios, Ella and Max had committed to planting a tree. Lizzie adored the thought of her six purchases adding partly to the woodland around Halesmere and the rest to a project Ella and Max supported in the South American rainforest.

It was almost time to head down to the church to meet Sandy, whose own studio would be open later. The door to Cal's in the old forge was still closed and a nearby bench looked inviting. Lizzie sat down, staring at her phone blankly, wondering how Gemma and Bea were getting on with him.

'Lizzie? Lizzie Martin? Well, as I live an' breathe, I don't believe it.'

She spotted an older man she recognised at once meandering towards her, a bobble hat covering what she knew was a bald head, despite the spring sunshine, and a green waistcoat adorned with several pockets, string poking out of one.

'Stan? Wow, how brilliant to see you, you look exactly the same.' She jumped up from her bench and they shared a grin. 'I thought you and Pearl might've retired to be nearer your daughters by now.'

'Course I'm still 'ere, what would I want with livin' in Germany or down south,' Stan scoffed. 'Never gonna get rid of me 'ere, reckon I'm too useful.' A pencil was sticking out of the hat beneath one ear and the usual bits of wood shavings she remembered were clinging to his trousers.

'Well, what are you doin' back 'ere, Lizzie? Thought we'd seen the last of you, after your mum an' dad sold up an' you went off to university.'

'So did I, Stan. I was in London for a while, working for a communications company, and then I moved to Carlisle and started my own business.'

Stan had been a highly skilled carpenter at Halesmere for years, even before she and Gemma had come along. He and his wife Pearl had always looked out for the girls, keeping an eye on their escapades, and hauling them out of trouble on a few occasions. Lizzie still had the little wooden carvings he'd made; her favourite was the family dog they'd had before her mum and dad moved away, a spaniel he'd managed to capture in miniature detail, even down to its floppy ears.

'So what brings you back 'ere?' Stan's head tilted to one side in the familiar curiosity she remembered. 'Come on, let's 'ave it. You didn't look 'appy, sittin' on your own just then. You were never miserable, Lizzie, you always 'ad a smile on your face. Reckon you an' Gemma an' all that mischief you made are the reason I went bald.'

'You've been bald as long as I've known you, Stan,' Lizzie retorted. 'You always used to tell us it was Pearl and your daughters' fault. Next you'll be saying it's this place, when we all know how much you love it.' She sighed, despite falling straight back into the banter they'd shared.

Stan had always been kind beneath the bluster, and a very good listener. Lizzie remembered him sitting her or Gemma in the battered armchair in his workshop and offering hot drinks and an ear as they poured out their teenage troubles. Usually involving boys, squabbles with friends or recalcitrant parents. He'd offered little in the way of advice, other than to remind them that everyone got stuff wrong from time to time, and staying friends was better than falling out forever. She suspected he'd known most of their secrets back then and he'd always cared.

'Would you believe me if I said I was here on a rewilding retreat for the weekend?' Lizzie's laugh followed as Stan's brows shot up to reach his bobble hat. 'I thought you might look like that if I told you.'

'Rewildin',' he said eventually, removing the hat to scratch his head. 'I can't believe me own ears, Lizzie. Things 'ave gone bad if you need to come 'ere to rewild yourself. You were always wild, the pair of you. I've never forgotten how you used to move the garden furniture around an' tell guests the gazebo was 'aunted with a grey lady.'

'Only when we wanted to use it for ourselves.'

He looked at her knowingly as he put the bobble hat back on. 'What 'appened to your camera? You always 'ad it with you.'

'Trust you to get to the heart of it, Stan.' Lizzie wasn't expecting the sudden wobble in her voice. 'Not much I want to look at in Carlisle, I suppose. Too many buildings, not enough fells or valleys.'

'Aye, or good-lookin' lads that catch your eye an' run off after summat else when things look like gettin' serious. I married our Pearl when I was twenty, you know.' He paused and Lizzie saw the sympathy in his expression. 'I take it by the way you're glarin' at me you know 'e's back?'

'We had the pleasure of Cal guiding us on a hike yesterday.'

'Oh, lass. I'd laugh if it were actually funny, but it's not, is it?' Stan's quiet understanding brought a furious tear to Lizzie's eye, and she blinked it away.

'What's he doing here, Stan?' Stan always had his ear to the ground and knew what was going on long before she and Gemma had. If anyone could explain Cal's presence here it was very likely to be him.

'You'd 'ave to ask 'im that, Lizzie. But seein' as you are askin' me, I'd say it's about 'im findin' out what's important.' Stan's look became beady. 'Just like you, I'd say an' all.'

'Right.' Lizzie forced a brighter note into her voice. 'So are you going to make me a brew then and tell me how hard you've worked to get the place looking so good? Moan about the new owners and all the work they want doing?'

'Moan? Me? You've got me mixed up with someone else, lass.' Stan threw her a wink. 'Looks like I still can't pull the wool over your eyes, Lizzie Martin. Max bought it last year, he's a great bloke. Bit quiet an' stiff upper lip but once you get to know 'im he's a good 'un. Lost 'is wife, so it's no wonder. Them kiddies of 'is are smashin', an' Ella's done them all the world o'good. She's 'is business partner as well now. Place wouldn't be the same without 'er.'

'You old softie,' Lizzie quipped. 'Ella's lovely, she organised the weekend for us and she's helping Gemma with the wedding, if all goes to plan.'

'Aye, I 'eard we might be 'avin' a weddin'. That'll be another list o' jobs comin' my way.'

'So you'll be seeing more of me, Stan, I hope you're happy to hear. I run a wedding planning business and I'm helping Gemma with hers. As a friend and bridesmaid, not a paying client.'

'Aye, lass, I am 'appy to 'ear it. So it's Carlisle, then, is it, where you're livin'?'

'For now.' Lizzie sighed. 'I have office space there and an ex-boyfriend whose house I need to move out of.'

'Right.' Stan pursed his lips to regard her thoughtfully. 'Well. Carlisle's not a million miles from Halesmere, now, is it? An' there's a flat goin' spare 'ere. Summat for you to think about, I reckon. An' wait til you 'ear I've 'ad my picture painted an' I'm goin' to be in a fancy exhibition. Max's mother is an artist, she lives 'ere when she's not livin' in France. She's French.' Stan grinned, as though being French explained everything, and Lizzie knew he was pleased by the prospect of the exhibition. 'Ella's certainly got plans for this place, that's for sure. Got 'er 'ands full what with the retreats, the family an' all.'

Lizzie suddenly realised the time and picked up her bags. 'Sorry Stan, I haven't got time for that brew, if you were actually thinking of making me one. We're off to the church to sort out the service for the wedding.'

'It'll keep for another time, lass.' Stan stuffed large hands in his pockets to give Lizzie a level stare. 'I reckon sortin' them retreats is a job that'd suit you, Lizzie Martin. You always liked people an' gettin' them organised. An' our Pearl always said anyone who could organise me 'ad the patience of a saint an' her undyin' respect.'

–

To everyone's relief, the church was charming, and the wedding booked by the time Lizzie, Gemma and Bea made their way to the White Hart for lunch. Sandy had been lovely, welcoming and helpful, and it was a huge load off Gemma's shoulders as she hurriedly called Simon to let him know. There was time enough before the wedding to read the banns and other plans could be re-made.

Lizzie took a deep breath when they arrived at the pub. It held so many memories, and not just the ones she'd made here with Cal. There was the stonewall where they'd shared that first unforgettable kiss at her eighteenth birthday party; the table outside where she'd wait to surprise him after work; the exact spot at the bar where she'd asked him for that cheeky photograph the night they met. She still had it in a drawer somewhere after printing it out years ago. For all that it wasn't technically great, she loved it for the way he was looking back at her. Amused, curious, aware, as though he too had realised something significant was already happening between them.

The pub was much more attractive now and it was packed; the three rooms she remembered now painted a warming shade of red. Wooden tables and chairs were newer, arranged between comfy old settles lining the walls, reupholstered in autumn colours, and there was no need of the real fire on such a lovely spring day.

Ella waved them over and introduced the three women to Max, Lily, and Arlo. The children were adorable, and Lizzie only realised they'd brought their dog Prim, who had been lying quietly underneath the table, when Lily asked her to stand up and then roll over, her latest trick. Max was lovely and very keen to hear more about Lizzie and Gemma's time growing up at Halesmere and what the house had been like then. Sharing those times was bittersweet for Lizzie as she laughed with Gemma through some of their stories, her memories bound up with her old home and Cal.

They moved on to the wedding and Gemma was excited by Lizzie's suggestion of a festival theme for the reception now that the more formal hotel they had booked was no longer an option. Gemma and Simon's original florist and photographer were already Cumbrian based and should be able to work around the change in location and style. Lizzie and Bea were in charge of the hen night and Gemma was very ready to have one now that the wedding was back on track.

Their meals ordered, it wasn't long before Stan and Pearl made an appearance, followed by Marta and her partner Luke, who farmed down the road. Tables were squeezed together, more drinks bought, and the superb meal was only just over when Ana and her girlfriend Rachael arrived. Sandy rolled up too, planning to throw pots in her studio later, and Ella and Max were the first to excuse themselves as the children were due to go to a friend's house.

To Lizzie's horror, Cal showed up just after Ella and Max left, and he wasn't alone. Another man and two women were with him, and he politely shrugged off Stan's calls that the four of them come and join their merry party. Lizzie felt trapped, back in her favourite pub, her gaze bouncing off the walls as she sneaked glimpses of Cal. His little group had positioned themselves in the middle of the three rooms and she had to pass them when it was her turn to go the bar.

'So this is weird.'

Lizzie would recognise his voice with that lilting accent anywhere and every muscle seemed to contract as Cal slotted in next to her. 'Yes.' She smiled at the barman as she reeled off her order. The noise was growing as more people arrived in search of a good meal after a day spent hiking on the fells or exploring the beautiful towns and villages beyond the valley.

'Still feels like I'm on the wrong side.' Cal tipped his head to the pumps. Someone shuffled up beside him and

Cal turned so he was facing her, one elbow resting casually on the bar, a glimpse of his tribal tattoo, the wolf at rest. She felt like prey, caught in his gaze like this. 'You don't wear it. I always wondered.'

'What are you talking about?' She was trying to focus on the drinks order and a glance was enough to catch his eyes drifting to her hands. Her heart seemed to leap into her throat; she knew now exactly what he was referring to.

'My Claddagh ring.'

'Why would I wear that?' Her thoughts raced back to those terrible moments that morning when she realised he'd run. She'd never forgotten the shock, the pain lodging inside her as she clutched his ring as though she'd never let it go. The barman was loading glasses onto a tray and Lizzie quickly added another drink she didn't need to the order. 'Why would I put a permanent reminder on my finger of you leaving me the way you did?'

'Ach, Lizzie, that's not what it was for. I wanted you to have it so you'd always remember I loved you.' He was staring straight at her, as though he could read her mind and the desire for him that had never gone away.

Her order was complete, and she handed over her card, unable to hold up the queue any longer. 'I'm not going there, Cal. There isn't any point.' Her body was at odds with her words, confessing everything she felt about going back to where they'd been. He only needed touch her skin with a finger and it would ignite, and she was certain he knew it too. She needed another pair of hands for the drinks and gave Gemma a pleading look across the room. 'I've got to go.'

Chapter 9

On Monday morning Lizzie, Gemma and Bea were all packed. They'd been more reflective last night, sitting on the terrace to talk through wedding plans and what they might do for a hen night, with Gemma favouring Edinburgh as a destination. Only Bea had made it out of bed in time for a yoga session with Ana first thing. Lizzie was staring out of her bedroom window, thinking over all that had happened since they'd arrived three nights ago. Gemma and Simon's wedding was secured, Lizzie would be working with Ella on the reception and Sandy had confirmed the first banns would be read next week.

And then there was Cal. Lizzie couldn't yet land her feelings on a place where they were steady after the shock of seeing him again. There was hurt, regret, sadness for how they'd ended and what they'd lost. Curiosity about the path he'd chosen and who might now share his life.

And desire. It was impossible to pretend she didn't still find him so very attractive. His eyes were telling her he knew it and wanted what she did. She understood him too well to mistake that.

Just like that, a decision was made. Picking up her handbag from the bed, she slipped something out of her purse and ran from the house. The studios were closed to the public on Mondays and only house guests were likely to wander in if the artists were at work. There was a pickup outside Stan's workshop and Lizzie was quick as she tried the door of the old forge; she didn't want him to notice her. It was locked and she turned away. She hadn't been sure what she was going to do until that moment in her room and she was disappointed now she couldn't see it through.

'Lizzie?'

Cal was walking through the arch and a blast of adrenaline followed at seeing him and knowing what she was planning to do. They met outside the old dairy beneath the flat where she and Gemma had used to camp out, pretending it was their own little home and cooking in the cramped kitchen.

'I thought you'd be on your way.' He halted in front of her. 'I didn't expect a goodbye.'

'I just came to return this.' Lizzie held out an arm and his gaze fell to stare at his silver Claddagh ring. It was sitting on her palm, and she felt as though she was holding the whole weight of their history in her hand. She had carried it almost everywhere for twelve long years, so many times dreaming of flinging it back in his face along with her scorn. Now the action felt pointless, empty and hurtful somehow. 'It doesn't belong to me, and I've never worn it.'

'I don't want it, Lizzie. It's yours.' His fingers folded hers back over the ring, securing it in her grasp. 'It was all I had to give you that meant something to me.' His arm shot out and he grabbed hers to yank her into the dairy, booting the door open with a swift kick. She had barely a second to wonder if her feet had actually left the ground before he slammed it behind them.

'What the hell do you think you're doing?' She was breathless with shock and anger as she steadied herself.

Her silk blouse had slipped down one shoulder and she straightened it, hearing a clink as the Claddagh ring fell to the stone floor. She spun around to open the door, reaching for escape, sense, reality. His arm moved past her head to flatten his hand against the wood.

'If you go back out there now then Stan will see you and this conversation will no longer be private.'

'That's why you hauled me in here? So Stan couldn't see us?' Her quick laugh was full of derision. She would have preferred Stan firmly wedged between her and Cal to the utter awareness of him right behind her. His breath was ragged, just like hers, and everything she remembered about his touch came storming back. How he'd expressed his love in gestures before words; his hand holding hers, a triumphant kiss the moment they'd reached a summit, arms tight around her when she'd leaned into him to watch the night skies.

'Lizzie, I need you to know how sorry I am for leaving you the way I did.' Gentle words, softer now, at odds with the powerful arm and the wolf tattoo almost brushing her face.

'Maybe you are but what you did that day was pathetic and cruel.' She dragged in another breath, her anger dissolving into despair for the hurt she'd carried down the years. 'And I gave up ever thinking I'd hear you say that, Cal. It's history, we can't change it.'

'I know, and I'm so sorry.' His index finger was tapping a light and anxious beat against the door. 'I didn't plan to leave that night. But I knew if I saw you again, I wouldn't want to go, and I just ran.'

'So why did you?' Her voice was a scratched whisper, an answer, finally, to the question she had longed to ask. 'Couldn't we have found a way?'

'That night in the restaurant with your parents, it was all about what you were going to achieve and the life you planned to have. I didn't see where I would fit.'

'So you're saying it's my fault you left?' She was just about clinging onto the furious tears threatening to fall and she pressed a hand to her chest.

'Of course it wasn't your fault. I made a choice.' He shifted and Lizzie flinched as his hands moved to her shoulders, sensing his tension even through the weight he was keeping deliberately light. She let him slowly turn her around and she saw the hurt of their history etched into own his face as their past hovered once again within reach.

'I left because I didn't trust us enough to find a way through if I stayed.'

'So New Zealand, when you asked me to come with you? You just threw that out there to test me and make me choose? See if I landed on you or everything I'd worked for?'

'I wanted you to come with me, Lizzie, I meant it. But that night I realised you were deciding between me or your future.' Cal's voice dropped and she was shocked to read his own pain as his fingers on her shoulders tightened. He'd never been someone who lied, and she understood the truth and intent in his words.

'It was the first time I realised you didn't think you could have both. Me and the life you wanted. You thought I'd tag along with you to St Andrews but if you came to New Zealand with me, you'd have been settling for less. I knew I wasn't enough for you and your dad was right. I was nothing then.'

Lizzie's legs were ready to give way as the truth slammed into her. Cal was right. She hadn't truly believed she could keep him at her side through university and into a new life as she pursued a career, securing her own future as best she could. He'd always belonged outdoors, in the mountains, the water, beneath a big sky. Even then she'd known he wasn't going to be bound by the nine to five and settle for a view that came through glass. She'd tried, just as he had, had hoped he might fit in her future, though somewhere deep inside then she had known that he wouldn't.

'My dad was wrong and I'm so sorry he said that,' she whispered brokenly, her chin quivering with the effort of holding back the tears. She had to force her hands into fists to prevent herself from touching Cal too, stroking her sorrow onto his skin. 'You were everything, and all these years I've blamed you for breaking us up. I assumed I was all you had, and it would be enough, that you'd just follow me. I let you down, too. I didn't stop to think what you might want.'

'Ach, I think we let each other down.' Cal ran a finger down her cheek, catching a tear before it landed on her lips. 'We were kids, Lizzie. We ran out of time.'

'I should have waited a year and gone to New Zealand with you. At least then we'd have known.'

'I could've gone with you to St Andrews. But we did what we did, no point looking back at what ifs. I just want you to know I'm sorry for hurting you and I've always regretted it. I had to go and make something of myself. It was the only way I felt I could get past not having a family.'

'And you did. Look at how far you've come.' Lizzie tried to smile, her heart aching. 'There's nothing you need to prove to anyone.'

'Maybe there is. I've written you a dozen emails I never sent.'

'Seriously?' That was a startling truth she had never dared hope for. 'Why didn't you send them?'

'Because I just couldn't seem to find the right words when I wrote them down.' His mouth quirked in something not quite a smile and he leaned closer, his hands still on her shoulders. 'Leaving you the way I did doesn't mean I didn't love you, though.'

'I know. I loved you, too.' She whispered her reply, recognising the unforgettable memory of their first kiss in his eyes as she gave herself up to the rightness of his touch on her body. She knew this one would be even better as she lifted her head to meet his. Twelve years of hurt and the love they'd lost were crammed into mouths furious and desperate on the other.

The pain, the separation, were all crushed by his lips bruising hers as she kissed him back just as urgently, the beard somehow a sign of his new maturity. Cal wrapped her long hair in one hand as his other pulled her into him. So very different from the first time, and somehow exactly the same. Even more skill born of more experience, the same soaring passion.

Her mind couldn't keep up with all she was feeling as her hands darted beneath his T-shirt, skimming over the glorious body once so familiar. He let go of her hair to tug the silk blouse free from her jeans, one arm tight across her back all that was holding her up. No one else had ever made her feel like this and she felt the roughness of his art against her skin, his hands no longer smooth.

She gasped as he began to unfasten the buttons on her blouse and his hooded eyes were lazy with desire as he parted the silk to reveal a primrose lace bra. His fingers went to the next button, and she covered them, trying to summon back sense.

'I've got to go. We're leaving.'

'When are you coming back?' Cal's hands slid to her waist, holding her, his voice a reluctant rasp. She could still feel the frantic beating of his heart pressed against her chest. 'Ella told me about the wedding.'

'I'm not sure.' Right now Lizzie was having considerable difficulty remembering what she was meant to be doing in the next few minutes, never mind the next few weeks, and thoughts of Gemma's wedding were a blur. 'We can't pin anything on what just happened, Cal. Let's call it our goodbye, the one we never had.'

'I guess you're right.' He smoothed a thumb across her cheek, and she was almost lost at the regret in his gaze. It was going to take a monumental effort to walk out of this room and leave him behind. 'You're still incredible, Lizzie. I knew that the moment I saw you the other night.'

'So are you.'

He reached past her to open the door and she peeped out, searching for signs of Stan or anyone else who might see her floating away from Cal with the imprint of their kiss still on her pink lips and grinning like the prize idiot she was. So much for goodbye, she knew it wouldn't have taken many more moments for them to have locked the door and remembered exactly what they'd been missing all these years.

If Stan spotted her, he wouldn't need to put two and two together to know what she'd been doing and with whom. Lizzie rushed across the courtyard, trying to convince herself she was in no danger from her feelings for Cal and wondering how she was going to pretend to Gemma that nothing had happened. She was lit up and practically glowing with a desire that had just been re-ignited, and how. Bea was trying to drag her case across the gravel with an armful of coats, and wiping the smile off her face, Lizzie rushed over.

'Want some help? Those coats are going to be on the drive if you don't put something down.'

'Lizzie?' Gemma emerged from the house, clutching her phone and keys. 'Where were you, I've been looking everywhere? Ella wants a word before we go.'

'Not quite everywhere,' Lizzie said dreamily, forgetting herself. She immediately realised her mistake as Gemma's eyes widened and fell to take in the buttons on her blouse she'd forgotten to fasten.

'Oh shit, Lizzie, seriously? You haven't?'

Chapter 10

Despite the familiarity of the city, Carlisle felt a bit like an old friend Lizzie couldn't get along with when she returned, just like Jack. It was as though she'd somehow shed the layer she needed to live here. The rewilding retreat with Gemma and Bea had brought her mind back to her real home at Halesmere and her feelings hadn't yet righted themselves since Gemma had first mentioned the weekend away.

Lizzie caught up with Jack after he arrived back from work, dodging his offer of dinner. Bea was right – Lizzie couldn't continue living in his house now their relationship was over, and she didn't want to stay for a minute longer than necessary. She spent the rest of the evening flat-hunting online and made two appointments for viewings this week, knowing she would need to dip into savings already depleted after lockdown.

And then there was Cal. Her mind was full of him and that crazy kiss they'd shared in those final few minutes before she'd left. After all the years without him, and the wondering, the worrying, the times her fingers had typed his name into a search engine and found no trace, he had suddenly exploded back into her life. She knew the kiss had been a massive mistake.

Whenever she thought of it her concentration would snap and she'd be right back there with him, hands running over each other as their mouths put their separation to rights. She'd told him it was their goodbye and she had to mean it, no matter how often her body reminded her it much preferred hello. She would be returning to Halesmere, probably several times, for Gemma and Simon's wedding and she couldn't look for another opportunity to be alone with Cal again.

Two days after the end of the retreat an email dropped into Lizzie's inbox. She read it through three times, her incredulity and excitement growing with each pass. She didn't need to read it a fourth time, she'd known from the first what she would do. Already she could see the plan in focus, as though she'd adjusted the lens on her own life. The email required a reply, and she sent one straight back.

–

'What do I think?' Gemma was talking to Lizzie early the next evening via a screen propped on a kitchen worktop as she put together a lemon curd trifle. Her soon-to-be parents-in-law were coming for dinner, and she was on the last minute with her dessert and kept disappearing from view. 'I think you're completely crazy and it's bloody brilliant. It's about time you sorted your life out and taking that flat is certainly one way of doing it.'

Lizzie's laugh was relieved as some of the tension slipped from her shoulders. 'I really hoped you'd say that. Twenty-four hours on, the decision still feels bonkers but somehow totally right.'

'And don't forget to remind yourself of that if you wake up in a cold sweat.' Gemma was back on screen, her voice clearer. 'The city was never really you, Lizzie. Living in London was like a test you put yourself through to make sure it was worth giving up Cal and New Zealand for.'

'You think?' Lizzie huffed out a breath as the uncertainty kicked right back in. Could she actually do this, make herself go through with it? Move her life and her business south and base herself at Halesmere for the foreseeable future? Give up the part-time hours she still drove at the supermarket to keep her income steady?

'Stop it.'

'What?' Lizzie refocussed on the screen to watch Gemma whipping cream.

'Finding reasons not to go.'

'Okay. I didn't know I was that obvious.'

'I know you, Lizzie Martin. You were biting your lip the way you always do when you're worried.' Gemma was spooning custard over sponge slices soaked in sherry now and Lizzie found the process very soothing and decidedly normal. Far more normal than giving notice on her office space and starting to pack. Just the thought of it had adrenaline racing through her body again.

'What did Ella actually say?'

'She was very keen to have me.' A spark of excitement replaced the nerves and Lizzie grinned. 'Apparently a little bird, obviously one with a very big beak, dropped in that I was looking for somewhere to live and did Ella think he'd made fancy new wardrobes in the flat for the mice to live in?'

'Oh Stan, bless his heart. He always did have a good one, getting us out of trouble the way he did.' Gemma disappeared again and Lizzie heard her open and close the fridge door. 'And you mustn't let giving up the driving job hold you back. There's bound to be something you can do to earn extra money if you need it. But you won't, I know your enquiries are growing and how much you love planning special days for people. There's loads of things you could do with your qualifications and experience if it doesn't work out. But it will work out, you'll see.'

'Thank you for having faith in me.' Lizzie's voice was small. 'I needed someone to give me a shove.'

'I have total faith and I'll shove you all the way back to Halesmere myself if necessary.' Gemma grinned at the screen, a blob of cream on her cheek. 'Please tell me you've heard back from Ella since you said yes?'

'Yes, right before I called you.' Lizzie flipped open the email to read it again, wanting to make sure the offer was real, pinned to her screen in black and white. 'She said they'd be absolutely delighted to have me, and the flat is mine for the next six months. She and Max are positioning Halesmere in the market for offering guests a more holistic approach to life and she's already asked me to take over a brand launch they're holding.'

'And you've said yes?'

'Of course I have, I'm not going to pass up an opportunity like that. We'll be bringing local businesses, customers, and media together, and it's a great chance to get my name out there as one of the organisers. Ella's planned quite a bit already but she's got room in the budget to offload the rest onto me.'

'What do you know about it?'

'Not much, just that it's a Cumbrian brand of clothing who are launching a range of luggage. I've had a quick google but that's all, I need more time on it. Ella's really excited about working with me, she didn't even want a formal interview after I sent her my CV. And Stan apparently told her to get on to me before…'

'Before what?' Gemma wiped the cream away. 'Go on.'

'Ella didn't say it was a secret, so I suppose it's okay to tell you.' Lizzie's voice dropped, even though she was alone. Jack had gone to play squash after work, and she briefly had the house to herself. 'Keep it quiet for now, just in case.'

'What?'

'Ella's pregnant.'

'Seriously?' Gemma grinned before disappearing from view again as she took the phone over to a breakfast bar and propped it against something else. 'Wow, how lovely for them. I thought she looked a bit peaky when she came to see us off that last morning.'

'Yeah, she and Max are thrilled, even though it wasn't planned. She was supposed to be starting a course in the autumn as she wants to teach at the catering college but she's going to defer it for a year and they'll both work around the kids. They're very happy with how the holiday business is developing but her real passion is for the catering students. Ella's mum and dad are moving over, too, and her mum's taking on the housekeeping side of things. It'll be the first baby in their family, even though they see Lily and Arlo as their grandchildren, too, and they want to be on hand. We talked for ages, she's lovely.'

'And the studio, Lizzie, that's amazing. I'm so pleased for you.'

'Thanks.' Lizzie felt a blast of real fear follow the excitement at that. What if her photography wasn't good enough to show in the old dairy beneath the flat? She knew there were ways she could earn extra money from her images, but every time she thought of it, the anticipation was followed swiftly by nerves. She should probably go on a refresher course – she was taking a serious risk, upending her life again, and dipping into her—

'Stop it. You're doing it again. I don't even need to see you to know you're biting your lip.' Gemma was firm as she wagged a finger. 'No doubts. You've absolutely got to give it a go. You can plan events and weddings from anywhere, you know you can.'

'Right. I can. You're absolutely right. I'm really going to do this.'

'You really are.' Gemma paused. 'So what does Jack say? I suppose you'll both be relieved to move on. He might even want to bring whatshername into the house once you've left.'

'Wendy.' Lizzie thought briefly of the friendly young woman who'd separated from her partner, and she had met once or twice at school events when she'd turned up to support Jack. Wendy was really nice; Lizzie knew they could have been friends if it wasn't for the small matter of Jack sleeping with her. Just the once, apparently.

'I haven't told him yet, Gem, I wanted to get your take on Halesmere first. It's not like he needs my share of the expenses, the house was his grandad's and he got it for a song.'

'I hope you're both all right.' Gemma paused. 'He's a nice guy, Lizzie. He made a mistake.'

'I know that. But it was one that shouldn't have happened in the first place, and I just don't feel the same way about him now. We both know it's over. And I'm looking forward to making a home at Halesmere again, at least for now. I'll worry about the rest later.'

'Okay.' Gemma's next words were delivered with a voice more casual than her sharp gaze. 'So are we going to talk about the elephant in the room? Or rather, the seriously hot, ex-model boyfriend who also has a studio conveniently close to your new flat.'

'What do you want me to say?' Lizzie hoped she was disguising the constant thrill she was feeling at knowing she would see Cal again. 'He'll be around, Gem, there's nothing I can do about that. We're definitely over and I suppose we'll bump into each other. We're grown-ups now, it'll be fine.'

'Fine? Are you kidding me? The guy broke your heart, shows up in your life again – looking like he does – and you say it'll be fine? And don't think I haven't noticed how he looks at you, either. He's like one of those bloody wolves he loves so much, just waiting to devour you. I know something happened between you that weekend. Please tell me he's not why you're doing this?'

'He's not why I'm doing this.'

'Don't you dare let him get close again, Lizzie. You've never been a fool in all your life, except where Cal's concerned.'

'Gem, I loved him and he loved me. It's not that simple. If you're asking me to say I don't have any feelings for him, then I can't. But if it makes you happy, then know I have zero intentions of starting anything up with him again, okay?'

'Okay.' Gemma seemed reassured and smiled. 'I'm so looking forward to having you as my eyes and ears on the wedding. Send me lots of pictures – I want to know everything – and we'll be up most weekends.'

'I can't wait, I'm expecting a regular delivery of baking. And this is just a reminder that I won't be putting up with any of that Bridezilla nonsense.'

'I'm your perfect best friend slash client. And thank you, I so appreciate all you're doing for us.' Lizzie heard Gemma's doorbell ring. 'Gotta go, they're here. Love you, I'll be there Saturday to help you move in.'

'Thank you, love you too. Bea and I will be in touch soon about the hen night.'

'Wonderful, can't wait.'

Lizzie ended the call and resumed sorting through stuff in her bedroom she could recycle, still thinking about Cal and trying not to measure her feelings for him against what she felt for Jack. She'd been truthful in her words to Gemma. She did have zero intentions of starting up anything with Cal again, even if she couldn't get that incredible kiss out of her mind. After they'd returned home from the retreat, Bea had shared images of the life-sized hawk sculpture she'd bought from Cal and given to her husband Matteo as an anniversary present, and he apparently loved the in-flight hen harrier made from steel.

Gemma had commissioned Cal to make Simon's wedding present and he'd agreed to have the sculpture of their adored Labrador ready in time. Bea had also let slip that she'd looked up the T-shirt Cal had been wearing on their hike and had ordered a couple for Matteo, dropping in that the brand was the company Cal had set up in New Zealand.

So without even trying he had somehow inserted himself into her friends' lives as well as her own. Lizzie had resisted this impulse for a long time, but finally caved, sitting on her bed and unlocking her phone to open up a browser, typing in 'Apera'. Within seconds her screen was full of links and images of the brand. And Cal.

She drew in a breath as she clicked on a couple of links, trapped like a bird against glass as the missing years of his life fell open before her. No wonder she hadn't found him whenever she'd searched for Cal Ryan. This man was Callum Lindsay, a public pseudonym he'd adopted as his profile grew to match his success.

She went deeper, pulling up shots from the early days of the company when he'd seemed a little awkward in front of the camera but still so gorgeous. She knew better than anyone that the camera loved him, and she found the more assured man coming out as she moved through the years, playing volleyball on the beach, dragging a board through surf, or laughing with the other equally beautiful young people around him. Sometimes he was staring straight at the camera, daring her to hold his gaze. In others, he'd be looking off to the distance, thoughtful, long hair blowing in a breeze she couldn't feel, always wearing his own brand.

She only needed to scroll through the company's Instagram to realise how successful he'd helped make it. Everyone had wanted to know who he was and where they could find him. He'd even moved to a new location when the beach house he was living in had been discovered, wanting to keep what privacy he could. He'd had the tribal wolf on his arm from the beginning of the brand and she saw how his ink had increased through the years until his right arm was full.

There was a post and some speculation from followers devoted to a new tattoo he'd got four years ago and she clicked on it. Her heart pinged as she stared at the enlarged image of a waterfall on the inside of his right forearm. She knew that place, now forever represented on his body. It was a remote river they'd discovered one unforgettable day, a series of deep pools formed between huge crags and rocks in a valley where hikers and climbers were the only visitors.

Lizzie could almost feel the clear, icy water as it fell from the mountain to form the pool they'd splashed around in the whole of that memorable day. She wouldn't ever forget as it was there they'd made love for the first time and Cal had confessed he loved her and trusted her with his heart, so rarely offered. Now that day was inked on his arm, a permanent reminder of what they'd felt. Was it etched on his heart, too, like it was on hers? If she closed her eyes, she could imagine herself back there with him, skin on skin through the cold.

She found other shots from his life in New Zealand: pictures of him partying with a series of stunning girls, arms draped around one another in bars, pulling silly faces, running through the surf or barbecuing on the beach. Each image vibrant in its own way, emphasising their youth and beauty, the best of life in their grasp. Nothing here of heartbreak and hard choices made, or family not found.

One woman appeared in more images with Cal than any other and she was incredibly beautiful. Small, athletic, with cropped dark hair, a dolphin tattoo on her left shoulder and a rose on one ankle. Lizzie saw them surfing, matching each other wave for wave, ride for ride. She was at his side in bars, at parties, the odd corporate event he'd attended, hands fixed together, smiling for the photographer in the formal dress that seemed at odds with their casual beach lives.

Lizzie felt a sudden, horrible jealously lurch inside her as she kept returning to the same questions. Did she love Cal still, and if she did, how might he feel about her too? This woman had held him, at least for a time, and had been a pivotal part of his life. Was she with him now, in Cumbria? Lizzie could read their relationship in these images as clearly as any words written in a book. He'd lived a bright and glittering life, oceans apart from hers, while she'd fixed herself firmly in the city and tried to convince herself it was all she'd worked for and wanted.

Not any longer. A different life was waiting and this time she was going to grab it with both hands. She put the phone down and began ramming clothes she didn't need into a bag.

'Lizzie?'

She jumped, the skirt she was holding falling to the floor. She hadn't heard Jack return and he was standing in the doorway of the spare bedroom. She was still thinking of Cal, sharply reminded of how she'd always liked that Jack looked nothing like him. He was a little older for a start, with a slighter build and laughing blue eyes behind glasses she'd always found attractive. They'd met at a wedding she'd planned, when Jack was the brother of the best man, and by the end of the day he'd had her number and her agreement to a first date.

'Are you packing?' Jack cleared his throat. 'You've found somewhere?'

'Yes.' She looked up. 'It's all happened very quickly. I've got the opportunity of a flat at Halesmere and I didn't want to pass it up.'

'Halesmere?' He raised a brow. 'Isn't that a bit remote? How much business do you expect to pick up around there?'

'I'm sure it will be fine, there are other things going on as well as weddings.' Lizzie stuck out her chin. 'I've already got a brand launch to plan and there's a room below the flat which I can use as a studio for my photography.'

'Your photographs? Of what?' Jack retrieved a top that had slipped to the floor and handed it to her. 'It's been a while, hasn't it, since you had your camera out? Wouldn't you be better off getting another job you can rely on rather than planning stuff people can cancel whenever they feel like it?'

116

'I suppose I'll find out,' she replied curtly, more stung than she wanted to admit by his comment about her photography and the career she was trying to rebuild. She didn't need doubts from him as well, she had enough of her own. 'And they can't just cancel, that's what contracts are for.'

'Sorry.' Jack cleared his throat awkwardly. 'And I am sorry too, about us, and what happened with Wendy. We didn't plan it, it was just one of those things.'

Lizzie raised a shoulder, her smile sad. 'Maybe it was, Jack. I know we've had our problems, but cheating is a deal breaker for me. Always has been.'

'And it's not like you've ever made a mistake, is it?' Jack said shortly. 'You're not big on seeing something through or second chances.'

Gemma's words from the retreat leapt into Lizzie's mind. 'One strike and you're out', she had said. It had always been Lizzie's way of protecting herself and she was doing it again with Jack. She probably hadn't loved him enough to truly let him in, and a stab of guilt followed.

'I just don't think we were right together, and I'm sorry too.' She spotted a sundress he'd bought for her and dropped it into another recycling bag, aware of him watching. 'I wish you all the best, truly. I've put what I owe in your account, and I'll leave the key.'

'Thanks.' Jack straightened from the door frame. 'So when are you going?'

'Tomorrow. Gemma and Simon are meeting me at Halesmere to help. I thought it was best to get on with it.' She was going home and she couldn't wait.

Chapter 11

As Lizzie didn't have much in the way of belongings it didn't take her, Gemma and Simon long to cart everything up to the tiny flat above the old dairy at Halesmere. Ella, Max and the children, as well as Prim, were on hand to welcome her with a hamper of goodies from the community shop, and invited the three of them to the pub as Gemma and Simon were staying over for church and the banns being read in the morning.

They had a lovely, merry evening, and after the church service on Sunday, when Gemma and Simon had left with fond farewells, Lizzie began to unpack. She hadn't realised just how little of her own beyond clothes she'd collected over the years, including the few bits from her parents' old home she'd wanted to keep, the boxes of her childhood memorabilia going under the bed. But other than that, she was shocked to realise, she could be starting out as a student, not rapidly approaching thirty and the beginning of another six-month flat stay.

Stan and Pearl popped by with a cake, Ana stuck her head around the door to invite Lizzie to yoga in the morning, and Marta brought a candle to welcome her. Lizzie couldn't shrug off her excitement at being back at Halesmere with the artists and so much more on her doorstep.

And Cal. He was now quite literally on her doorstep too, less than fifty metres away in the old forge. She had no idea what he felt about her moving into the flat, if he even knew, though she presumed he must – Stan would have made sure of that. She had an excellent view of the courtyard from the mezzanine bedroom above the sitting room, especially in the roll top bath. Stan informed her that Max had installed it for Ella as a surprise after having the floor reinforced when she'd lived in the flat before moving into the cottage with him and the children.

Used to city living, the size of the newly refurbished flat didn't bother Lizzie; her first London house share had been smaller than this. A compact white kitchen was offset by walls painted palest grey throughout. A neat staircase lead to a bedroom covering half of the lower floor where the woodwork was stripped back to natural oak, reflected in the beams above her bed and wardrobes in the eaves she knew had been expertly built by Stan. The steps down to the courtyard were narrow with an elegant wrought iron handrail and matching spindles creating a feature both practical and beautiful. She suspected Cal might have made them.

Lizzie was out of bed at dawn on Monday and off exploring the once-familiar grounds with her camera. The light in May was exceptional and she didn't want to miss a moment. When she joined Ana for yoga in the barn at seven, she had to disguise her exhilaration at seeing Cal there, laughing with Ana, who quickly excused herself to welcome Lizzie, Sandy, Ella and a couple of locals.

The session lasted half an hour and, when they'd finished, Lizzie felt energised and fresh, loving how much she had already packed into her morning. Back in the city she would grab a bowl of cereal as her go-to food whenever she was on the run, driving the supermarket delivery van during mostly unsociable hours.

She couldn't deny she also liked the sense of danger her latest move had brought, the nerve-racking realisation that she had to make her business a success and finally think about creating a home of her own. Her parents were very supportive, and Lizzie spoke with her mum most days, already looking forward to their next visit.

Outside in the sunshine she was watching Lily and Arlo charging across the cobbles to feed the chickens before school, Prim hot on their heels and Stan waiting for them with a bucket. Yesterday Lizzie had laughed when Ana tried her best to persuade him to join them for early morning yoga too. He was having none of it and informed Ana cheerfully, as he clutched his back and gave Lizzie a wink, that his day began with a bacon butty and a brew, and he was quite sure all that bending would be very bad for him.

'What about ye, Lizzie? How's the flat? Settling in?'

She spun around to find Cal behind her. The last time they'd spoken she'd run from his arms out of the dairy, and seeing him now, she was already remembering him pressed against her as they'd kissed, the door at her back, the naked desire in his eyes, fingers unfastening buttons on her blouse. She swallowed, aware of a flush that hadn't come from the yoga. She had to make herself get past this, past him. They were over and she had to mean it. 'It's lovely, thanks. Getting there.'

'Bit sudden, wasn't it? The move?' He stuffed hands in the pockets of his shorts.

'It's not because of you, if that's what you're thinking,' she quipped.

'Ach.' A hand went to his chest, smile widening into a grin. 'I suppose I deserved that.'

'I'm grateful to Ella and Max for giving me an opportunity to work with them on the retreats and grow my business from here. And letting me have the flat, of course.'

Lizzie wondered if he knew about Jack and her recent break-up. But why would he, she admonished herself, it was none of his business and she didn't imagine Ella would gossip about someone else's personal circumstances.

'And what about the studio?'

Lily and Arlo were on their way back from the chickens and Max was at the arch, calling something about getting ready for school and they'd better hurry up.

'What about it?' Another tremor of fear darted through Lizzie at the reminder.

'Are you going to use it for your photography?'

'Hopefully. Maybe. I'll see.'

'Make sure you do. You're grand, Lizzie. You deserve a chance.' Cal glanced at the dairy, and she wondered if he too was remembering their last meeting. 'So I guess it means I'll be seeing you around. I'd better go, I've got a wedding present to make.'

For a second, she thought he was going to say something else, but he offered a quick nod and walked away. She was caught staring at the bottom of the steps to her flat when he reached the forge and raised a hand, that sexy smile and idle curiosity still lingering.

As the week moved on, Lizzie found the beginnings of a new routine as she worked on the weddings and a romantic proposal she had coming up – one that should hopefully result in an engagement. She also had some enquiries and arranged to meet other prospective clients interested in her services. She went to see a local venue, a converted barn and farmhouse beside a river, and loved it at once. The owners were keen to work with her and she made an appointment to return with two clients looking to marry in the autumn.

Lily and Arlo popped by one afternoon after school, curious to see inside the flat. Lizzie made them drinks and shared between them the cupcakes Gemma had left, as Arlo merrily confessed he'd broken his arm in here before Christmas after falling from the old ladder up to the bedroom. Much to her brother's disgust, Lily said cheerfully, their dad had now taken over the cooking at home because Ella couldn't stand the smell of onions or garlic. Lizzie sympathised, she'd seen Ella belting to the bathroom with a hand over her mouth a couple of times as her morning sickness made itself apparent.

Lily also confided that Stan had bought some ginger tea especially for Ella so she could still have a regular brew in his workshop. He wasn't big on deviating from his beloved builder's tea and the ginger one was resolved solely for her. Her bump was slowly growing, with the baby due in late November, and Lizzie had also noticed Stan rushing across the courtyard to help Ella onto the nearest bench after he spotted her leaning against a wall with her hands on her knees. Lizzie had smiled, some things never changed, and Stan clearly thought the world of Ella, as he had of Gemma and Lizzie back in the day.

He gave Lizzie a merry wink when she popped into his workshop, informing her she'd have to make do with regular tea or Bovril as he didn't often run to coffee, and she'd come to the wrong place if she thought he'd be offering her iced blonde lattes with super skinny double shots and oat milk. But he was still a mine of inform-ation about Halesmere, as well as being someone who appreciated keeping busy and making himself useful, and over her laughter and their banter, he'd be a great support while she settled in.

Halesmere House was full, with eight guests staying, and it seemed perfectly normal to see them around the courtyard and exploring the studios, given her history here. Max's mother Noelle, a portrait artist who divided her time between a flat in the house and a cottage in France, invited Lizzie to supper on Thursday night and promptly invited her to sit for a painting.

Forewarned by Max and already eyeing a pair of exquisite nude portraits on the wall, she politely declined. Noelle wasn't dissuaded for long, suggesting Lizzie might like to think about it, that the offer was always open and why didn't she pop along to Noelle's monthly drawing class? Lizzie accepted the invitation, deciding it was probably the lesser of two tricky evils, and it was very late when she returned to the flat, feeling a little unsteady after several hefty gin and tonics.

She only saw Cal twice more those first few days, and they didn't speak. He was a glimpse in the courtyard through her window, a shadow one night in the dark as he locked up the forge. She refused to give in to the desire to find him and work out how things should be between them now. She knew very little of his life here and had no idea how he spent his time when he wasn't at Halesmere, whether there was a partner, or children, waiting for him somewhere else. She couldn't help doubting that after the madness of those moments in the dairy and the kiss they'd shared. She wouldn't describe his character as straightforward, but he had always been loyal.

On Friday afternoon Lizzie was going over the final details for the proposal she'd helped her client plan, scheduled for tomorrow morning. She still felt a little dulled after the late night with Noelle as she double checked the itinerary she'd already emailed her client, which he'd confirmed a few days ago.

Doug Barnes and his partner Christy were over from the States and holidaying in the UK for a few weeks, having met in Cumbria nearly thirty years ago. They'd enjoyed a summer romance before going their separate ways, and their paths had crossed again after divorce and widowhood. They'd resumed their relationship and were revisiting all their favourite places in the Lake District. Unbeknown to Christy, Doug was also planning to propose and not let slip this second chance at happiness together.

Lizzie had met him online when he'd got in touch and liked him at once. He was friendly and jolly, cheerfully admitting that he didn't have a romantic bone in his body and very much wanted her expertise to ensure all would go well on the day. His only stipulation was that he wanted to propose on Windermere as he and Christy had first met on a lake cruise all those years ago.

Satisfied all was in place for him and Christy, Lizzie checked her inbox. A new email had the colour draining from her face – the yacht that was supposed to take Doug and Christy out onto the lake tomorrow was no longer an option. She went straight to Google for help, scrolling through the first of thousands of results in her frantic search. She clicked on a few, dismissing them, before a sudden brainwave followed. She grabbed her phone, shot down the steps and across the courtyard, and shoved back the door into Stan's workshop so hard it bounced back and just missed giving her a black eye.

'What is it, lass?' Stan was tightening a piece of wood in a vice, and paused to rub his chin. 'If you'd run in 'ere any faster you'd 'ave crashed out t'other side. What's goin' on?'

'Stan, I need your help,' she blurted out. 'Please. I've just had an email saying that the yacht for tomorrow has had engine failure.'

'What yacht?' He scratched his bald head.

'The one I've booked for a special proposal on Windermere for an American couple. It's all arranged and now I'm being told the yacht is out of action. They're offering a refund but...'

'But that's no good, is it, with your Americans about to roll up an' this fancy day out all set.' Stan gave the vice a final turn. 'Sit down. Nowt worse is gonna 'appen while you get your breath back.' He put the kettle on as Lizzie sank into a worn armchair. She hoped he was right, but couldn't resist checking her phone again for any more horrors that might be lurking.

'How can I tell them it's cancelled, with Doug wanting to propose to Christy on the lake? I haven't got time to try everyone I've found on Google for a replacement, and I thought you might know someone. Ella's gone for a scan with Max, so I can't ask them.'

Lizzie felt winded, ambushed by the sudden change in her carefully executed plans. She was never like this usually. Work had thrown everything at her in the course of her career and she'd coped, had found a way smoothly through. But this felt personal, and she so wanted Doug and Christy to have the proposal they deserved after many years apart.

'I might 'ave a solution.' Stan passed a steaming mug of tea across, which Lizzie accepted gratefully, hope flaring in her face.

'You do?'

'Aye. But you're not gonna like it.'

—

The house was as difficult to find as Stan had warned and Lizzie drove past the entrance twice before she realised her mistake. She spotted the track, not even a proper lane, on her third attempt and bumped along it for a quarter of a mile before reaching a narrow two-storey building clad in pale timber and set among trees. If she didn't know better, she would have assumed it was nowhere near the lake. A plain grey van was hooked up to an electric charging point and her smile was wry. It was so like Cal to tread lightly, even down to his choice of vehicle.

Once out of the car, the landscape was silent and still, and she caught a glimpse of the fells between the trees, sharp green and grey ridges jabbing across a blue and cloudless sky. With a nervous knock on the oak door, she pushed sunglasses into her hair and waited, biting her lip when Cal didn't answer. Perhaps he wasn't in, although the presence of the van suggested otherwise. She hadn't seen him for a couple of days and butterflies were swirling in her stomach. She knocked again, realising she should've called ahead or let Stan, she hadn't thought...

'Lizzie? What's the craic?'

The door was pulled back and her polite, prepared smile became a gape. Cal was soaking, barefoot, wearing only a pair of shorts and her eyes jumped to the wolf on his arm, her breath suddenly a stutter.

'Sorry if I've kept you waiting, I'm just out of the water.'

She could see that, and she was doing it again: thinking about their kiss, those moments alone, his hands in her hair, fingers tracing his wolf tattoo. 'You didn't. I, er, it's about...' She was trying her level best not to follow the glistening drops running down his chest.

'Want to come in?' His surprise had become amusement as he swung the door back, revealing a narrow hall, white walls, more oak, and a glimpse of blue lake. 'See if you can remember why you're here?'

That he had noticed her distraction sharpened her focus at once and her reply was cool, more considered. She had not come here to make a fool of herself, and she straightened her shoulders. 'Are you alone?'

'Does it matter?'

'It does if I'm disturbing you.'

'You're not. Go through.'

Lizzie followed the hall to emerge in a stylish sitting room, the wall overlooking the lake made entirely of glass, the bi-fold doors pulled back. She was familiar with Windermere, but it tended to be somewhere she usually avoided because it was so busy, and she hadn't been this close to it in a while. She saw a square patio with seating for two, a lawn between the trees leading straight to the water and a small jetty where, nestling against the wooden planks, bobbed a yacht, bright in the sun pouring down. The view was exceptional and a few moments later, she sensed Cal nearby, a T-shirt already damp covering his chest.

'I'd offer you a drink but—'

'It's fine, I'm not staying.'

'If you'd let me finish, I was going to say, "but you're driving". Would you like a glass of water?'

'You have alcohol?' He'd never bothered with it when she'd known him before. His mum had tried to numb her pain with a bottle, and he'd hated what it had done to her.

'I keep some for guests. Yes or no?'

'Yes. Please.' She might need to be sociable to get him onside with her request. Admiring the beautiful house, she couldn't help wondering if he was alone here now, was he always?

The boathouse was tiny. The sitting room, dining area and kitchen were one square space divided into three and made for two. The kitchen comprised two rows of oak cupboards, shelves fastened to the back wall above one, the remaining storage fixed beneath thick beams to separate it from the sitting room. Cal was opening the fridge next to a Belfast sink and a contemporary range. The art on the white walls was all modern and a wooden staircase wound its way to the first floor. Everything was functional yet still stunning. Exactly Cal.

'Cheers.' He passed Lizzie a glass filled with iced water, cucumber and mint. He raised his own and they shared a quick smile at their new awkwardness, the social niceties they were performing and had never needed before. 'Shall we take it outside?'

'Okay.'

He ignored the two chairs on the patio, carrying on to a pair of Adirondack seats further down the lawn, just above the waterline. Lizzie was already too hot in the jeans and rugby shirt she'd been wearing when she'd crashed into Stan's workshop little more than an hour ago.

When he had suggested his solution to her problem of the broken-down yacht, she'd leapt on it like a lifeline, jumping straight in her car and racing to Cal's secluded boathouse to throw herself on his mercy. He settled in a seat, and Lizzie refused to let herself be drawn by how good he looked – relaxed, one hand around the glass, gaze fixed on hers, as though she was his view and not the water or the boarders paddling past.

'So what brings you out here?'

Lizzie took a deep breath. 'Is there any possibility of you taking two people out on the lake tomorrow? Please?' She glanced at the white and blue yacht bobbing against the jetty, righting itself from the swell of a ferry chugging past loaded with passengers. 'I promise I wouldn't ask if there was another way but it's a crisis situation and Stan thought you might be prepared to help. You can name your price and we'll pay it. It's very important – an engagement is at stake.' Not to mention her reputation and possibly the potential for growing her business, but she didn't want to confess every detail and relinquish any remaining credibility she might still have.

'Sure.'

Lizzie nearly dropped her glass and water sloshed onto her knee. 'You'll do it? Just like that?' She had been prepared for Cal's refusal, not this straightforward acceptance and the wry amusement lingering on his face.

'You said I could name my price.'

'I did. You can.' Damn. He'd never been hungry for material possessions but perhaps the success of his company had changed him. If he demanded an unreasonable fee, she'd make up the difference herself. Anything to keep Doug and Christy's weekend and their proposal on track.

'And I have one other condition.'

'Okay.' Lizzie gulped a mouthful of water, coughing on a piece of mint. How had making a simple request of this man reduced her confident city-career self to this dithering wreck? She strongly suspected it was because he'd answered the door soaking wet and had said yes to her request without hesitation. Neither had been expected. 'Let's hear it, then we can talk terms.'

'Bring them here at five forty-five and we'll set out at six.'

'PM?'

'AM.'

'Cal, I can't do that.' This time Lizzie did put the glass down and turned in her seat as much as she was able. 'They're expecting a relaxing and special weekend. I can't drag them here before breakfast at silly o'clock.'

'You can.' He tilted his head to the view, a hand on his bare knee. 'It'll be worth it, I promise. It's going to be a perfect day.'

'Is it up for discussion?'

'Tell them the early start is part of the private experience you've laid on just for them. You'll think of something.'

Her initial euphoria at his agreement was already disintegrating as frustration set in. She'd have to find a way to smooth Doug and Christy over and get them to agree. They were expecting breakfast in bed and a leisurely chauffeur-driven visit to the lake, not some madcap dawn adventure sprung on them at the last minute. But she could do this; she'd faced much worse in her career before now. 'And how much will you charge for taking them out?'

'Nothing.'

'What? Don't be silly.' Yet again Lizzie was wrong-footed. 'I've already had the refund from the other yacht. We can pay and you should take it. There'll be a cost surely, to taking it out.' She glanced at the jetty. 'Fuel or something. Electricity.'

'My price isn't money.'

Oh, hell. Why didn't that surprise her? A glimmer of triumph on his face told her he was enjoying this, and she wished she could wipe that smug suggestion of a smile off his lips, caught by his stillness as he sipped from his drink.

'I want you to come with me. That's my price.'

'What, on the lake? With them? You?' Her head jerked back as she laughed, but it was her smile that was wiped away as she realised he was actually serious. 'I can't. I'm not playing gooseberry and when Doug lets you know he's ready to propose to Christy you'll have to make yourself scarce.'

'And how am I supposed to do that? It's only a small yacht, there aren't many places to hide.'

'I don't care! Tie it up to a tree and throw yourself overboard or something.' Hopefully drown at the same time, but then how would she get her clients back? As long as Cal returned them safely to shore, she could drown him herself.

'You mean drop anchor?'

'Whatever. You're doing this on purpose. It's ridiculous.' She leapt up to glare at him. 'There's no good reason why I should come with you, and you could just take the money like a reasonable person. Or have said no in the first place.'

Her glass fell over when she caught it with her foot and she was storming back to the boathouse, her plans and her equilibrium in tatters. Stan had only been trying to help and now she was wishing she hadn't asked him in the first place and had stuck to trawling online for another yacht instead of having Cal toy with her for his own amusement.

'Lizzie?' He caught her hand, letting her go as they drew to a halt. 'I'm sorry, okay? But I do want you to come with me and that's my price.'

'Why?' The brief touch of his fingers still lingered.

'Because there's something I want to ask you, and if we're on the lake then you won't have much choice other than to hear me out.'

'Ask me what? And you can't do that here, now? I'm a good swimmer, I reckon I can make it to shore if I need to.'

'I know that.' His gaze drifted down her body and she almost gasped at the lazy interest he wasn't bothering to hide.

'You can't make me go on the yacht with you.' Her pulse was still spiking, the air between them simmering.

'I know that, too. But you need me for this trip and ach, it's all I've got to bargain with.'

'What about the proposal? How would we both disappear if the yacht's that small?' She was wavering, certain he understood she wanted this crazy trip with him as much as he apparently did her.

'We're not, they are. There's a tiny island where we can drop them off and they'll have it all to themselves at that time of day. We'll give them an hour, more if they want. I take it you're organising a meal for them?'

'It was supposed to be a champagne lunch. If Christy says yes.' Lizzie hadn't thought of breakfast.

'Leave it with me, I'll sort it. Part of my price.'

'Okay. I suppose I should thank you.' She was already fizzing at the thought of a morning on the lake with

Cal, the hours together, the high of his company that had always swept her away. He'd been unpredictable at times, surprising her with an adventure, an experience he thought she'd love. If she could give herself up to this one then she might actually enjoy it, the pressure of the proposal, her clients' future happiness and the success of her business notwithstanding.

'So I'll see you at five thirty?'

'Five thirty,' she echoed faintly. What had she agreed to?

Chapter 12

When Lizzie returned to the boathouse at five thirty the next morning, she knew Cal had been right to suggest this most perfect time of the day for the sail. She walked through a side gate he'd left open, pausing to lift her camera and frame a shot of the garden and that view.

Last night, to her immense relief, Doug had been excited rather than alarmed by the sudden change in her plan and he'd promised to explain the new start to Christy without giving the game away. Lizzie had offered to take photographs of their trip and he was quick to accept. Now, the lake was reflecting the outline of the fells above it, the sun not long risen to greet her.

The meadows on the opposite shore, dotted with grazing grey sheep, sloped to the water's edge and a pair of early morning hikers were marching between them. Three paddle boarders were out, and she knew she couldn't have set up a scene like this for Doug and Christy in the middle of the town where the sail was supposed to have begun. Her worries about the day were fading, as she watched the yacht sway in the water. Cal jumped from it onto the jetty and give her a grin.

'Okay, you were right.' She framed him in her lens and he pulled a face, making her smile as she took the shot. 'It's pretty amazing here right now. They're gonna love it.'

'Told you.'

'Do you have to be so smug?' It felt very easy to fall back into the teasing they'd used to share. 'Don't you have a Captain's hat or something? I'm sure you'd like everyone to be clear on who's in charge here.'

'I'm not in charge of the yacht today, your clients are.'

'Doug and Christy? He told me they've never been on a boat like this, I don't think they'd know how to sail it.'

'It's not difficult, I'll keep an eye on them.' Cal's bare feet padded from the jetty onto the grass and Lizzie's fingers stilled on the camera. She'd forgotten how he'd used to look at her, as he was doing now, as though he could read her every thought and knew what she wanted before she could voice it herself.

'Thank you for doing this,' she rushed out. 'Doug just wants everything to be perfect for Christy and I was dreading having to find another way for him to propose.'

'You're welcome.' Cal halted and she caught the scent she'd always thought of as his, as fresh and clean as the early morning spring air. Had he showered before she arrived or swum in the lake? She was fighting her own fingers to prevent them from finding out if his beard would be as soft against her palm as it looked. She liked how it suited him, holding onto the memory of it against her skin when they'd kissed. His eyes were on her mouth, and she knew he wanted the same thing she did – another memory to make. How were they going to get through this day on a yacht, she wondered, when they couldn't seem to hold an ordinary conversation without revealing the attraction that had never truly gone away?

'Have you sorted out breakfast?' She made herself take a step back, sliding the cover over her lens. 'Is it in the boathouse? I'll go and get it.' The rest of her kit was in her rucksack, which she swung off her shoulder and dropped to the grass.

'I've already been out to the island and left it ready, and there's champagne on board.' Cal grinned at the expression on Lizzie's face as he picked up her kit. 'Relax, it's all going to be fine. I'll take care of it, okay? I'll look after them.'

'And what about your price? You do know you don't need me today?' Her voice sounded stretched, high. She wasn't sure she could trust her own self around him.

'It's too late for that. I figured the best way to get you to help me was for me to help you first.'

'Make me an offer I couldn't refuse,' she retorted. She heard a car pulling up on the drive behind them and Cal laughed softly.

'Something like that. Come on, they're here.' His hand was brief around her fingers. 'Let's give them a trip they'll never forget.'

Doug and Christy were elated when Cal invited them onto the yacht and gave them a quick tour. Gleaming white in the early morning light, hull edged with blue, the saloon inside was all cream leather, pale wood finishes, and gorgeously snug and comfortable. Lizzie chose a seat in the cockpit, enjoying listening to him explain that the yacht, an Oceanis Clipper with a lifting keel suitable for even the shallowest of jetties, had been on the lake all her life. The payoff for such a beautiful, still morning, he explained, was that they were unlikely to raise the sails and would be under power most of the day.

He showed them how to start the engine and Cal took the helm to sail smoothly from the jetty. Lizzie caught his eye and gave him a grin of pure exultation that he returned just as quickly. The city and her break-up with

Jack seemed a million miles away in this moment. At this hour there were no ferries full of passengers or pedal boats pottering around, and even the hotels hadn't quite woken up.

After a few minutes Cal encouraged Christy to take the helm as he pointed out their course and what to avoid as Doug recorded everything on his phone, the water rippling gently in the yacht's wake. The couple hadn't seemed to mind Lizzie's presence and her camera was busy as they followed the lake south, Christy swapping with Doug after a bit so he could take the helm.

With Cal guiding him, Doug sailed close to the shore and Cal shared some of the history of the houses on the lake; the families who had lived here for generations and others who'd swooped in to secure their own little piece of paradise. Two people were having an early morning swim outside a boathouse and a couple breakfasting on a balcony offered hands and cheery calls in greeting.

After an hour and a half, when they'd crossed the lake and were gliding north on the opposite shore, he suggested that Doug and Christy might like to explore an uninhabited island, rarely visited and formerly home to monks, with a ruined chapel its only building. A history major, Christy loved the idea and as they drew alongside an old jetty in water so clear and shallow Lizzie could see the bottom, Doug threw her an anxious glance as Cal secured the yacht.

'Everything's ready for you,' she murmured, watching Cal giving Christy a hand to step onto the wooden jetty. 'Breakfast is at the chapel door, just follow the path through the trees.'

Doug nodded and he followed Christy from the yacht. He took her hand and they soon disappeared. Cal untied the rope, jumped back on board, and pointed to the helm.

'Come on, your turn. We've got an hour.'

An hour alone with Cal seemed to Lizzie both an eternity and simply not enough. He was beside her as she cautiously reversed the yacht from the jetty and turned it. The sun was high and warm, the sky a vivid cornflower blue as they sailed away from the island, heading south again to avoid the bustle of the towns already beginning to wake up.

'Cal, I think you've made Doug and Christy's year, never mind their day. Thank you, they're never going to forget this.' The light breeze was a pleasure on Lizzie's face as she tried to keep the yacht steady, loving how it responded so smoothly to her careful guidance.

'As long as Christy accepts the proposal.' There was a wry note in his voice as he settled on a seat, confident in her abilities as always, and Lizzie laughed.

'I don't think that's in any danger, have you seen how they look at each other? It's so lovely.'

He reached across to increase the speed and she felt the yacht surge forward. There was a strict limit on the lake, and they were close to it now; they couldn't go much faster. Her loose hair was blowing across her face, her hand following to push it back.

'May I?'

She nodded as Cal stood, holding her breath as he gathered her long hair in his hands. She kept the yacht steady as she found a band in her pocket and passed it to him. He'd never tied her hair before, he'd always much preferred loosening it from whatever held it back.

'So what did you want to ask me that needed to be said in the middle of a huge lake from which I can't escape?' She'd thought of this half the night, excited and nervous in equal measure.

'Let's drop anchor, then I'll tell you.' He raised an arm and Lizzie glimpsed his tattoo of the waterfall again. Their history, and now another chapter of the story, not yet ended. 'Keep right, mind that buoy just ahead. See it?'

'Yes.'

'Aim about twenty metres this side of it. Dead on.'

Cal cut the engine, silencing the sound, and she heard the anchor fall as the yacht was secured. They were moored between two small, wooded islands, the yacht drifting in the breeze before settling, sunlight bouncing off the white. It was warmer now they weren't moving, and she tipped her head back to enjoy it as he jumped down the steps into the saloon.

'Drink? Lemonade squeezed by my own fair hand this very morning?'

'Is that another offer I'm not going to be able to refuse?'

'Absolutely. I was making it for Doug and Christy anyway so...'

'You made lemonade for them?' She hadn't thought of checking what he'd brought for her clients to eat and realised she probably should have done. She'd trusted him when he said he'd take care of it for her and she took the two glasses he was offering through the door.

'Yes, and breakfast.' He raised his voice, back in the saloon. 'What did you expect? That I was going to feed them and starve you?'

'You made some for me as well?' Lizzie had swallowed down some yoghurt before leaving the flat this morning, too tense about the day ahead to eat anything more. She was famished now, though the early start was worth every single minute just for the view alone.

'Made some for *us*,' he corrected, a grin following as he held up a plate. 'So we've all got the same. Bananas with granola, frozen yoghurt and berries. I hope they like the egg and bacon muffins – I didn't make those, in case you're wondering. Fresh coffee and smoothies to drink, and I left them a martini cocktail on the table I set up for two outside the chapel, with freshly picked wildflowers. And there's raspberry, chocolate and hazelnut bread if we're still hungry. I did make that, I like baking.' Cal was laughing as he took in Lizzie's expression. 'Have I passed the romantic proposal planning test? Will it do?'

'You did all that? For them?'

'Actually, I did it for you. You said it was very important and that it should be special. I thought it needed a bit of effort and would be nice for them.'

'Nice?' Lizzie's laugh was incredulous, her thoughts caught on why he said he'd done it for her. 'Now I'm really worried about why you brought me out here after going to all this trouble for the proposal. Come on, you're killing me. Just say it.'

'What's Ella told you about the launch party she's organising at Halesmere?' Cal was serious now as the teasing fell away and Lizzie's pulse jumped. He passed her a bowl of granola and she thanked him.

'Not much, we're having a handover meeting on Monday. Why?'

'Because I'm involved with the brand that's being launched.'

'You?' All the questions running through her mind hadn't arrived at this one. 'But why? How?'

'I'm already using some of their kit and they got in touch after they saw my Instagram. It makes sense for both of us now I'm a qualified mountain leader. The company liked what I did in New Zealand and thought we could help each other.'

Lizzie could see it at once. She'd already looked up his Instagram, she just hadn't quite got as far as following him yet. So, he'd be working with another clothing line made for the outdoors; sustainable, and as stylish as it was functional. She'd be advising the client to do exactly what Cal was suggesting, linking their social media posts to create interest in the brand through his profile, and drawing attention to his own business at the same time.

'So you brought me out here to make sure I wouldn't back out of the launch because you're part of it.' She tried the granola. 'This is delicious, thank you. And don't worry, I need the work. It'd take more than you being involved to make me give it up.'

'That's not quite everything.' He had already finished, putting his empty bowl on the floor.

'Oh?' Her spoon paused halfway to her mouth.

'I need some great content for my Instagram before the event.' He leaned forwards, hands clasped between his knees. 'I brought you out here to ask you to take the images for me. Please. You're the one I want to work with on it.'

'Cal, I'm not the right person for that!' The spoon clattered back into the bowl. 'You need a professional, someone who knows what they're doing.'

'You do know what you're doing, Lizzie. We both know you're good enough.'

'Why me?' she rushed out, her hand going to the camera as if seeking reassurance from its familiarity.

'Because you know me better than anyone and I want to work with you,' he said quietly. 'If you'll have me?'

Lizzie's mind had jumped straight back to the online images she'd found of Cal in New Zealand: him on the beach, in the surf, with the beautiful woman who'd shared his life. 'I can't.' It seemed the only rational response. 'I've got to focus on growing my business. I need it to be a success and I think you should find someone else.'

'I don't want someone else, Lizzie. I want you to do it.' His voice was soft, the lilting Irish accent he'd never lost filling her senses, her soul. The camera slipped on the seat and they both lunged to retrieve it. Her fingers found his, desire falling into her stomach. She leaned back, trying to focus on anything other than the way he was looking at her. 'You always got me, right from the start, that night at your party. It's like you could see through all the bullshit and underneath you knew I was better. Someone you could love. Someone I didn't know how to be then.'

Lizzie was remembering her party too, the emotion and excitement racing through her, the moment at the bar when she already knew she'd lost her heart to him, his smile when she'd taken that first photograph. 'You just needed to be who you are for me to love you, Cal,' she said quietly. 'No filter.'

Her gaze went to the blue lake, letting the light blind her vision before she saw too much. 'Why did you come back? I heard what you said to Bea. Was it true, about it being home?'

'Honestly? Yes.' His smile was hopeful, a little sad. 'I can't explain it any better than to say I feel like my heart is here, for all sorts of reasons. I want to make a real home here. I didn't plan to stay in New Zealand as long as I did but life was grand and I got used to it.'

Lizzie was instantly reminded of that lovely woman again – at his side, the relationship they'd shared – feeling the unwelcome blaze of jealousy before she forced it away. 'I saw some of the shots for your company, they were stunning.'

She hadn't needed to find every image to see how perfectly he'd defined his passion for the outdoor life he represented. The new models were just as beautiful, but they weren't Cal. She'd sensed they didn't have a love of the landscape flowing through their veins in quite the same way he did.

'Thanks, Lizzie. I never meant for it to attract so much interest. Modelling was just a bit of fun that got the brand started and I packed it in the minute we sold up.' He smiled and she noticed the new lines around his eyes, his mouth, the evidence of their fourth decade coming upon them. 'So you have been looking me up.'

'Bea liked your stuff, she bought some T-shirts for her husband. So you didn't want to stay on, after you sold the company?'

'No, it was never really me, that corporate life. Not like you. It was always what you wanted, what you worked for.' He leaned forward to clasp his hands between his knees. 'So where have you come from, Lizzie Martin? Where have you been these past twelve years?'

'You probably already know the answer if you've seen my website. And my life doesn't compare with yours, Cal.' She tried to laugh off his question and the casual attempt to fill in the blanks of their time apart, what little there was other than work and looking after those she loved. 'I haven't surfed my way around New Zealand or had my picture on the front of magazines. So this is you now? Fancy yacht, expensive boathouse? New brand, new business?'

Cal laughed softly. 'Ach, you know me better than that. The yacht came with the house, I'm renting it for the summer. I'm not really a yacht person, much as I like taking it out.' He ran a hand along the smooth edge of the hull, his eyes suddenly bruised as they met hers. 'I made some changes after my grandfather in Ireland got in touch last year, not long before he died. Someone he knew had seen a picture of me in the local paper as it mentioned my having family there. He was already ill and I came back to see him before it was too late, and we talked. He told me how much they regretted cutting my mum out of their lives the way they did, because of me.'

Reaching for Cal's hand to offer her sympathy felt as natural as breathing to Lizzie. His fingers were quivering inside hers and she didn't need to see his face to understand the hurt in his voice. 'I'm so sorry. That must have been such a shock.'

'It really was.' He said my grandmother had written me a card every year around my birthday and Christmas but didn't know where to send them. He still had them. They'd adopted my mum and had no other family apart from distant cousins.' Cal's voice caught. 'He told me he was proud of where I'd got to on my own and my mum would've approved because she was a free spirit who always did her own thing. He knew they'd let us down and made our lives harder than it should have been.'

Cal turned his hand so their fingers were entwined, and Lizzie wished she could banish away his sorrow. It felt so right, to be at his side like this. 'I'm sorry. I'm glad you had the chance to talk.'

'So am I.' He let out a long breath, and slowly their hands separated. 'It helps, to know they cared in some way.'

'And he didn't know anything about your father, something he could share?'

'Nothing. My mother never said a word about him, at least not to them.'

'You haven't found him?'

Cal shook his head very slowly. 'But I'm still looking. One day maybe I'll get lucky.' He paused. 'So have you decided yet? We both know my content will generate some interest and I can help you, too. I'll tag you in everything, make sure your name is out there as the event planner and my photographer.'

'And what if I don't want that? You'd be there, every time I pick up my phone or my camera.'

'That's your decision, of course. And I'll respect it.' His eyes were fixed to hers and she was falling; she'd been falling since the moment she'd seen him in the courtyard that first night. 'You want to know what I was thinking, when I was on a beach somewhere having my picture taken or getting another tattoo?'

She knew it. She didn't need to hear the words to know he was going to say he had been thinking of her. How twelve years ago she had framed his joy so naturally with her camera when they'd reached a summit, or he'd hauled himself up the side of a rock face and roared with triumph at the top, waiting for her follow. The times when they'd swum alone in their waterfall and had laid back to dry out in the sun, sharing teasing kisses.

Lizzie's throat was tight as her gaze went to the waterfall inked on his arm. They'd been over for years, ever since he'd vanished from her life as quickly as he'd landed in it. They couldn't be having this conversation alone on a yacht in the sunshine of a beautiful day in the middle of a glistening blue lake. They shouldn't be having it anywhere and she forced a lighter tone into words already quivering with emotion.

'If I said yes, how do you plan to help me?' Her eyes were telling him yes already and she was certain he knew it. 'You'd need to make it worth my while.'

'I'll totally make it worth your while in any way you like. Whatever it takes to grow your business too.' His grin was suddenly cheeky. 'How about I do a themed shoot, just for you? Anything you like.'

'Anything?' She raised a brow, her voice falling to match his.

'Anything. Wedding, proposal, we can use the boat-house and the yacht if you want. Dress me up however you like.'

She'd been about to say she'd much rather undress him but that wouldn't be the right start to this project. Excitement was fizzing through her veins, a warmth on her skin that hadn't come from the sun. Her hand went to the water, the coolness dissipating some of the heat.

'Cal, there's something I need to know and I'm sorry if I have no right to ask.' She was staring at the water, the ripple around her fingers, wondering if he understood quite how important his next words would be. 'I don't think I can do this if...' She paused, tried again. 'If there's someone...'

'There isn't, Lizzie.' He shifted on the seat so he was opposite her. 'I wouldn't have asked you if there was.'

'Why not?' She wanted to hear him say it out loud, tell her what her heart already knew.

'Because I couldn't work with you and go home to someone else.' The quick laugh disappeared as he raised his shoulders. 'It's not how I am. Especially when I can't get that kiss we shared out of my mind. How about you?' Cal's stare was unflinching, and he must know she lived alone in the flat. But she understood he was asking her so much more, just as she had. He was asking about her heart. Lizzie knew this path was leading her into all kinds of trouble but it was already too late.

'It's over. He was lovely but we weren't right together.'

Gemma had been correct. One strike and Jack was out. It was all the reason Lizzie had needed to run away. They hadn't loved each other enough.

'I'm sorry. I know how that feels.' Cal leaned back, breaking their moment of sadness. 'So don't think about my offer too long, remember you owe me. Right now there are two people madly in love and busy getting engaged on their own island, all thanks to me.'

'Thanks to you? I had nothing whatsoever to do with it?' Lizzie was indignant and her hand was still in the water. She flicked her fingers and missed as he ducked out of the way. He caught her around her waist, tugging her backwards until she was in his arms, then knelt on the seat to dangle her over the lake, the yacht swaying beneath them.

'Don't make me throw you overboard for insubordination. This is still my yacht for now.' His gaze wandered down her body, taking in the summer top and shorts she was wearing, as though assessing how quickly she might dry out if he dunked her.

'You wouldn't!'

'You think?'

'Cal, don't you dare!' She was laughing, trying without success to escape his arms tight around her.

'Say yes. I want you out there with me, Lizzie. Let me help you too.'

'Put me down.'

He lowered her a little further and she shrieked as one foot touched the cold blue water. 'Say yes or I drop you and you can swim to shore. You're not a duffer, you won't drown.'

'I'll do it if you jump in with me.'

She was falling, screaming as she hit the water, bobbing back up to find a soaking Cal beside her. Both laughing as they trod water, he ran a hand over his face. She turned, swimming away from the desire in his eyes to haul herself back on board.

Chapter 13

'You two look cosy.'

Lizzie wasn't expecting to see Gemma when she and Cal arrived at Halesmere together. Doug and Christy had floated back onto the yacht when Lizzie and Cal returned to the island, beaming and with a beautiful diamond ring on Christy's left hand. Congratulations were offered, champagne uncorked, and Cal took the helm for the sail back to the boathouse.

In their happiness and distraction Doug and Christy hadn't seemed to notice that Lizzie and Cal's clothes were damp, and she couldn't restrain her grin after the hour alone with him. Once she'd seen her clients into a taxi and promised to email the images she'd taken, she realised she'd drunk two glasses of champagne. Embarrassed by her most unusual unprofessionalism, she'd asked Cal, as they'd tided the yacht, if he would run her back to Halesmere.

'Hi, Gemma. You're early, sorry I wasn't here when you arrived. Have you seen Ella yet?'

'No, she's on her way. Something to do with Arlo's birthday, she won't be long.' Gemma shifted a cake tin to share a hug with Lizzie. 'You look well, you've caught the sun already.'

'Have I?' Lizzie's laugh was self-conscious, her gaze wandering to Cal and the wolf on his arm. Was she his prey? It felt that way, after the sail and his determin-ation to work with her on social media content. The tremor of excitement flared again, thoughts still lingering of all they'd shared this morning and the anticipation of capturing him with her camera in the landscape they loved. 'So much for the factor thirty. Probably wind burn, we've been on a yacht all morning on Windermere.'

'"We"?' Gemma's tone was cool. 'Who's "we"?'

'Cal was good enough to help me out of a difficult situation with clients, that's all.' Lizzie made her reply casual on purpose. 'Are you staying over tonight?'

'At Mum's, Simon's on shift. So how did the proposal go?'

'It was brilliant, thanks to Cal stepping in at the last minute to save the day and providing them with the most amazing breakfast. Plus I have some great shots of a gorgeous and newly engaged couple on his yacht.' Lizzie's hair always dried curly if she left it alone, and Gemma was eyeing it suspiciously. 'Do you fancy a coffee while we're waiting for Ella?'

'Lizzie?' Cal's hand briefly touched her arm. 'Can we get together and talk about locations? I've got a few suggestions and we'd like to get some images out there as soon as possible.'

'That's fine.' Her nod was professional, smile practical, eyes dancing.

'What images?' Gemma gave Cal a sharp glare. 'What's going on with you two?'

'Cal's asked me to shoot some social media content for a company he's working with.' Lizzie rubbed one foot against the back of her other leg. This wasn't going well, she'd intended to let Gemma know in her own time. 'It's part of the brand launch I'm planning.'

'What the actual—' The cake tin crashed to the cobbles and Gemma scrambled to pick it up. 'Have you lost your mind? You've barely been here a week, and this is what you do? What happened to zero intentions and being over him? Are you actually back together? And if those brownies are in bits don't blame me.'

'Of course we're not back together.' Lizzie was about to add that she had more sense, but wasn't sure she could be quite so untruthful to her best friend. Sense didn't have very much to do with how she still felt about Cal.

'Would it be so bad if we were, Gemma?' Cal's voice was quiet. He made it sound so simple and Lizzie gasped.

'What do you think?' Gemma rounded on him, and Lizzie paled at the fury in her face. 'You broke her heart into a million pieces! She loved you and you walked out on her without a word for twelve years, you fu—'

'Can we stop this, please?' Lizzie quickly stepped between them. 'It's history, Gem. Cal and I both made mistakes. We've made peace and we're moving on.'

'Mistakes? Is that what you're calling it now?' Gemma sighed, ignoring the phone ringing in her bag. 'I know what a massive mistake it would be, and you do too, Lizzie.' She glanced at Cal. 'I'm sorry, I just don't want her to go through anything like that again.'

'Neither do I, Gemma, that's the last thing on my mind.' He bent towards Lizzie, dropping a quick kiss on her cheek, 'Glad I could help you today.' The lightness of breath and familiar touch of his lips had her head inching up, wanting more. Cal straightened, wrenching his gaze from hers but not before she'd read the same desire. He looked at Gemma, the chill between them not quite abated. 'Are you quite sure you still want me to sculpt Simon's present? It's not too late to change your mind. I've only done the drawings so far.'

'Bit late for that seeing as I've already paid the deposit.'

'Then I need to go and do some work in the forge.'

He turned away and Gemma was soon following Lizzie to the flat. 'He's trouble, Lizzie, I'm telling you,' she muttered crossly. 'Just you make sure you won't regret all this time you're apparently going to be spending together.'

'Come and calm down with a drink while we talk about the theme, and you can look over Ella's suggestions for food. They're stunning, perfect for the informality you're after and she's very happy to arrange a tasting.'

'That sounds wonderful. Never mind coffee, though. I could do with a whopping great gin after what Cal said about working with you.'

'Would it be so terrible if we did get back together?' Lizzie's voice was small as she unlocked the door. 'He's not a bad person, Gem.'

'I guess it wouldn't be awful, not if you really loved each other and were planning to make it last this time. And what's this about a yacht? Bloody show off.'

'The yacht came with the boathouse he's renting, that's all. It's not actually his.' Lizzie stood back to let Gemma go through first. 'What do you think? So much nicer than it was in our day.'

'Love it, especially that bath. Big enough for two, I see.' Gemma gave Lizzie a meaningful stare as she left the cake tin on a worktop, and Lizzie laughed. The thought *had* occurred to her.

'Remind me what it was you said, about moving back here and not doing it because of Cal.' Gemma planted hands on her hips. 'What's actually going on between you two? And don't say nothing, either. I leave you alone for five minutes and you're, what? Giving true love another chance? Sleeping together? Dating? I've seen the way you look at him, Lizzie. It's dangerous and he knows it.'

'And how do I look at him?' Lizzie sighed as she rolled her eyes. Best friends or not, this conversation had not been in her plans for today.

'Like you want to devour him as much as he does you.'

'It's not like you to be so judgemental about someone, Gem.' Lizzie was stung and she squeezed past her to switch on the coffee machine and find mugs. 'Nothing's happened, beyond one kiss that weekend. We didn't plan it and I'm not expecting it to happen again.'

She wanted it to, though, and there was that delectable shiver again as she thought of spending time with him. A mug clattered onto the worktop, and she stood it back up.

'You're right, and I'm sorry.' Gemma slipped her arms around Lizzie, hugging her quickly. 'Please just promise me you'll be careful. Fooling around, sleeping with him is one thing. Getting your heart smashed again is quite another, Lizzie. And you've never been big on the sleeping without involving your heart thing.'

'I'm going to take some images for his Instagram and the brand launch, and that's it, Gem. I've got six months in this flat to grow my business and that's my focus. Cal's paying me, and it's another way to get my name out there. I need work I can rely on.' Lizzie raised her voice over the beans grinding. 'Don't worry about me, please. You have enough to think about with the wedding. I'm a big girl and I'm going to make certain it's wonderful for you and Simon.'

'I know you are. And thank you. Just take care of yourself, please. I'm so excited to see what you've been planning.'

'You don't look it.' Lizzie passed Gemma a cappuccino.

'No? This is my best "I'm worried about my friend and excited about my wedding" face. Can't you tell?'

There was a knock at the door and Gemma went to answer it. Ella had arrived and Lizzie made her a cup of ginger tea. There wasn't room for three around the table so they sat on the small sofa and two armchairs to talk through the wedding reception Ella and Lizzie were creating.

Ella had already booked a yurt for the garden, which Gemma adored. Large enough for the guests as well as a dance floor and bar, it was the perfect space for a festival theme. Gemma, who wasn't often lost for words, was rendered almost mute by Ella's menu. Designed for communal dining, and guests helping themselves, the simple and elegant meal would be a hot buffet with waiting staff on hand to make sure all ran smoothly, with street food vendors for hungry festivalgoers later in the evening.

Lizzie had tracked down two Cumbrian bands, one of them a local group with whom Simon had briefly been a bass guitarist back in the day. An acoustic set during the guests' arrival would be followed by rock and party classics. She suggested keeping the first band's identity as a surprise for Simon, and Gemma was quick to agree.

Lizzie had also met with Marta, who had the candle studio at Halesmere. She and her partner Luke had recently set up a campsite at their farm down the road and Lizzie thought it might be nice to offer guests the opportunity to stick with the festival theme and camp for the night if they wished. Luke's brother Will was Simon's best man and they'd all hung out together back in the day. Gemma loved the new plans and as the afternoon went on Lizzie was relieved that the disappointments of the previous wedding cancellations were already becoming stories they could laugh about.

The next morning, Lizzie joined Gemma and Simon to hear the second banns being read by Sandy. It was a lovely old village church, snug, with a centuries-old tower recently repaired and set in a beautifully kept garden, mostly tended by Sandy, who loved gardening as much as she loved ceramics, her new parish and Strictly Come Dancing. As Lizzie's car was still at Cal's boathouse, she later walked down to the pub to have lunch with Ana and her girlfriend Rachael, and it was almost five before Lizzie returned to Halesmere.

On Monday morning, after yoga in the barn with Ana, Lizzie settled down to go over the details of the brand launch Ella had emailed. Ella's morning sickness wasn't great, and she'd already sent an apologetic message to say she couldn't make the meeting she'd arranged with Lizzie.

A knock at the door had her leaping up with a grin. 'You're early, I thought you said you were busy first thing.' She raised her voice, taking a quick step back when she opened the door. 'Cal! Hi, I was expecting Stan. He's supposed to be fixing a cupboard door for me. Not one he fitted, he made sure to point out.'

'I'd offer to help but he'd never invite me into his workshop again if I made a mess of it.' Cal ran a hand over his cropped hair. Lizzie was getting used to it; she'd always liked it longer, but the short style suited his face, especially with the beard.

'Better not, then. You don't want to be excommunicated.'

'Is this a good moment to talk? It's fine if not, we can arrange something else.'

'Actually it's a very good one, I'm just going over the details for the launch.' Lizzie took a further step back. 'Do you want to come in?'

'You don't mind?'

'No, you need to know what's going on.'

Cal ducked through the door, the space around them seeming to shrink to almost nothing. She was wondering where they stood on greeting one another now and made the decision for them, her hand light on his shoulder as she reached up to kiss his cheek. She was barefoot, smaller than him without heels and he returned the kiss, lips light on her face.

'Would you like a drink?' She cleared her throat, trying to remove the husky note their welcome had produced. 'I made a banana and oat milk smoothie after yoga. I'm hoping to persuade Stan to try it when he turns up.'

'Good luck with that. I saw him heading off to the shop for his bacon butty on my way in.' Cal settled in a chair. 'I think the only oats he consumes come covered in butter and sugar. The smoothie sounds great, thanks, if you have enough. I wouldn't like to deprive Stan of a new experience.'

'No, there's plenty. You know him well.' Lizzie was in the kitchen, still smiling as she returned to the sitting room. 'Here you go.'

'Thanks. You made yoga this morning then.'

'I did.' She'd been disappointed Cal hadn't and she'd found it harder to ease her mind into the movements after the anticipation of wanting to see him had faded. 'Why do you sound surprised?'

'Only because I thought you might have been out with your camera instead.'

'Not when Ana's doing yoga. It's a great way to start my day, especially when it's literally on my doorstep.'

Already, there was an ease developing between them as they got used to one another again. Twelve years ago they'd been in a hurry to see everything, go everywhere, and they hadn't often stood still. She was enjoying this time with him and the smile on his lips told her he felt the same. They'd never hidden their feelings and he knew her too well for Lizzie to start now.

'It looks grand in here.' Cal was checking out the flat and his glance went to the mezzanine and the view of the roll top bath in front of her bed. 'A lot different to how I remember it. Weren't the walls yellow?'

'They were.' Lizzie dragged her mind back to his comment, her thoughts stuck on the vision of him in the bath, with her. She wondered if he'd noticed, like Gemma, that it was big enough for two. 'Ella said it was revolting when she arrived and she had to live in the house until the flat was renovated. So, the launch.' Lizzie put her glass on the hearth. She had to focus; this event was important to everyone. 'I love the theme of "Into the Wild". I've looked up the company, but I'd like to hear your take on their story.'

'Sure.' Cal's glass was empty, and it joined Lizzie's before he crossed one ankle over a knee. 'Oliver Holme is the founder and joint MD with his partner Sarah. I met with them after Oliver got in touch. He grew up in Cumbria but left to travel and met Sarah in Canada. They spent a few years in Ontario before deciding to settle here and set up their clothing business. It's all sustainable, using recycled products and organic cotton in everything they can. They're launching a luggage line along the same ethos, designed to be multifunctional, for anything from commuting to climbing.'

'Perfect for you.' She looked up from her notes and Cal smiled. 'I've only seen a few images online of the brand and already I'm picturing you on the fells with one of their rucksacks on your back, scrambling to a summit.'

'See, that's why I wanted you. To work with, I mean.' He quickly corrected himself but Lizzie had heard his other meaning. The one confessing he still wanted her as much as she did him.

'So the yurt Ella's booked for the launch – she's lined up a bigger one for Gemma's wedding – will work well if the weather's not cooperating on the night, and there'll be a mobile bar serving Cumbrian ales and spirits with soft drinks, keeping to the local theme.' Lizzie was busy with her laptop. 'I've been in touch with someone who runs workshops on living at nature's pace and how we can better connect with the natural world. I've made a provisional booking, which I'll confirm once I know you, Oliver, and Sarah are happy with it.'

'I think that's grand, Lizzie. I'm sure they will, too.'

'I'll send you all the link. It'll be a short session on forest bathing, how to be calm and quiet amid the trees and observe nature with mindful breathing. I haven't gone quite that deep before in a forest but it's great for boosting well-being and reducing stress. I think we should tie some of that into your shots so it's not all about bouldering and fells. There's so much out there.'

'I'll make sure to show up on the night and do my thing.' He shrugged, as though a few pictures of him was all that was required.

'You're not just someone they've brought in to make their products look good, Cal.' Lizzie hoped to make him understand. 'You love this place and that's at the centre of everything you're doing here, just like them. People want to follow you and that's the whole ethos of your new business. You're leading others into the landscape you love and helping them find what you already know – and we're encouraging them to want to use the kit you use. That's what we need to get across at the launch, with the right guests. You're more pivotal to the brand than you maybe realise.'

'You think?' Cal's laugh was awkward. 'I don't want all that stuff to take over again, Lizzie. I've been there, done that. I'll do what I can and that's enough.'

'I understand. I can help.'

'Thanks.' His smile was telling her he trusted her, that she had his confidence and they'd look after each other on this project.

Her phone was ringing but she let it go to voicemail.

'Sorry, I'm keeping you.' Cal glanced at his own phone, and a wistful look was fleeting in his expression. He moved on the chair, as though he was about to get up, but changed his mind. 'I had some news yesterday, about the search for my father.'

'Cal, that's brilliant! What have you found out?' Her enthusiasm seemed to iron out some of the worry on his face.

He unlocked his phone, shifting to her side and sitting on the floor next to her chair so it was easier for Lizzie to see the image on the screen. 'This is the best lead I have so far.'

'Is that your mum? She was beautiful. Marianne, wasn't it?' Lizzie caught her breath at the image as Cal nodded, sliding down to sit next to him on the floor. Marianne's blonde curls were loose around her face, glowing blue eyes full of laughter. How terrible for life to have become such a burden for one so vibrant and young. Lizzie didn't think, her hand moving to cover his resting on his thigh, one finger tapping a quick beat.

'I'm sorry for what happened to you both. It must have been so hard.' An ache for his sorrow seemed lodged in her throat.

'Thanks, Lizzie.' Cal's gaze was on her hand holding his. 'Ach, I guess I was used to it. It was all I knew. But I really need to know who I am, where I came from, who he was. What their story was, him and my mum's. It's something to do with Cumbria, I can feel it. I know that sounds crazy.'

'But what if you don't find out?' Lizzie was trying to summon back the few details they'd discovered twelve years ago. 'And if you do find him, he could be anywhere. Disappeared or...' She didn't want to say it out loud, not yet.

'I know.' Cal's head bowed. 'Dead, or he might not want anything to do with me. He never got in touch or tried to find me. Mum always said that he wouldn't be interested, that he had his own life, and it didn't include us. That was how he wanted it. But if I find him then at least I'll know some of the truth and that's got to be better than always wondering. Half of my history is a blank page, Lizzie, and I really want to fill it.'

'I understand.' She couldn't mistake the sadness in his voice, remembering her own family's unwavering love and support, no matter the circumstances, and comparing it to Cal's fractured family. The years he'd spent in care, the determination to stand on his own two feet and make a success of his future. She wished she could wrap her arms around him, tell him everything would be okay and that'd he find out where he fitted.

Chapter 14

Cal threaded his fingers between Lizzie's, accepting of her sadness for his broken family. She saw the waterfall on his arm, the reminder of their love that he'd chosen to keep close. His hand released hers and she looked at the image of his mother on his phone again.

Marianne was sitting on grass, her arms wrapped around her knees. But it was the man holding her from behind that caught Lizzie's attention this time. His short hair was already flecked with grey, long legs revealed by navy blue shorts. He and Marianne were laughing, his chin on her shoulder, seeming confident and assured in the pose. And if Lizzie knew anything at all about couples, they were in love. Connected and together, separate from the blur of figures behind them by more than just distance.

'Do you know who he is?' Had Cal, too, picked up on the similarity of his eyes and the shape of his face to this man's?

'No.' Cal's sigh was deep as he ran a hand over his chin. 'But I need to find him, or at least who he is. Or was.'

'It looks like they're at a festival, I think I can make out a stage and some stalls. In summer, judging by that sky.'

'Yeah, I thought that too. I know she sang at festivals the year before I was born. I found setlists for a couple and it turned out she was part of a folk band called Bluegrass Bobby. I managed to track down Bobby, the founding member, in Wales. He called me back yesterday but there wasn't a lot he could tell me about our guy.'

'So this man she's with wasn't a member of the band?' Lizzie understood Cal's frustration. One door opened and then another banged shut.

'No. I emailed the image to Bobby, and he confirmed he saw this man and my mum together a few times, but he wasn't a musician, not as far as he could remember. So that's another dead end.'

'And you don't think your father could have been another member of the band? If she was with them all the time, maybe it was possible. Were any of them called Jim? I remember you said that was the name your mother used for him.' But still Lizzie couldn't dismiss the similarity between this man and Cal. Were they really staring at his father and yet might never know who this man actually was?

'Well, it wasn't Bobby,' Cal said wryly. 'He's been very happily married for forty years and swears he's never been unfaithful and I believed him. And the guitarist was in a relationship with the double bass player, so I doubt it was either of them. They're both in the States now, I could find them if I want, but Bobby doesn't think they'd know any more than him.'

'Okay. So this man, with your mum. Are we calling him Jim?' Lizzie wondered if Cal had noticed her using the term 'we' in that sentence.

'I think we might as well.' She liked how he used it, too, making her smile as he continued. 'He's my best lead, but without knowing exactly where this was taken, I've still got nothing to go on. Even if we do find out, if he's not on a setlist or identifiable in some other way, I might never track him down.'

'But it's worth a try. You could maybe share the photo on social media and see if anything comes up. Someone, somewhere, knows who he is.'

'Or was. There's that to think of as well. And I like your idea in theory, Lizzie, but I don't want to stir up a load of crazy stuff. Ach, there's a reason why my mum wouldn't say any more about him. "Jim" tells us nothing, not really.'

'Your middle name is Hamish, isn't it, not James? So she didn't name you after him.' Lizzie was biting her lip, her mind running over the ways they might learn more. 'Let's go back through Cumbrian festivals and look for more setlists and images. It's possible we might be able to identify which festival this was from the background, and we know the year.'

'I'm presuming it's the one before I was born. Thirty-two years ago.' He paused. 'I like how you said "we", Lizzie. Makes me feel less alone.'

It was only a second before she leaned into him. Cal felt different now to the boy he'd been. Stronger, his shoulders broader, and she sensed the weight of his search resting on them. 'You're not alone, not if you don't want to be. I'll help you.'

'Thank you. I know I have no right to ask anything of you.'

She soaked up the warmth of her arm pressed up against his, the glimpse of the waterfall telling her what she already knew − that they weren't done, their story wasn't over, and they were beginning a new chapter. He touched his lips to her hair, dropping a light kiss on the top of her head. It wasn't enough. She wanted more than his mouth brushing her forehead, the second when his beard had skimmed her ear.

Lizzie's phone pinged a notification and she eased herself away from him. They both had work to do, they couldn't sit on her floor side by side all day. 'I'm sorry, I have an online meeting and it's due to start in ten minutes.'

Cal got to his feet, offering a hand to pull her upright. She took it, bumping against him when she stood. They both laughed, easy and awkward all at once, and she followed him to the door, watching as he ducked beneath it.

Stan was whistling as he strolled past outside. 'Now then, 'ave you two been tryin' out that bath,' he bellowed, Lizzie presumed in case the whole courtyard wouldn't hear him. He added a wink for good measure. 'I'll be back in a bit to sort that door for you, lass.'

'The bath is fabulous, Stan. Perfect for two, I'm glad Max thought of it,' she called back, and Cal laughed.

'Aye, well, I'll 'ave to take your word for it, my knees an' Pearl's 'ip bein' what they are.' His whistling resumed as he marched away, hands in pockets.

Lizzie rolled her eyes, smiling at Cal as he spoke. 'So do you want me to run you back to the boathouse for your car later?'

'Please. I'm going to need it soon.'

'Come and find me when you're ready, I'll be in the forge all day.' He ran down the steps and turned to give her a wink. 'I could probably use a bath when I'm done.'

'Stop it.'

After her meeting with a lovely couple who wanted Lizzie to plan their wedding in a Cumbrian castle, and then two telephone calls, she was delighted to have Gemma's florist, known for her natural, country garden style, on board as a supplier she could work with again. She also spoke with Gemma and Simon's photographer who loved to offer a departure from formal images and delve into the adventure of the day. He had a brilliant reputation and Lizzie was thrilled when he pointed her in the direction of a new venue who were holding a wedding showcase in a few weeks' time. She fired off an email introducing herself straight after, excited to receive an invitation to join the event in return.

She also received an email from Bea, letting Lizzie know that one of her colleagues in chambers had just got engaged and that she'd passed on Lizzie's contact details as they were considering getting married in Cumbria. Delighted and excited at all these new opportunities, Lizzie composed a reply to the colleague and sent a grateful one back to Bea.

The afternoon was almost over when she made her way to the forge. On the lake with Cal on Saturday, caught up in the romance of the yacht and the day, she hadn't really given much thought to the reality of working alongside him to take the shots he wanted for social media. As she crossed the courtyard, she assured herself again that she was in no danger of breaking her promise to Gemma because she really did have zero intentions of starting anything up with him for a second time.

She pushed open the door to see the forge was more of a large workshop than a studio, a small gallery area separated from the workspace by a pair of metre-high wrought iron gates. A vaulted ceiling curved to meet stone walls lined with shelving and a dizzying array of tools. A huge metal table stood in the centre, a board behind it fixed to a wall and sprayed with the form of a life-sized dog. It must be Gemma and Simon's Labrador; the breed was unmistakable. Two high doors built into the wall at the far end were open, allowing in more light to the already bright space.

Cal was at the table, a visor over his face, one thick glove covering the arm supporting a long piece of glowing metal he was hammering into shape over an anvil with the other. She was in no hurry to disturb him, and he only noticed her when he raised the visor and measured the metal against the drawing on the wall and turned back.

'Hey. Sorry, didn't hear you come in. How long have you been there?'

'Only a minute. I was just enjoying watching you work.' She liked his grin before he pulled the visor back down.

'Give me time to finish this before I lose the heat?'

'Of course.'

He resumed hammering and over the noise she decided it wasn't a good idea to keep staring at the play of muscles in his upper body while sculpting the metal, turning instead to explore the gallery area. A plain white counter stood in one corner, business cards and a charging station on top. Drawings on the walls of sketches more assured but just as natural as she remembered, flowing simple lines implying energy and life to each animal he'd portrayed: a pheasant, head raised in familiar alarm, as though it were about to squawk; a heron poised and serene, and a hare, big ears alert to danger, long legs ready to leap.

'Oh!' A life-sized sculpture of a wolf stood on the stone floor. Watchful, alert, it was brought to brilliant and vibrant life in metal with a lean and narrow body, its head tipped back in a silent howl. It was stunning, and Lizzie saw at once how Cal had somehow captured an air of menace and incredible power even in its utter stillness. She touched a hand to a piece of curving metal forming part of its back, almost expecting to feel breath and sudden movement beneath her fingers. Like the tattoo on his arm, here was another reminder of the wolf characteristics of strength and protection he'd wanted to embody.

'I've still got it if you were wondering.'

In her awe she hadn't noticed the hammering had stopped and she whirled around. He'd removed the visor and glove and was standing behind the gates still separating them.

'That's nice.' She was thrilled he'd kept the small bronze wolf sculpture she'd gifted him as a reminder of that unforgettable time they'd spent with the animals twelve years ago. When he'd unwrapped it, he had shown her without words what it meant to him. She thought of his Claddagh ring, dropped that day in the dairy, wishing now she hadn't returned it.

'You always did love them, their wildness and strength, how they took care of the pack.' Her hand went to the metal wolf again, its head cold to her touch. 'What have you sculpted it from?'

'Steel. Eventually the surface will have a coat of rust and I like that better, it's more natural.'

She understood. Made from metal, strong, permanent, and yet he'd worked into those sweeping lines a softness to the form that gave life to the wolf. 'You're very good.'

'Thanks.' A lift of his lips was enough to reveal his pleasure in her compliment, his eyes told her more.

'I'm sorry if I interrupted you.'

'You didn't. I'm done for now.'

'How's the present coming on?' She glanced at the life-sized drawing of the Labrador on the wall.

'Yeah, dead on. Gemma said Simon loves the dog almost as much as her.'

'She might say so but there's no doubt who the big love in his life is, and it's not the dog. Are you sure you're ready to go home? I don't want to stop you working.'

'It's fine, I'm grand.' Cal was tidying up and he turned a dial on a tall gas bottle.

'That sketch of the hare is incredible, I bet the sculpture is beautiful. I wish I could fit one in the flat, but I don't think there'd be room for both of us.'

'I wouldn't make you a hare anyway, Lizzie.' He had his back to her as he put tools away, closing the doors at the far end.

'Let me guess, you'd make me a grumpy badger or a prickly hedgehog.'

'Nope.' He slid the leather apron from around his waist and hung it up.

'Go on then, spit it out. The suspense is killing me.'

'I'm more about showing than telling, so if I ever sculpt it then I guess you'll find out.'

A flash of awareness and desire ran through Lizzie. That was Cal exactly and she watched as he pulled off a dirty vest and ran it over his face, replacing it with a T-shirt as he walked towards her.

'I'm so glad you've found what you love to do,' she rushed out. 'I'm sure your sculptures and the mountain leader business are going to be a big success.'

'I hope so. At least I've sold everything I've made so far.'

Her gaze drifted to the wolf. 'Everything except this.'

'I made that for me. I'll never sell it.' He opened the gate and suddenly he was in her space. Their kiss was in his eyes again and she wrenched herself free from the longing. His hand went to the wolf's head, almost as though he was reassuring himself it was still there, still a part of him.

The tiny gallery area seemed far too small with Cal and the wolf so close. She backed out of the door into the courtyard so he could lock up.

'Lizzie! I will see you tonight, *non*?'

She whirled round, smiling as she saw Noelle hurrying over. Grey hair was piled on her head in a messy bun, a pencil sticking out of it. Bangles were rattling on both arms, and she lowered huge sunglasses to give Lizzie a meaningful look. 'You are joining me, *oui*?'

'Tonight?' Lizzie's mind was a blank. 'Sorry Noelle, did we have something arranged?' Was it supper? She had no idea. She was pulling her phone out to check her calendar when Cal reached them.

'Ah, *non*. You have not forgotten me, Lizzie? You promised to come to my drawing class, and it is tonight, seven thirty in the barn. You will be there, *oui*?'

'Hi Noelle.' Cal lowered his head to kiss Noelle on both cheeks.

'Cal, *mon chéri*, how delightful. I must visit you in your studio and see how your sculpture is coming along.' Her look became sly, and she threw Lizzie a wink. 'I was just reminding Lizzie about my drawing class this evening. She must join us, Cal, *non*?'

'You're going to be there?' Lizzie rushed out the words, too surprised to disguise her amazement. 'You know how to draw.'

'Of course he knows how to draw, but it is never a bad thing to keep on practising.' Noelle's shoulders were raised in a very expressive shrug. 'And it is never too late to learn a new skill. After all, Lizzie, it is either attending my class or you must sit for me. You promised, remember.'

'I'll be there,' Lizzie said hastily. She'd always liked art and had been good at it, and a drawing class was infinitely preferable to getting naked in Noelle's studio. Cal and Noelle both laughed as they shared a look. 'I'll see you both there then.'

Her sudden evening plans meant there wasn't time for Lizzie to linger at the boathouse when Cal drove her back; she didn't even go inside for the drink he offered. She returned to Halesmere and ate a quick dinner before making her way to the barn, meeting Rachael at the door.

Noelle had already assured her at supper last week that Lizzie need bring no materials, she could supply everything that was required. Lizzie was trying to cover her nerves as she chatted with Rachael, watching as four more women and a man walked in, and Noelle came over to welcome and introduce everyone. Lizzie already knew from Ella that places were limited and in demand as Noelle was a portrait painter of some renown. Eight easels were placed in a semi-circle around a low dais and the wide windows set into deep stone walls let in plenty of spring light.

There was an excited buzz around the barn as everyone settled onto stools, and Lizzie thanked Noelle for the charcoal and paper she'd provided. Noelle explained the ninety-minute class was untutored. Cal was cutting it fine, and Lizzie eyed the empty easel to her left, ready for him.

'Everyone, this is Cal.' Noelle clapped her hands for quiet as the door behind Lizzie opened. She turned a shoulder, already anticipating the evening alongside him as well as the photography session they'd planned, on the way back to the boathouse, for tomorrow morning. His smile was a general one for the group and he gave her the merest wink as he ignored the spare easel and made his way to the dais in the centre instead.

Noelle greeted him warmly, kissing him on both cheeks. 'This evening we are very fortunate to have Cal as our model. Cal, welcome, *bienvenu*.'

'Thanks, Noelle. Hey, everyone.'

Lizzie's cheeks were already burning. Surely he wasn't actually naked underneath that robe? Her breath faltered as he casually removed it and tossed it onto an empty chair. The air shot out of her lungs, but she wasn't sure if it was in disappointment or relief when her gaze landed on a pair of tight, black trunks. A murmur flew around the barn, and Noelle's voice became a buzz in the background Lizzie was unable to make sense of. The charcoal slipped from her grasp and she almost knocked over the easel trying to retrieve it, heads turning her way at the clatter.

'Sorry.'

Noelle was busy instructing Cal as he settled on a stool. He was beautiful and Lizzie already knew exactly how she wanted to shoot him to represent his own brand as well as the clothing one. Noelle had him turn so that he was in profile to the group and Lizzie's eyes widened. He had another small tattoo, a dolphin on his right shoulder, which she recognised at once.

She had seen it before, on the shoulder of the woman with whom he'd been close in New Zealand. A sign, then, if she needed another, that it had been a significant relationship. She was playing with fire, spending all this time with him, coming close to the flames, knowing they could burn her.

He was leaning forward, hands clasped between his thighs. This man was different to the one she'd first known twelve years ago: sure of himself, more aware of the world now, even as he still sought his place and his family in it.

With some difficulty, she dragged her attention back to Noelle, desperate not to miss any more instruction.

'This is not a tutored class, as you know, but an opportunity for you to develop your drawing skills with the benefit of having a life model to observe.' Noelle was strolling between the easels. 'Remember, it is very important to take your time, do not rush the process of observation. You will spend more time observing than drawing. Think of it this way: picture an item from your home and then imagine yourself drawing it from memory. You will find there is only so much detail you can remember, and you will want to observe it again. This is the same. Look at our model, and look again, *oui*? Observe not simply his outline but the detail that makes up the three-dimensional form.'

Lizzie did as she was told. She looked. She saw the scar on his wrist when he'd fallen from a rock and had needed stitches, the elegance of his hands despite skin roughened from so many years outdoors and his sculpting. The width of his shoulders, the muscles running between them. She picked up the charcoal, aware she ought to try to draw. Noelle was saying something about character and Lizzie found her photographer's eye had instinctively caught the shape of his torso, and she drew something in her first attempt she felt resembled his form if not his persona.

He managed to combine a sense of urgency with complete stillness, and again she was reminded of a wolf – the impression of utter awareness disguised in a desire to not waste energy. She knew she didn't possess the skills to draw this aspect of his character in charcoal; she needed her camera to capture that.

In the ten-minute break Lizzie didn't know what to do with herself. Should she go and chat to him, like some of the others were doing now he'd put the robe back on? Or was it better to hide behind the easel and hope he wouldn't want to see what she'd drawn?

She opted for the latter and after the break Cal resumed his pose. Lizzie concentrated on his face now, trying to replicate the outline of his jaw, the shape of one eye. Once the ninety minutes had passed, more quickly than she expected, she had three discarded sketches she'd crumpled up and one she felt was slightly better than terrible. She was chatting with Rachael beside her, aware of Cal approaching.

'Let's see, then.'

'Absolutely not.' Lizzie hurriedly stuffed the rejected sketches in her bag before he or Noelle could inspect them. Rachael made her excuses and said goodbye to them both.

'That's not bad.' Cal pointed to the best of the four, still on her easel. 'I didn't realise my nose looked like that.'

'I'm thinking of adding a wart. It would serve you right.' She'd tried to read his face as Noelle had suggested, finding new texture, character in the lines around his eyes, ones he'd never had back then. 'You knew I was coming tonight, and you didn't think to tell me?'

'You knew I was going to be here, too.'

'Oh, that's right, I did. I must have forgotten the bit when you told me you were going to be the model. The nearly *naked* model.'

'I was hoping it might be a nice surprise.'

'Oh, it was definitely a surprise.' And an utter distraction. Lizzie waved to the last two people heading to the door and snatched the sketch from the easel, sliding it into her bag with the others. She was still thinking of the dolphin on his shoulder and what it represented. 'So how long have you been doing this?'

'It's my first time. I'm a life model virgin.' He gave her a cheeky grin. 'What can I say? Noelle is very persuasive. And it's not like it's going to end up on social media.'

'Lizzie, I'm so happy you came to class tonight!' Noelle joined them, chuckling gently. 'May I see your work?'

'Oh, sorry, it's terrible. I'm better with my camera than with charcoal.'

'Cal is an excellent model, *non*?' Noelle gave her a wink. 'If I had time to paint him, I would put him in my exhibition. Next time perhaps, Cal?'

'Maybe, Noelle. I did enjoy it, more than I expected.'

'Then we will talk, *chéri*. I consider that a yes.' Noelle bent to kiss Lizzie. 'Come to my class again next month, Lizzie. Perhaps then you could be our model and we will observe Cal's drawing skills.'

'I'm not sure I'd be doing much drawing, Noelle,' Cal said, and she giggled as Lizzie glared at him.

'You're on,' she said sweetly. 'How hard can it be?'

'I guess we'll find out.' His grin was unabashed this time and Lizzie flushed as Noelle roared.

Chapter 15

Lizzie knew exactly where she wanted to take Cal for their first photo shoot. They'd previously agreed it was better not to use two vehicles for something that only needed one, so they met in the car park at Halesmere at five the following morning, hoping not to disturb anyone else with their early start. Clouds were floating across the sky, and she was optimistic about the light. Better this than bright sunlight making every shot look the same.

'Morning.' He jumped out of the van to help load some of her kit. He'd already given her a bag from the brand he was working with, and she'd packed it carefully, making sure she had spare batteries, lenses, and her trusty tripod, along with everything else. He slid a cool bag into the footwell between them. 'What have you got in here? I thought it was only supposed to be breakfast?'

'Just enough to keep us going. If you're still the Cal I know then you'll be starving long before we're done.'

'I'm always hungry.' His smile was a sideways one and she laughed at their familiarity. 'So where are we going?'

'Head northwest and I'll let you know when to turn off.'

It wasn't hard to compare the anticipation of the day ahead with those they'd shared in the past, and thirty minutes later Cal was driving along a single-track lane, pulling over for the occasional farmer on a quad bike, collies clinging to the back. They passed an inn and a clutch of cottages, and two miles after that he parked on a patch of gravel just off the lane beside an ancient pack-horse bridge. Lizzie was quickly out of the van, assessing the light.

'So I was thinking we'd head along the river, and I could get some shots of you bouldering. I saw the mat in the back and there are some great rocks along here.'

'Sounds good. I'll get the kit.'

They set off along the rough path beside the river, loose scree beneath their feet making the ground trickier. A couple of times they had to scramble between boulders using their hands as well as feet. Cal had his climbing gear in a backpack like hers, graphite to her olive green, the mat fastened on top. Once they'd found a suitable location, a short walk off the path, he changed his boots for climbing shoes and attached a chalk bag to his belt as Lizzie set up her tripod. She wouldn't need it for every shot and the light was ideal, and for now it seemed they had this spectacular valley all to themselves.

'What do you want me to do?'

She was busy adjusting her camera settings and gave him a grin of pure exultation. 'Just do your stuff, work out the problem. Forget I'm here.'

She took a few warm-up shots of him placing the mat, finding the best spot for it to rest for if, or more probably when, he came off the boulder. She knew the mat's two different layers of foam should help with any impact and lessen the risk of injury.

It was a mild day, despite the clouds, and Lizzie watched through her lens as Cal covered his hands with chalk. Sweating would make the holds he found slippery, so he'd need plenty of chalk to help. The boulder was around four metres high, with ridges and sharp edges that, to Lizzie, looked nearly impossible to climb. Cal was assessing the route he wanted to take first, understanding the grading afforded to these short, hard ascents much better than she did.

'What's this one called?'

He turned to give her a grin. She was ready and took the shot, checking it quickly. His excitement in the challenge that lay ahead was clear and she knew this image was one she'd keep. He looked so alive, alert, his energy contagious, and it wasn't difficult to imagine she'd pressed reset on her own life now she was once again with Cal in this valley.

'Gideon's Gorge. Apparently, there was a vicar who used to climb around here and he named his first ascent after a sermon he'd just preached. Either that or he was greedy.'

Cal set off and Lizzie ignored the quick squeeze of anxiety. He'd done this so many times and soon her photographer's instinct took over and she was focussing only on getting the best shots, going wide to capture some of the surrounding landscape and zooming in on others, altering the aperture to record the power and strength it took for him to haul himself up an unforgiving rock face. It wasn't a straight line to the top and he hit the mat a couple of times as she moved it to follow his progress. With one last stretch of his arms, legs following, he reached the top of the boulder more quickly than she was expecting.

'Well done. You didn't hang around.' She liked the jubilant grin he was giving her. 'But don't look at me. It's about you and what's around you.'

'I like looking at you.'

'Yeah, well, I like looking at you too but that's not why we're here.'

'It sort of is.'

'You need this.' She laughed as she grabbed his bag and launched it up to him, easier now it wasn't quite so full.

She took some gorgeous images of him sitting on the boulder, the rucksack beside him as he looked out across the valley. If anything, the camera loved him even more than it had twelve years ago and he was experienced at this now, knowing what was required.

Back on the ground he went for another ascent on the same boulder using a different route, so technical and difficult, even on so low a climb, that he was practically upside down and horizontal at times. She captured everything – the sweat running down his face, the hand reaching behind his back for more chalk to help him grip, the seconds before he reached the top, muscled arms holding his body steady, one foot above his face as he hooked it into a hold, grimacing with the effort of clinging on, reaching up, going higher.

'Breakfast?' She had to shout and saw him nod as he raised a triumphant arm.

'I thought you'd never ask.' He was soon back on the ground, his T-shirt soaked in sweat. He reached into the bag for another one and her camera was ready as he pulled the first over his head.

'I was going to say we need some different images somewhere else, but I've changed my mind now.'

'Oh?' The new T-shirt was dangling from his hand, and he was grinning as she clicked the button, zoomed in on his face, refocussed, and clicked again.

'Yeah. Just post this and you'll be grand. I think you'll have all the attention you can handle.'

179

'You want me to climb, like this?' He turned, one shoulder to the rock, hand raised.

'Well. If you're offering. Don't wear yourself out.'

'It'd take more than that, Lizzie.' He went for the first hold, the muscles across his back, arms and shoulders straining to keep him steady as his swung his left leg higher, reaching for a better grip. 'Want me to prove it?'

'Not really.' *Yes, please* was what she wanted to say, her mind not quite on the job as Cal made a third ascent. She took lots of shots and knew some of them would be good enough for his social media, though she wasn't certain he would want to use these last few, however much attention it would bring the brand. And him.

Safely back on the ground, clean T-shirt on, they sat down to enjoy the breakfast Lizzie had brought. She poured him coffee from a flask and handed him a cup.

'Do you remember that time the tent nearly got blown away and I did my ankle going after it.'

'Yeah.' She sipped her coffee, liking the strong taste, needing no caffeine to wake her up. 'You were mad because you couldn't work for a couple of days and refused all attempts to get it X-rayed. I'm still not convinced you didn't break it.'

'It was grand, it got better.' Cal accepted the tub of overnight oats Lizzie handed him. 'Thanks. So do you think we've got enough bouldering shots now?'

She raised a brow. 'Is that a serious question?' She shifted position to sit next to him and swapped her porridge for her camera to show him the screen. 'See for yourself.' She scrolled through the images, deleting a few, zooming in on some.

'Wow, okay. You're right, we have.' His smile was a little self-conscious. 'Don't think I'll use the shirt off ones. That's not the image we're after.'

'I understand. There's attention for all the right reasons and then there's attention for the wrong ones.'

'Exactly. Just delete them.'

'Why would I do that?' she retorted. 'They could be some of my best work. Maybe we should pick just one. It would stand out and be different from the others.'

'You think?' He leaned back, propping himself on his elbows. 'I just thought I might be able to distract you.'

'After last night and you and Noelle duping me into the drawing class? You're kidding, right? I've already seen far more of you than I expected.'

'You've seen everything, Lizzie. You *know* everything.' The smile fell from his lips as he stared at her.

'Cal, I...' It was too late to worry about risking her heart for him, despite what she'd promised Gemma. She and Cal had been here before, on the fells, the landscape spread out before them. The last twelve years seemed to matter less somehow, in this moment. As though Lizzie hadn't packed her time with study, long hours at work and professional success just to fill the space he'd left in her life. Missing him, wondering about him.

'Was it serious, with your ex?'

Lizzie wasn't expecting such a blunt question and she settled on a shrug. 'For a while. I thought it was going to last but he met someone else through work. Jack's a teacher and lockdown was pretty crazy for both of us. It didn't work out.'

'I'm sorry.'

'Thank you.' If only her sorrow over breaking up with Cal could have been gathered into so few words. 'Looking back, all those lockdowns meant we were stuck with each other in a way. My work disappeared overnight so I found another job and we were both really busy and under pressure. Now I can see we were just drifting along – or drifting apart, I suppose.' Lizzie thoughts turned to the dolphin tattoo on Cal's shoulder and the woman who'd shared his life.

'What about you? I saw pictures of you with someone in New Zealand.'

'Tash. We'd known each other for a while before we were a couple, we hung around with the same crowd. She's a pro surfer so she always travelled.'

Lizzie knew exactly what he meant. His surfing buddies, the mates on the beach, at the bar; they seemed always together. Had he run away from Tash too or was it the other way around? Was she back in New Zealand, patching up a broken heart or had she shattered his? And now Lizzie had a name to attach to those vibrant, beautiful images of the woman who'd been in his life.

'And it was serious.' She didn't need a reply to her statement. She understood the months and years he and Tash had shared, the beach house, early morning surfing, the late-night swims. So very like the life Lizzie and Cal had created when she was eighteen, although she only had weeks together to remember, not years. She couldn't – shouldn't – be jealous, but still it stung, thinking of the life she might have had with him if she'd been brave enough back then to make a different decision.

'For a while.' Cal had finished his breakfast and he put his bowl on a flat stone. 'Tash was kind of the reason the brand took off the way it did. We were messing around on the beach one day and she posted some stuff on Instagram that got noticed. Then we got busy with the business for a while and when the US offer came in, it was life-changing for everyone. They were prepared to relocate us to the States but I didn't want that. My business partner went with his family, and I had some choices to make.' He shifted on the ground to stare at her. 'I'm done running, Lizzie. I want a home, a place of my own.'

'All the things you ran away from before.' Her voice was a whisper, surprise racing through her mind.

'Yeah. Kind of ironic, isn't it.' He shrugged. 'Even though you lost your house, you still had a home with your parents. You had that security, and I threw it back at you. I'm sorry for doing that, for not wanting to meet them.'

'That's okay. I think I was pretty pushy.'

'You were, but I know why you did it.'

Was he going to say the words out loud? Remind her how much she'd loved him, how he'd been very nearly her whole world and she'd wanted him in every part of it.

'I was frightened of them, Lizzie. Worried they'd see straight through me and know I wasn't good enough for you. And worried if they didn't, I'd grow to like being part of your family and I'd stop looking for my own.'

'I'm sorry you felt like that. They wanted to give you a chance.' Lizzie and Cal were still side by side and she shuffled lower until her head was on his shoulder. 'I've done nothing but run since you left. Gemma thinks I won't settle down with anyone because I'm afraid I'd lose everything, like my mum and dad did.'

'There's just one big difference, Lizzie.' His arm shifted until he could slide it around her, and she saw the wolf resting on her side as his hand sat lightly on her hip. 'They had each other and it was enough to get them through it.'

'What happened to Tash?' Saying her name made his ex-girlfriend feel even more real to Lizzie.

'She moved on. She wasn't done travelling and competing, and I didn't want that life. We were both sad, but it was okay.' He turned his head to fix an unwavering gaze on Lizzie. 'I didn't run away and break her heart if that's what you're wondering. I don't make a habit of stuff like that. It only happened once, and I've always been sorry.'

'Why didn't you get in touch if that's how you felt?'

'I wanted to.' Cal's hand tightened on her hip, and she liked it there, keeping them together. 'But the longer I left it the more I thought you'd still hate me for what I did. I didn't think it was fair to walk right back into your life and maybe mess it up for you again.'

'I never hated you, Cal. I was mad at both of us. You for leaving the way you did, me for not being brave enough to go with you.'

'But the choice you made *was* brave, Lizzie. Going to university, seeing your plans through, and making a good life for yourself. It was a lot braver than taking off the way I did because I was too scared of getting hurt again if I'd stayed with you.' He paused. 'There is something I have to tell you. I hope you're not going to be angry with me.'

'That sounds exactly like the sort of comment someone makes right before they know someone else is going to be angry with them.' Her tone was light, disguising the spike of worry. 'Have you been waiting to get me halfway up a hill so I can't run away?'

'You remember those emails I wrote you and never sent?' He waited for her nod. 'You were right, what you said about my being able to find you if I'd wanted to. I did. I had.'

'What do you mean?' Her words were shaky as she wriggled to her knees to face him, and his arm fell away.

'I'd googled you, Lizzie, and found your business.' Cal's hand reached for hers as he rushed on. 'I wrote you all those emails, trying to find a way to ask you to be involved with the launch. I still hadn't sent any of them when you turned up for the retreat.' His smile was wry as he pleaded with her to understand. 'The moment I saw you that first night, I just wanted to tell you how sorry I was about what I did, how I still felt. Then Ella came to me after the weekend and said she'd met this amazing event planner and they were moving into the flat. She told me it was you and that's when I came up with working with you on the content as well as the launch.'

Lizzie scrambled to her feet, knocking the flask sideways. 'So all this Mr Nice Guy, "I'm so sorry about what I did back then", it's… what? Just a way to get a cheap photographer, someone gullible enough to trail round after you for days on end and make your social media look good?'

'Of course not.' Cal sprang up, hands agitated at his side. 'I meant every word. You are the only person I want to work with. Because it's you, Lizzie. It's always been you. I knew it that night.' His arm reached out and his finger went to her chin. 'Look at me, please?'

Lizzie knew she'd be lost if she did. The softness of his voice, the truth in his tone was almost more than she could bear. 'I'm not going back there, Cal,' she whispered. 'I can't.'

'I'm not asking you to go back. I don't want to go back either, to be that kid again, uncertain, afraid. I might not know who my father is, Lizzie, but I know myself better now. What I want, what I'm capable of. I had to leave so I could find my way home again.'

His hand cupped her chin and this time she let him lift it, her mind spinning with longing, her soul with love. 'I'm asking you to think about it. Moving forward, with me.'

—

'I can't wait to hear what you're thinking.' Gemma was flitting in and out of shot as usual and Lizzie smiled when she heard the clatter of a tray hitting the worktop. 'We've got a charity bakeathon thing at work tomorrow and I'm up to my elbows in flour.'

'Sorry I'm late.' Bea jumped onto the video call, glasses on and a pile of papers spread before her. 'Still at work, have I missed anything?'

'We were just chatting before you and Lizzie tell me what you've got planned for my hen night. Hit me with your ideas.'

'We've booked it for this weekend as time's tight and it was the original date anyway.' Bea flipped an iPad open. 'I'm sending you links now. We've tried to find something that will appeal to all ten of us as much as possible. Lizzie? Do you want to explain as you did most of the research?'

'We're spending Saturday driving four-by-four vehicles on a private estate not far from me. Then clay pigeon shooting before cocktails and dinner with a personal chef. If we're up for breakfast, then it'll be a leisurely one before we hopefully make it back in time for the final banns being read.'

'That sounds brilliant, I love the idea of cocktails and a personal chef. You're beaming, Lizzie, the way you do when you've got something up your sleeve. I didn't know four-by-fours got you that excited. What's going on?'

'Nothing.' Lizzie couldn't keep the happiness from her voice or the light from her eyes. Yesterday, bouldering with Cal, was a thrill still keeping her warm. They'd posted the first shots on both their Instagram accounts and their follower numbers had jumped, as well as the clothing brand's. 'Stan made me laugh, that's all. You know what he's like.'

'Go on then, tell.' Bea took her glasses off. 'He's very wise, is Stan. Like an old sage.'

'When he heard we were planning a hen night, he said he'd got the perfect solution and why didn't I arrange another drawing class with Cal as the model.'

'I'd be up for that.' Bea grinned as she sat back. 'Do you think he'd do it?'

'Another?' Gemma screeched and her pink face appeared back on camera. 'What do you mean, "another"? Don't tell me you've been drawing him in all his glory? *You have!* I can tell by your face.'

'Lizzie Martin, I'm shocked. And very impressed. I saw your posts, I'm following him as well.' Bea was laughing and disappeared as a few papers fluttered from her desk. She quickly popped back up and stuffed them in a folder. 'Was he actually naked?'

'Not quite.' Lizzie was dreamy.

'And how did he look?' Bea always got straight to the point.

'I'd offer to show you but I'm crap at drawing. I have got an interesting post lined up for tomorrow you might like. But can we just get back to the hen night, please?' She didn't like every conversation about Cal turning into a battlefield with her best friend. 'We need to make a few plans.'

Gemma was busy sliding scones so gorgeous looking onto a cooling tray that Lizzie's mouth actually watered. 'Just tell me when and where to turn up. I've got ten minutes before the next batch is ready and I need to focus. I'm in this bakeathon to win.'

'Seriously?' Bea's brows shot up. 'You're actually letting us arrange everything?'

'Yep. I've got enough to think about.' Gemma was back on screen, and she huffed out a harassed breath. 'Has Matteo mentioned what Will's arranged for the stag night, Bea? I know they're going this weekend as well. Barcelona and Camp Nou got cancelled when the first wedding went south.'

'He said they were on it and Will, as best man, was in charge. Do *you* know what they're doing?'

'Yes, Will emailed me to help with packing as it's a surprise for Simon.'

'Okay, what's going on?'

'I found out today they've booked Cal to take them hiking in the wilds.' Gemma paused to take in Lizzie's reaction.

'Sounds great, Gem,' Lizzie replied quickly. How easily he seemed be slotting back into all their lives, especially hers. 'He'll make sure they have the best time.'

'Oh, I don't doubt it. They've got that hostel for the night, the one that's only accessible on foot and he's arranged for a chef to stay over and sort all the meals. It's all top secret so Simon doesn't find out. Wild swimming, stargazing, even some bouldering, all that stuff. Simon's been saying how much he misses the fells, he's going to be like a pig in clover. You okay with that, Lizzie?'

'Of course I am.' Lizzie couldn't wait to get more shots of Cal at a ruin beside a tarn they'd chosen for his next setting, and she was impatient to head out again. 'You don't have to creep around me where Cal's concerned, I promise. We're fine.'

'You look fine, too.' Gemma narrowed her eyes. 'You light up every time his name's mentioned. Anyway, we haven't forgotten your thirtieth is coming up soon, Lizzie. I know it's the day after the wedding, but we've got to do something.'

'I'm not bothered about celebrating, it's just another year.' She'd barely given her birthday a thought. She supposed turning thirty was a big event, but she had so much else to deal with right now. 'Let's get back to the wedding. The florist is coming over on Monday afternoon to see the garden. She's got some incredible new ideas you're going to love, Gem.'

'Thanks Lizzie, that sounds perfect. Simon's back on shift but Mum and I will be there.' Gemma was busy filling a sponge cake with buttercream and Lizzie's stomach rumbled greedily. 'This wedding is going to be amazing, thanks to you and Bea, and Ella and my mum, of course. I can't believe I'm actually saying this but I'm so happy the other two got cancelled.'

Chapter 16

Lizzie was settling into a routine at Halesmere and tried to always end her working day at six unless she was meeting potential clients. Her new enquiries had so far resulted in four bookings: one for the autumn, one at Christmas and two next spring. Some venues were only just getting going again and she was finding a few dates were still available for this year.

She didn't see Cal every day, but he was around, in the forge or busy in the office he'd set up above his workshop. She looked forward to those glimpses, the moments when they'd share a smile or stop for a quick chat. They weren't together, not in any sense of the word but their relationship was evolving, and she was enjoying their new friendship.

They were following each other on social media and his was really taking off as he shared his own images of trips with clients on the fells alongside hers from the bouldering. Last night he'd posted just one of the shots of him bouldering without his T-shirt, and his followers had leaped. Interest was growing and the brand were reposting everything, clearly delighted to have him on board with their line. Cal credited Lizzie's images and tagged her in everything, and she was surprised to receive a couple of enquiries about her photography, which she turned down for now. She'd think about that once Gemma's wedding was over.

Lizzie was also researching the history of Cumbrian music festivals and sharing what little she'd found with Cal. They'd learned nothing new on his mother or any certain information about the festival from the photograph and she was equally as frustrated as him by the lack of progress or decent new leads. He'd mentioned that he planned to visit a few festivals over the summer and Lizzie agreed to join him; it was the best they could do for now.

Stan liked to invite her into his workshop for a regular brew and she'd begun baking again, something he was very keen to encourage. Lily and Arlo also popped in to the flat sometimes with Prim, who would sit obediently on the rug in front of the fireplace, hoping to hoover up crumbs.

Arlo had just celebrated his fifth birthday with a sheep-themed party, arranged by Ella and Max, with the young guests treated to a short sheepdog trial and a chance to have a go at running a dog themselves. Arlo had been overjoyed to discover his present: a tiny flock of sheep of his own in the meadow, half a dozen beautifully bred Herdwick ewes.

The sheep were under the watchful eye of Luke from the farm down the road, and he was passing his shepherding skills on to Arlo, who lapped it all up and was already having serious discussions with Luke about the merits of breeding tups, the male sheep. Arlo was desperate for his own sheepdog, too, and Lizzie overheard Max telling Arlo he'd have to write to Santa about that and see what he thought.

Lizzie loved her early mornings, either out with her camera or practising yoga with Ana or Rachael, sometimes with Cal too when he joined them. The house was busy with guests on retreat and learning new skills in the barn, and Lizzie was ecstatic when Ella asked if she would consider managing all the events at Halesmere so Ella could plan for maternity leave. Little by little everything was slotting into place and Lizzie was beginning to believe she was creating a new life she could build on for the future.

Gemma's hen weekend was brilliant fun and they all loved driving the four-by-four vehicles across the estate. Cocktails were served until late and even Bea, used to Matteo's cooking, raved about the fabulous personal chef who had trained at the local college. Only Lizzie and Gemma made it to church on Sunday for the final banns being read. In the afternoon Lizzie had a lovely, long bath after Gemma returned to her mum's, and fell into bed to catch up on sleep.

Two hours later, she groaned as she was woken by a knock on her front door. It was probably Stan, or Lily and Arlo, and Lizzie was not getting up. She couldn't remember how many cocktails she'd drunk last night but it must have been quite a few, judging by the state of her head. She pulled a pillow over her face at the second knock.

Her phone was pinging as well, and she was cross that she'd forgotten to turn notifications to silent when she went to bed. She rolled over and unlocked the screen, smiling when she saw Cal's name, and opened his message.

I'm outside. Get up, I know you're in there.

How? I could be miles away.

You're not. You're in bed. Still outside.

Still in bed. Not getting up.

Yeah, you are, I'm your hangover cure. Are you getting up or do I have to ask Stan for a spare key?

How do you know I've got a hangover?

Bea told Matteo who told me. Still outside. Are you getting up or not?

Depends on how you're planning to cure my hangover.

Get up and I'll show you. Actually, scratch that. Stay there and I'll show you.

Lizzie was laughing so much she almost fell out of the bed, and she swore when her phone bounced all the way down the stairs. She followed more slowly and pulled the door back inch by inch. Her phone had thankfully survived the fall and she picked it up.

'Oh, aye. Look at you. You need some air.'

'What's the matter with me?' She squinted at Cal, aware she was in short pyjamas and her hair was tied in a careless knot on her head. 'You look disgustingly fresh for a man who's just spent the night on a fell with a bunch of wild stags. The men, obviously, not the animals.'

'I got about three hours sleep. I had to make sure everyone else was grand before I went to bed, they were my responsibility.'

'So what are you doing here?'

'Once you're dressed, I'm taking you out for the best hangover cure you'll ever have.'

Lizzie had two choices but she only needed one, already buzzing with anticipation. 'Give me ten minutes. Do I need boots?' she called over her shoulder as she ran up the stairs. Cal ducked his head and closed the door behind him.

'Not walking ones. Bring your camera though, the location is practically a cure on its own.'

'Are we eating?'

'Yep.'

She chose a multi-coloured summer dress, more suitable for a festival than a fell, with its three-quarter length sleeves and floaty skirt. She teamed it with ankle boots and rearranged her hair into a messy knot at her neck, doing her make-up quickly. Cal was waiting when she returned more slowly down the stairs and his smile told all her she wanted to know. She found her camera and grabbed the old trilby she kept on the back of the door. 'I hope this is worth it. I could still be asleep.'

'It will be, I promise.'

'Have you checked the forecast?' She glanced up once she'd locked the door. 'It doesn't look great.'

'No. Catch yourself on, Lizzie. I don't care about the weather. Right now I'm only interested in being with you.'

That was a thrill as they got into the van and he drove them north into the high fells, close to where a narrow lane ran into moorland and only hikers and sheep could carry on. An isolated farmhouse had been converted into a tiny pub at the top and he had to leave the van a quarter of a mile below it, as there was no parking at the pub. Each of the three snug rooms only sat around eight people and Lizzie bagged them a corner while he ordered their food. It was already five thirty and food service stopped at six on a Sunday.

'Even I haven't been here before. How did you find it?' Lizzie smiled her thanks for the drinks he offered.

'Get that down you. A bloody Mary and a glass of water. I came here first time with a couple of clients after a day on Scafell Pike. I love it. Food's grand and it's remote, dead on. If you know, you know. And they do the best avocado and eggs on toast you've ever had. Everything's organic, it's a proper pick-you-up.'

'I could have made eggs at home.' She smiled at the face Cal was pulling.

'You could but where's the fun and spontaneity in that? They're full of vitamins and protein and will do you good after the night you had.'

The eggs on toast were poached to perfection when they arrived, served with smashed avocado, lime and chilli on top of wholemeal sourdough, and they demolished the lot.

'Well?' Cal was leaning back, triumphant.

'Has anyone ever said you do smug very well?'

'You, several times. So how was it?'

'Perfect. Just what I needed.'

'Do you feel better?'

'Much. Thank you.'

It might be very early summer, but the fire was lit to cheer the day turning gloomy, and they ordered more drinks as the afternoon slipped into evening. They were in no hurry, and it was close to nine when they decided to leave.

'See, I said you should've checked the forecast. I didn't even bring a coat.' Lizzie shuddered at the rain sheeting sideways from the fell and pulled her trilby low, hugging her camera in its case very close. 'We're nearly the last ones here. Stunning location or not, I'm not taking pictures in this. Some mountain leader you are, we're going to get drenched.'

'Now who's smug? Make a run for it?'

It was one of those downpours that soaked in seconds and their clothes were plastered to their skin by the time they leapt into the van.

'Boathouse?' He started the engine and turned up the heat, wipers flipping furiously. 'It's closer than Halesmere and you can warm up with a hot shower. I can lend you something.'

Her teeth were chattering as she nodded. Mud from puddles they'd run through had splashed up her legs and she took her trilby off, hoping it wasn't totally ruined. 'When we get back, we could just stand outside to shower in the rain. I don't think I could get any more sodden and it would at least get the mud off my dress.'

'Sorry.'

'It's fine, and you were right. It's definitely cured my hangover.' Lizzie looked across. Cal was focussed on keeping the van steady through deep puddles gathering on the narrow lanes. 'You've got mud on your face. May I?' She held her breath as she raised a hand.

'Please.'

Raindrops were nestled in his throat, and she dipped her thumb, catching a couple. She ran it over his cheek, smoothing away the splash of dirt, loving the feel of his beard against her palm, the graze of it both rough and soft at once.

'Lizzie, if you do that again I can't promise to keep the van on the road.' The words were ground out from somewhere deep inside him and she felt a rush of longing.

'Sorry.'

'Don't be. We won't be long.' The lanes flashed by as he drove as quickly as possible, eventually bringing the van to a sharp halt outside the boathouse. He killed the electric engine, shifting a shoulder to face her. The rain pelting down was quieter than the racing of Lizzie's heart in the new stillness surrounding them. 'Do you want that shower?'

'Is there any point?' She looked at her mud-spattered legs, the dress halfway up her thighs. 'I don't know if I can even get these boots off. I can't wear them in the house, not with all that white.'

Cal hit a button on the key fob and the side gate slid open. 'Through there, we can take our boots off outside.'

'I think you're going to have to help me.' Lizzie was first out of the van into the rain, half laughing, half shrieking as she ran into the garden, aware of Cal right behind her. She dropped onto a chair on the patio and held out one leg. Her skin felt as though it was on fire, despite the coolness, as he knelt before her. She couldn't tell if the boot really was so troublesome to unfasten or if he was just taking his time to undo it. Unzipped, his hand followed the shape of her calf as he slowly slid it off.

His hands went to her other leg, and she was dizzy with desire when the second boot came off, watching as he tucked them underneath a table. His T-shirt was stuck to his chest, the rain pouring off his face. One hand was on her knee and her breath was a scorched whisper.

'You need to get *your* boots off too.'

'Then you do it.'

He pulled her upright and they exchanged places. Lizzie knelt as he had, his eyes amused and desperate all at once when she looked up. The stone was cold beneath her legs, her shrunken dress clinging to her body. She slowly unlaced his first boot, exploring his calf, just as he had hers, feeling the muscles beneath his jeans.

'Get the other one off, Lizzie, please. I can't stand this much longer.'

She refused to rush, the night dark around them, clouds bringing yet more rain, and a few moments later his boots joined hers under the table. Barefoot, she held out a hand and he took it, tugging her against him as he stood up.

'I don't think we need that shower.' She tipped her head back to let the rain fall on her face and run down her throat to gather in the neckline of her dress. 'If we stay out here much longer the weather will wash off the mud. And we really can't go in the boathouse like this, we'll ruin it.'

'So what do you suggest?'

'Let's go in the lake, it won't be that cold.' She wriggled free, already running down the grass. She threw him a glance over her shoulder, laughter bubbling as he took off after her.

Cal caught her up at the water's edge and she lifted her arms, spinning round, aware of him watching as the soaking dress rode higher. 'I feel very hot.'

'That's because you are.' His hands reached for hers and he folded her fingers over the hem of his T-shirt, moulded to his body. 'Would you please take this off?'

'Do you actually need the help?' She was slowly inching it up, and he forced out a reply.

'No.' He took one of her hands to slide it onto his chest and this time it was Lizzie who gasped. 'But I'd like it.'

She dragged the T-shirt up and over his head, her mouth dry as the atmosphere between them shifted again. She drank in the sight: their waterfall tattooed on one arm, the wolf on the other; his lazy smile telling her he was enjoying the view his T-shirt on the grass afforded her. Her hands were on his face, running to his shoulders and along his arms to his stomach.

He reached out, trailing a slow finger from her wrist to her elbow and the heat from his simple, questioning touch was surging through Lizzie's veins. His gaze went lower to take in her short dress, the mud still clinging to her skin, before returning to linger on her lips and then her eyes. She saw the passion blazing in his, wanting her, and Cal moved the same moment she did. He pulled her into him, one hand unfastening her hair, holding her steady as they kissed again and again, each frantic to rediscover the other.

'My turn.' His voice was low as he murmured against her ear. 'You don't get to do all the staring.'

He hooked a finger into the neckline of her dress and Lizzie was lost and already arching into him when it edged beneath her soaking bra. He raised her arms with one hand to yank the sopping dress over her head and her stomach plunged in desire as his eyes swept over her.

'You're so beautiful, Lizzie,' he muttered, holding her close to undo her bra. 'You always were.'

'So are you.' She slid the straps to her wrists and let them fall as the rest of her underwear and his jeans swiftly followed. His arms went to her thighs to lift her, and Lizzie had a final second of thankfulness that the boathouse was so private as Cal carried her into the lake.

–

'Am I allowed to stay all night?' It was after midnight and Lizzie was sleepy, her head resting on Cal's shoulder. Her hand was on his chest, his arm tight around her, hand resting on her hip. They were in his bed and she was smiling at the luxury of it not being on a mat in a tent somewhere on a fell in the dark.

'I'd really rather not get up and drive you back so…' She sensed his own smile, the low note in his voice telling her all she needed in this moment. 'So that's a yes, if you would?'

'Depends. Do you think we'll be able to sleep in an actual bed?'

'Also depends.'

'On what?'

'Your ability to utterly distract me whenever I'm with you. Especially when you're naked. I think it's your super-power.'

'Oh?' Lizzie wriggled from his arms to lean over him. 'What else do you like about me?'

'Everything. The way you smile, how we laugh together. How kind you are, how you always try and see the best in me. And your hair, the way it falls down your back, and I just want to unfasten it whenever you wear it up.'

'Like this?' She sat up, scooping her hair from her neck, knowing she was holding him with her smile, this gesture. She let it fall, tilting her head so it rippled down her back.

'Exactly like that,' he muttered. 'You're the sexiest woman I know, Lizzie, and I love how we are together.'

'And how are we together?' Suddenly her voice was small and the laughter and the teasing fell away as she tried to get his take on this night. How it had swiftly ended up with them naked in the lake and still unable to make it upstairs the second time they'd made love. What they were now to each other, that first summer and the past twelve years history as they hovered on the edge of an uncertain future.

'I think we're pretty incredible.'

That she already knew, and she wondered if more would follow. And when it didn't, she curled into his arms again, thinking perhaps he was right not to suggest anything more in these heady moments. Was this all he'd meant about moving forward together, when they'd been bouldering? Maybe an affair that was even better second time around was all they would share, and a few more weeks of this would finally be enough to detach them from one another.

And yet. She knew she'd always remember his look when he'd carried her from the lake and run upstairs to bring a blanket, wrapping it around them as they snuggled on the tiny sofa to warm up. The familiarity of their kisses, the feel of his shoulder now beneath her head, her face resting on him, the wolf on his arm across her back. Holding her, protecting her with his strength. Would it be enough? Could she ever let him go? Whatever was happening between them, she knew her heart was already entwined around his once again.

'This wasn't why I brought you back here tonight, Lizzie.' His words were soft, and she sensed his utter relaxation in her own limbs, weightless around his. 'Just so you know I didn't plan it.'

'Sure about that?' She ran a teasing finger from his chest to the outline of the hardened muscles of his stomach. 'Because it definitely crossed my mind.'

He laughed, turning swiftly to place a hand either side of her head and she saw his eyes darken as his mouth found hers.

–

Cal was still asleep when Lizzie woke, the lines of his face softened by rest. It was dawn but she was too alert to doze again, thoughts of the past few hours warming her. She slid quietly from the bed and pulled on a T-shirt of his she found on the back of a chair.

Her camera was still in the van, and she fetched it, savouring the warmth of the rising spring sun after the rain, and the dampness beneath her feet as she strolled to the edge of the lake. The day, the hour, even this single moment, felt utterly fresh as she framed a shot of the white yacht, silent and still against the jetty.

Every glimpse around the garden was a reminder of last night. Clothes strewn where they'd abandoned them, their wet boots still beneath the bistro table, the blanket slung over a seat. She wanted all of this with Cal, she already knew that one night and a morning would never be enough. She turned back to the lake to stare at the ripple of the water between the trees, thoughts of this new day and all that might come after it for them pounding through her mind. He was such a part of her that she doubted she'd ever be fully free of loving him. But what did last night, this morning, make them now?

'Hey.'

She hadn't heard Cal approach and his arms went around her. She couldn't prevent a smile when he kissed her neck, his chest bare against her back. 'I hoped I'd find you out here. When I woke up and realised you weren't still in bed, I was worried you'd left.'

'Wearing just your T-shirt?' She was surprised by the suggestion of hurt in his voice. Her hands covered his, letting him know it wasn't her intention to leave without a word. 'I forgot to hang up my dress last night and I couldn't exactly call a taxi dressed like this.'

'I think you look almost perfect.'

'Almost?' She turned and raised an eyebrow. His mouth quirked into a grin as he slid her hair across one shoulder, tugging gently at the T-shirt.

'You looking perfect would involve me taking this off and I'm starving. I think I should make you some breakfast.'

'You don't want to drive me back yet? I'm hoping the dress will be okay if I hang it in the sun while I shower. My hair is desperate for shampoo.'

'Do you have to go?'

She heard the lighter note in his voice. He was freeing her if she wanted to leave. She knew it was going to take more than a long hot shower to wash away the gloss on her skin and the light in her eyes. 'Not yet. But I'm meeting Gemma's florist with her later.'

'Then how does bacon and eggs sound?'

'Almost as perfect as you in shorts.' Lizzie slid her arms around his neck, taking her time to kiss him good morning.

'Breakfast, before we end up on that yacht,' he said reluctantly, untangling her to take her hand. 'I don't fancy the lake this morning, there are too many tourists about already.'

Lizzie gathered their clothes and laid the patio table, made coffee, and poured juice while Cal cooked. The view of the lake, in this light, was extraordinary and she was distracted by boats and paddle boarders idling past, the occasional swimmer and walkers mere dots on the opposite shore. It wasn't long before Cal reappeared, and Lizzie pulled out chairs as he set the plates on the small table.

'Thank you. You were right, I am famished.'

'My pleasure.' He bent to kiss her quickly before he took the seat opposite hers. 'I think we're both in need of some sustenance. Probably a very good thing I'm not scaling a summit today, I need more sleep.'

Lizzie helped him clear up once they'd finished and they shared a long, luxurious shower before they set off for Halesmere. She'd run out of the flat yesterday afternoon for some adventure with Cal with no thought of today and she already felt like a different woman from the one who'd left then.

'Are you still okay for tomorrow?' He pulled up in the car park and turned to her.

'Of course.' They'd made plans to hike out to a ruin for more social media shots. 'I'm looking forward to it even more now.'

He was smiling as Lizzie's hand found his. 'You remember there's the festival next weekend at Ellthwaite?

I'm taking bouldering groups out both days and there's loads going on. The craic will be grand.'

'I do, I looked it up.' He'd mentioned it before when they were searching for his father, and she hadn't forgotten. 'Couldn't find any setlists or names of bands who performed there, though.'

'I'm wondering how you feel about coming with me?' There was an uncertain note in Cal's voice. 'I'll be there Friday morning to Sunday night, and we might find a new lead on my father. It's worth a try, plus we can get some different content shots.'

'I'd love to.' Lizzie didn't need more than a moment to consider. 'I've got a wedding on Friday though, so I'd have to drive over afterwards and meet you there.'

'That's okay, come as soon as you're ready.' He lifted her hand to kiss her palm, smiling against her skin. 'No fancy boathouse this time, I'm camping. Do you have a tent?'

'No.' She gave him a look that made it clear she'd much rather share.

'Good, I want you in mine. Don't bring anything except your camera.'

'And thermals, obviously. It might be summer, but it can still be perishing at night in a tent.'

'You definitely won't need those.' The smile was reflected in his eyes holding hers. 'I'll keep you warm.'

Chapter 17

'So the wellies have arrived, and Simon's utterly perplexed by the notion of bridal ones. He said the difference between those and proper ones is that they're useless because they're white and cost twice as much as ones that look better with mud on them.'

Lizzie was laughing, slightly relieved that she, Gemma and Bea were speaking online so the shimmer in her eyes wouldn't be immediately apparent to her two friends. Sunday night and the morning after with Cal was still a secret she was hugging to herself, too lit up with hope and happiness to worry about what her friends thought for now.

'How's things with Cal? I'm following you both on Insta. The content is stunning, Lizzie, and your numbers have jumped.' Bea was at home in her kitchen, a glass of red nearby. 'You really are very good, I can totally see why he wanted to work with you. Those shots yesterday were beautiful, the way you caught him sitting against the ruin in that light, just him and the landscape beneath those skies. And the kit, of course. Already ordered a rucksack for Matteo.'

'Thanks Bea, that's lovely of you. And we're good, everything's fine.' Lizzie flushed with guilt, wondering if Gemma could read her thoughts. She hadn't broken her promise because she really had had no intention of starting up anything with him again.

Their early evening hike to the abandoned farmhouse had been a joy and a complete contrast to the morning they'd spent bouldering. They had both been distracted and happy, the walk taking longer than expected as they paused for lingering kisses and silly selfies on their phones.

'Actually, I was thinking of inviting him to the wedding if you and Simon don't mind, Gem?' Lizzie said nonchalantly. 'Seeing as I'm already down for a guest and Jack won't be there.'

An exasperated smile spread across Gemma's face, and she wagged a finger. 'So you are seeing him again. I knew it. All that "we're fine" stuff isn't you, Lizzie. I know you. You don't do casual.'

'And?' Lizzie almost didn't dare ask.

'And I think it's complicated and if you want the truth then I'm worried that it's just unfinished business between you both and someone's going to get hurt.'

'Me, you mean?' There was a sharp note in Lizzie's reply. 'I hurt him too, Gemma. I didn't stop to think what he might want.'

'Yes, but he's not exactly big on hanging around and happy endings, is he? I know he had a tough start, and I'm being a bit harsh, but it's true. He left Ireland, he left you, then New Zealand and Tash. What's next?'

'Gem, you don't know him like I do.' Lizzie had to try to defend him, but couldn't deny she had wondered, too. If he might pack his life into the van once he'd left the boathouse and set up somewhere else. And if he did, this time would she be with him or left behind again? 'You know there was nothing in Ireland for him then. I think here is where he wants to be now.'

'Let's hope so.' Gemma blew her a kiss. 'We're here for you, hon, always.'

'We are.' Bea offered her own kiss too.

'I know, and I love you both for it. Thank you. What about the wedding, are you okay with me bringing him?' Lizzie needed to be sure Gemma was on board before she officially invited Cal, she didn't want any more battles.

'Actually, Simon's already invited him.' Gemma shrugged. 'They had a brilliant stag weekend with him and one of Simon's mates from work has already booked the same experience for the autumn. Didn't Cal mention it?'

'No.' A prickle of alarm darted into Lizzie's mind, but she dismissed it. 'We haven't talked about the wedding. I suppose we've both been focussed on the launch and the social media content. What did he tell Simon?'

'That he'd let him know. That's all Simon would say.'

'Okay.' Lizzie let out a breath. She'd find the right moment to invite Cal as her guest and it would be fine. Maybe he was already hoping she'd want to bring him to her friends' special day and that made her smile.

'Just checking in on the final dress fitting, too.' Gemma unlocked her phone and Lizzie presumed she was eyeing her calendar. 'Eleven a.m. a week on Saturday, and then I thought we could do lunch somewhere nice.'

'Sounds perfect, I can't wait to try mine. I changed my mind on the shoes and I've got a new pair.' Bea was topping up her glass of wine. 'Lizzie, about your birthday, while we're thinking about planning. We took your advice and decided against doing something on the day. Gemma and Simon will be heading off to their secret honeymoon destination and the rest of us will be going home at some point. It's probably best to arrange a get-together when the happy couple return.' Bea pulled a face. 'Matteo's gone all wild man after the stag weekend and bought a tent. We're camping down at the farm for the wedding. It'll be a beard and shaggy hair next and washing in streams. Ugh.'

'Oh, Bea, that's the best thing.' Lizzie was laughing at Bea's outrage, and a shiver ran over her at the thought of camping with Cal at the festival this weekend. 'Never ever did I imagine Matteo would get you in a tent. How's he going to cook?'

'No idea,' Bea replied gloomily. 'But seriously, I'm far more concerned about where all my shoes are going to fit.'

—

The rest of Lizzie's week was a blur of work and blissful anticipation as she prepared for her clients' wedding on Friday. She hadn't planned the whole event but had been brought in as a coordinator to make sure all ran well on the day. She had dinner with Ella and Max the night before to discuss a programme of winter retreats in the house, delighted by their confidence in allowing her free rein to decide and plan accordingly. Her business was steadily growing and her social media and links with Cal's Instagram were bringing in regular new enquiries.

Max's landscape practice was busier than ever, and he'd recently been commissioned to design a garden for a new hotel, a huge project he was delighted to be leading and one which was going to be featured on a television series about the Lakes and Dales. He and Ella had laughed about the small matter of a new baby while all this was going on and they were very relieved to have Lizzie taking care of the retreats.

Arlo was apparently spending nearly every waking moment when he wasn't at school with his sheep, all of whom had names and whose ancestry he could recite off the top of his head – a technique Max said dryly, that would be especially useful to apply to his times tables. Lily was training Prim with Ella's help, and Lizzie often saw them walking Prim to heel around the courtyard after school and using a whistle for recall. Prim would race back to sit at Lily's side and the little girl would make a huge fuss of the dog who joyfully lapped it all up. Noelle had gone to her cottage in France to paint for a few weeks, but not without first reminding Lizzie with a wink that she'd promised to sit for a drawing class.

Lizzie had also spent a little time researching the upcoming festival, hoping to find out more of its history. Part family fun, part wild outdoors, it offered everything from camping to comedy, culture and climbing, and it had grown over the years, with all of the food and drink supplied by Cumbrian producers. She couldn't wait to be there, especially after Cal sent her an image of his tent on Friday morning, just as she was about to leave for work. Two sleeping bags zipped together, like before.

The wedding was beautiful, and she loved every minute. It took place in a tiny chapel on a private estate for a couple who farmed there, and the bride's bouquet of pale pink and white flowers had all come from the garden. Lizzie looked after everyone, making sure the bride, groom and guests were exactly where they needed to be, and she was on her feet most of the day. There was much laughter, a very relaxed atmosphere and she wasn't the only one wiping away a tear at the groom's speech and the one given by the bride's mother, who'd walked her down the aisle. Once the cake was cut and the dancing about to begin, Lizzie said her goodbyes, thrilled to have another enquiry for the same service at a wedding already planned for late summer.

She was fizzing with anticipation at seeing Cal after a day spent filled with romance and happy new beginnings as she drove straight to the festival, the landscape achingly familiar. She passed through a tiny village, just a cluster of cottages and a centuries-old pub, busy with diners enjoying the sun outside. The river she followed meandered through the valley and some of the boulders she spotted were huge, just one of the reasons why this festival was so popular with climbers who loved to work out problems and search for first ascents on routes still yet untried. She passed a few hikers loaded with gear, probably headed, like her, for the campsite higher up the valley.

So impatient was she to see Cal, she hadn't thought to change before she left the wedding, and she was still in the pale blue wrap dress and the nude court heels she'd worn all day when she arrived. She might look out of place in her work clothes among the hikers and climbers in these wild and rugged surroundings, but she was utterly at home here.

Once glance at her phone was enough to confirm zero signal and she shielded her face from the low evening sun as she stared at the array of tents. She knew Cal's was green but that wasn't much use in narrowing down the ability to identify it. Music was thundering from a stage somewhere in the next field, and as it wouldn't be dark for a while, she decided to change her shoes and go in search of him at the festival. She popped the boot to find something else for her feet.

'You've made great time. I wasn't expecting you yet.'

Lizzie melted as a pair of familiar arms went around her waist and Cal was turning her. She had a second to see his own exhilaration before they were kissing.

'Should I go then and come back later,' she murmured. 'It'd be worth it for a welcome like that.'

'Catch yourself on, Lizzie, that's just hello. I haven't even begun to welcome you properly.' Cal's lips drifted to kiss the sensitive skin below her ear. Her blonde waves were held back in a high ponytail, and he unfastened it to let her hair spill over her shoulders. 'I'm so happy you're here.'

'So am I.' Her arms were around his neck and a hand went to his hair to run her fingers through his short crop. 'I think your beard is longer than your hair now. It feels that way when you kiss me.'

'Maybe you need to be sure.' He took her hands and placed them on his face. They were staring into each other's eyes and a rush of emotion swiftly followed at his look. Maybe it was the wedding and the romance she had just left, the bride and groom, so in love and setting out on a new future together. Maybe it wasn't. Maybe it was simply Cal and she knew deep in her soul it had always been him.

'So how are you planning to welcome me properly?' She tried to laugh away the feeling of falling once more before it gave her away. 'Songs around the campfire? Dinner with fifty other climbers?'

'Nothing quite so public.' Cal grinned, nodding at a passing camper. 'You going to change your shoes or walk to the tent in those?'

'Change.' Lizzie swiftly swapped the heels for a pair of trainers, and he grabbed her bag.

'This it? Grand, you pack as light as me.'

'I'll take that as a compliment. You said not to bring anything, but there are some essentials in there.' She collected her handbag and camera, hand around his as they set off. The campsite was packed, merry chat and laughter floating across the evening air in between songs from the stage next door.

Cal had pitched his tent at the back of the field close to a stonewall. A pair of fold-up chairs and a low table sat outside it, their temporary home for the weekend as comfortable as canvas ever got on a flattish patch of rough ground. Their backdrop was the fells and high crags some of these people had come to climb, and she was excited to be joining his bouldering groups over the weekend. The river was crashing into pools somewhere between the trees lining the lane, the noise quietening when Cal unzipped the flap, and she ducked inside.

He'd laid out the tent as neatly as she remembered from before, his few belongings carefully stored, and Lizzie loved how he placed her bag next to his. The tent was roomy enough for a couple of nights and a definite upgrade on the ones they'd used to camp in. A mesh window at the back was uncovered and Lizzie fastened it shut. She gave Cal a look over her shoulder.

'Are you going to wait outside while I change?' She smoothed her hands over her dress. She hadn't thought to bring something to hang it on, it would have to go back in the car if she didn't want it to end up a crumpled heap.

'Only if you'd prefer me to?' His voice was a murmur right behind her.

'I wouldn't. Could you help me then?' She heard the flap closing as she lifted her hair out of the way, swallowing as his fingers inched her zip down. He slipped the dress from her shoulders, dropping a kiss on one, then along her arms. The skin he'd barely touched felt scorched and her pulse was pounding as she lifted each leg in turn to step out of the dress.

'What do you want out of your bag?' His words were a hoarse whisper as he hung the dress from a hook holding an unlit lamp.

'Nothing yet. I want you to welcome me properly.' She couldn't think beyond his promise made a few minutes ago.

'It will have to be a very quiet welcome,' he muttered, and she smiled as she heard his T-shirt coming off. 'This tent might be insulated but it's not exactly soundproof.'

'I can be quiet,' she whispered, using one foot and then the other to remove her trainers.

'Ach, you think? You weren't very quiet at the boathouse last week.'

'The boathouse is completely private. I didn't need to be quiet.'

'Hush.' His voice offered both laughter and gentle reprove as he kissed his way from one shoulder to the next. 'Silent, remember.'

'If you really want me to be silent then you should have thought of a different way to welcome me.'

—

'Are we going to the festival?' Lizzie's hand drifted across Cal's chest. She wasn't sure she'd ever want to stop touching him, loving the reality of having him beside her, instead of a mirage in her mind.

'It's nine thirty. Do you really want to get up again?' He was sleepy, and she smiled.

'I suppose you do need to save your energy for tomorrow, those boulders look pretty tough.' She snuggled into him, her head finding his shoulder. 'I don't want to tire you out.'

'Are you suggesting I haven't welcomed you properly?' Cal rolled Lizzie onto her back, and she was laughing at his look of pretend outrage. 'Because if you are…'

'I think you made me very welcome. It might even be worth getting up and going out, just so you could welcome me like that all over again.'

He lay back, gathering into her his arms to hold her tightly. 'I've missed you this week. We've both been busy.'

'I missed you too. How did the Rannerdale trip go? The images were gorgeous.' She could feel his smile on her head nestled into him.

'Thanks, Lizzie. It was grand, a mixed group but they all loved the navigation skills and two of them have booked for the next level.'

'That's brilliant. It's all taking off for you. I'm so pleased.' She loved how much was anchoring him now to Halesmere, maybe even to her. 'I did some more research on the festival. There wasn't much on setlists, but I do think it's a definite maybe that the photo of your mum and Jim could've been taken here. I'm sure those trees in the background are elders and they're flowering so it's definitely late spring onwards.'

'Right.' Cal sighed and his hand tightened on her waist. 'I've been doing some thinking this week and I've made a decision.'

'Okay.' Lizzie tried to keep the alarm from her voice.

'I appreciate your support with finding my father more than you know, but I've decided to stop looking.'

'But why?' She propped herself on an elbow to look at him. 'We're only just beginning, I'm sure there's more we can do. I know it's frustrating, having so little to go on, but don't give up, please. We're not done yet.'

'I think I am.' Cal eased her back into his arms. 'I need to move on, not cling to this crazy dream of finding out who he is. I don't want him to define my life for ever, Lizzie, one way or the other. I feel more complete now I'm back here and making a good life. It's better to look ahead, not back.'

'You're sure?' She hated giving up so soon when she knew what his history and his search for a family meant to him. 'I wish it was easier and we had at least a name or something more to go on.'

'I'm certain. It's time to let go, it's over. I don't want to know any more. I want a home, a family of my own eventually. That's the future I want to think about, not my past and what happened with him and my mum.'

'I understand. But if you change your mind I'll still help.'

'Thank you.' His kiss was gentle, before Lizzie wriggled away. 'What are you doing?'

She found her bag and slipped a hoodie from it, smiling at Cal's sleepy contentment as he watched her. 'Finding my torch and some clothes for the shower block. I don't want to put my dress back on, it's chilly.'

'Take my torch.' He lifted it from a pocket hanging beside him, laughing as he watched her trying to get into jeans lying down.

'Shush,' she hissed, squirming awkwardly on her back. 'Be quiet or have you forgotten?'

'Sorry, but you're all arms and legs and it's funny. Want some help?'

'No,' she muttered, giving him a look she failed to make more of a glare. 'That definitely would not help.' Jeans finally on, she threw something onto her pillow.

'What's that?'

'Thermals.'

'Have you forgotten what I told you?'

'No. You said you'd keep me warm.'

'And I will.' Cal grabbed the pale pink top and matching leggings and stuffed them under his own pillow. 'You'll have to come and get them if you want them.'

'Oh? Is that a challenge?' Lizzie was crouching at the flap. She recognised that happy and satisfied gleam in his eyes; it was in her own, her heart full in these moments.

'I'll keep you warm, I promise. Whatever it takes.'

'Just be here when I get back,' she whispered, and he nodded.

—

Cal was up before Lizzie in the morning, and she was content to huddle in the sleeping bag for a few more minutes as he dressed. He'd kept his promise, had kept her snug through the night and she could already see the glare of the rising sun outside, signalling a glorious day to come.

'Hello. You're up early.' She blinked sleepily at him.

'Sorry. I did try not to wake you, you looked so comfortable.'

'I am comfortable.' She stretched, aware of him watching, his gaze filled with a lazy, languorous light. 'Do I have to get up now?'

'Not yet, if you don't want to.' He crouched down to kiss her, and she wound her arms around his neck, unwilling to let him go. He was smiling as he reluctantly backed away. 'Breakfast at eight, then there's a briefing at nine before we head out, and I have to shower.'

'Fancy a swim instead?'

'I'd love one.' His eyes narrowed. 'But it'll be more like an ice bath in that river at this hour.'

'I don't care. I'm still warm from last night.' She crawled from the sleeping bag, reaching for her clothes.

'Ach, you wait until you're in the water. And if we don't get dressed right now, I'll be lucky if I make the bouldering, never mind the briefing.'

The dew was glistening beneath their feet when they emerged from the tent to a spectacular morning. The blue sky was cloudless above them, too bright for Lizzie to bother with her camera, and she returned Cal's exuberant grin. They passed a few other early risers enjoying the best part of the day as they left the campsite to reach the river. They walked down the lane until the river disappeared between trees and found a quiet glade to undress beside a deep pool. It was much cooler in dappled shade and Lizzie shivered.

'Whose crazy idea was this,' she muttered, walking steadily into the water, trying to breathe normally and not gulp in a shocked breath. They'd have to be quick; they might not be the only ones having an early morning skinny dip to set up their day.

'Yours, as I recall.' Cal found her hand. 'And I love it.'

'I'm not sure I do. Let's go back and have a hot shower instead.'

'Too late for that, we're in.'

This part of the river was a series of waterfalls dropping from higher ground, and he ducked underneath, rising to shake the water from his hair. Lizzie did the same, nearly screaming from the chill. They kept moving, swimming a few metres to kiss underneath falling water that felt more like ice pouring over them. He smoothed her long, wet hair back from her face and her gaze went to his arm and their history, the waterfall inked on it.

'Why did you choose that?' She had to raise her voice over the rushing water as they kept moving, tried to keep the cold at bay.

'I won't ever forget that day.' His mouth was against her ear as they held each other. 'I see it every time I look down. I see you and me. I want you to know you can trust me, Lizzie. With your heart, your life. Everything.'

He'd been back in her world only a few weeks and she wanted more. She wanted tomorrow with him, she wanted to trust him. She nodded hurriedly and the kiss they shared was brief as they shivered. They ran from the water laughing, dressing as quickly as possible and adding layers to warm them.

Back at the festival they devoured outstanding coffee and toasties filled with grilled halloumi, fried egg, tomato and spinach. Stalls were opening as people wandered around, some fresh and bright and others looking very much as though they hadn't yet made it to bed after last night. A band was sound checking on stage and Lizzie and Cal hung around to listen, and she was reminded of the search for his father, the decision not to continue. It still saddened her, even as she understood it.

She joined Cal for the bouldering briefing, standing at the back of the group and loving how professional and passionate he was, making the day and the problems ahead sound both exciting, challenging and a lot of fun. No one had ever made her feel the way he did and surrounded by the festival and filled with the same energy and excitement, she wanted only to give herself up to everything and cherish each moment with him.

Back at the tent they collected their kit and set out with the group to a rocky outcrop about a mile up the valley that Cal had already recced and decided was right for the day and the group's abilities. Lizzie was up front with him when she halted on the rough path, giving him an apologetic grin as she hurriedly checked her bag.

'Sorry, schoolboy error. Just realised I've come without spare batteries. I'll have to go back, this one's not going to last all day.'

'Okay. I can't leave the group, sorry.'

'No, it's fine. I'll catch you up, it's not far and I know where you're going. I'll be as quick as I can.'

She ran back to the campsite, quieter now with most people out on the fells or at the festival. She found the spare batteries in her car, where she'd left them. Music from across the field was loud and vibrant, and it made her feel happy, at peace with the world around her. The warm sun seemed to be filling her bones with ease as worries about the future slipped away. Not for now, plans about what she'd do when her time in the flat was up, and Cal left the boathouse. Her thoughts were all of him, and she was impatient to return to the group and take the shots she'd promised.

Two men were chatting near the shower block, and they stepped off the narrow path as she approached to let her through. She thanked them, dividing her glance between both as she walked past. Something caught in her mind as she reached the lane and she spun around, shock landing like a punch in her stomach. She snapped the lens cap off her camera and sprinted back, forcing herself to slow down as she reached the two men. They'd resumed their position on the path and the younger man gave her a wry grin as he made to move out of her way for a second time.

'Forgotten something?'

'What? Yes, batteries.' She couldn't think beyond the importance of her camera in this moment as she skidded to a halt, scree flying out from beneath her boots. She tried to laugh away her urgency, desperate not to reveal how fast her heart was beating or the new clumsiness in her fingers.

'Would you mind?' She raised the camera. 'I'm taking photographs all weekend and I'd love some of both of you. I like how you were just chatting, with the festival and the fells in the background. It would make a great shot.'

'Alec? I don't mind if you don't?' The younger man grinned as he looked to his companion.

His answering smile was one she would have recognised anywhere, and her fingers tightened around the camera.

Chapter 18

Lizzie's attention was fixed on the older man. Alert, watchful, her camera poised. She felt like a wolf in this moment, ready to capture her prey in any way she could. She guessed he was probably in his sixties, attractive with very short steel grey hair and fit, muscles in his forearms revealed by his dark blue T-shirt, rangy, lean, long-limbed. Probably a shade below six feet with a suntanned, lived-in face. Craggy, almost, she would have said, laughter lines softened by amusement as he regarded her.

'Of course not. What would you like us to do?' His voice was lovely, too: polite, deep, with a rich Scottish accent that Lizzie didn't know whether answered another question or added to the mystery.

'Just pretend I'm not here and you were talking, like before.' Her pulse was roaring as she framed them, realising that the two men had lost some of their ease while they resumed their conversation. She took several rapid shots, moving around to capture them from every angle and lowered her camera before they could ask her to stop, she couldn't delay them indefinitely.

'Thank you so much,' she said casually, working hard to keep her voice even. She was desperate to stare at the older man and make out every detail. She knew now she had the means to do so in private, on her camera. Alec, the other one had called him. 'I could send the images on to you both. I'm with the bouldering group today and we've already swapped emails.'

'That sounds great.' The younger man went to his pocket and produced a card he handed to Lizzie. 'Jason Poole.'

'Thanks, Jason, nice to meet you. I'm Lizzie.' She was already turning to Alec, and he shrugged.

'Sorry, I don't have one of those.' He glanced at the card in her hand.

'Would you like to write your email address on this one?' She held out the card, trying to keep the frantic note from her voice. *Please say yes*, she willed. *Please say yes.*

Alec hesitated and then took it from her. 'Why not?' He found a pen in a rucksack at his feet.

'Will you be at the Q&A later?' Lizzie was gabbling, remembering a session planned for this evening. 'I've heard loads of people will be there, those two climbers are such local legends. It's going to be unmissable if climbing's your thing.'

'Not for me, I'm afraid.' Alec propped the card on his thigh to write. 'I have another commitment today and you caught me just as I was leaving. There you go.'

'Thank you.' She took the card and scanned the line he'd written. 'Alec Sutherland,' she read out loud. 'Perfect, thank you both so much. I'll get the images to you as soon as I can.' She quickly remembered Jason's presence and shared a smile between the two men, hoping she hadn't made her interest in Alec too obvious.

'You must let me know how much I owe you,' Alec said, and Lizzie was already shaking her head.

'That's so kind,' she rushed out. 'It's really not necessary. I'm not a professional, I just love taking photographs and I thought you'd make a great shot. Both of you,' she added, glancing at Jason. 'But I mustn't keep you, thank you so much for your time.'

'You're welcome.' Alec held out a hand. 'It was nice to meet you, Lizzie…?'

She accepted it, feeling the rush of excitement as their fingers connected. Was this the past meeting the present? Was she right, and was this man really the one from the photograph of Marianne at a festival all those years ago, the year when Cal had been conceived?

Might Alec Sutherland hold the key to Cal's story? The only way she could find out would be to ask. But not now, not like this. First, she had some searching to do, and adrenaline was pumping through her limbs at the thought of having a name and a possible image of the man now to compare with the old one. 'Lizzie Martin. I'll be in touch.'

She wanted to fly back up the fell, find Cal and blurt out what had just taken place at the campsite. But he needed to focus on the job he had to do today, and she couldn't let him be distracted by news like this. Instead she forced herself to walk slowly, her mind raking over the bare details of the man in the photograph with Marianne that she'd stored on her phone, to compare them with Alec Sutherland. She wanted to scream at the lack of signal that hadn't mattered until this moment.

Finding Cal's group, she hung back to stare at him offering instructions beneath a huge boulder. A second burst of shock sped through her, stilling her feet, as she dragged in a long breath. There was a definite similarity between Cal and Alec in the shape of their faces, the two pairs of hazel eyes. But she mustn't read too much into this and search for a connection that might not exist. She needed to tread carefully, she didn't want to alert Cal to something that might amount to nothing, especially after his decision not to continue the search for his father.

He spotted Lizzie, giving her a quick grin as he raised a hand. It was as though she was seeing him through a different lens and her eyes were racing over his face. She didn't think her equilibrium was restored enough to talk to him yet, and she concentrated on working with the group, switching herself to autopilot to take hundreds of images she could share with them all later.

Surely Cal's father couldn't have been just across the field from them at the festival, already gone from their grasp to make the prior commitment he had mentioned. But now Lizzie had something precious, and she felt in her pocket for Jason's business card. It wouldn't matter now if she lost it, she'd already committed his and Alec Sutherland's email addresses to memory. The moment she returned to the flat she would begin searching until she had enough to share with Cal and they could find a way to confirm her suspicions together.

Soon, it was time for lunch, and Lizzie was full of love for Cal all over again as they sat side by side to eat. He had come so far on his own without a family to guide, support and love him, and she was so proud of all he'd achieved. There was a lot of laughter and craic in the group. Lizzie was captivated when he was asked about his climbing in New Zealand, and he shared stories of his favourite ascents in Kawakawa Bay on the North Island, and Arthur's Pass on the South.

When the session was over and the group hiked back down to the campsite, they all promised to meet for drinks later, and everyone wandered off with 'thanks' and 'hope to do this again's. Cal wanted to see Lizzie's images, planning to use some for his social media so she scrolled carefully through them, palms clammy as she made sure to avoid the ones of Alec. Even though she knew he had already left, she was constantly searching him out as she and Cal strolled around the festival until dark. She held Cal very tightly in the tent after they'd made love and he fell asleep in her arms long before she drifted off.

The next day was different, an even more technical boulder with a more advanced group and Lizzie took hundreds of shots, the light better this time, as clouds scudded across the sky and offered patches of sunlight falling onto the landscape. She and Cal were both tired as they packed up the tent and though Lizzie hated having to leave him, for once she was glad she could drive home and have some time in the flat alone to begin her search.

'Sure you don't want me to come back with you?' Cal kissed her again, still holding her hand as he reluctantly backed away. 'I could use an early start on Simon's present.'

'No, really.' She loathed making up an excuse, especially as she'd love nothing more than to wake up with him again in the morning. 'We'd probably end up sleeping late after this weekend and then your early start would be gone. And I've got to work too.'

'Call me when you get home.'

'I will.' She kissed him a final time and got in her car. 'It's going to take me hours to go through all those shots.' That much was true at least, and right now there were only about a dozen she was really interested in. 'I'm already missing you.'

'Me too.'

Her phone started buzzing with notifications as soon as she left the valley and she drove home as quickly as she could, nearly screaming at some of the slower tourists meandering along. She dumped her bag the minute she was through the door in the flat and microwaved something quick to eat as she called Cal to say goodnight. It was unlikely she would want to get up again any time soon and she settled down with her laptop. She'd waited almost thirty-six hours to do this, typing Alec Sutherland's name into Google. She gulped a mouthful of water, excitement and relief filling her mind as thousands of results followed.

Here he was, and Lizzie leapt straight onto his Wikipedia page. Everything from when he'd been born in Edinburgh sixty-one years ago to the death-defying climbs he'd completed all over the world, and so much more in between. She brought up images of him at dizzying heights on countless Cumbrian fells and Scottish Munros, arms and legs stretched wide to reach for the next precarious hold. She saw him staring into the camera on the summit of snow-covered mountains, his face barely visible behind the kit required to climb in sub-zero temperatures, arms draped around others who had made those terrifying ascents with him.

She tracked him down the years of his life as best she could, bookmarking anything she thought might help, and making notes to share with Cal later. She couldn't ignore how the landscape he adored might well have been passed on by his father. that seemingly shared need to be outdoors, to push and climb and rise.

And then there were Cal's eyes – hazel, like Alec's – and Lizzie recalled those few minutes standing in front of him and how she'd instantly known without explanation who he was. She had carried the image of Cal in her heart and mind for too many years to mistake his eyes in someone else. Tears followed and Lizzie's hands covered her face in part shock, part triumph, and part fear at what might come next when she told Cal all she had learned. How would he handle this new information, the possibility of discovery, so many years later?

She couldn't be certain, not without asking Alec directly if he was Cal's father, but in her mind, she was as sure as she could be. She needed to step very carefully and think about what best to do next. Frustrated by Alec's lack of social media, Lizzie clicked on a link to a literary festival in Derbyshire and saw he was due to speak at it next weekend. She had to go and see him. She had to try to bring him and Cal together somehow.

In between finalising plans for the brand launch, setting up meetings with newly engaged couples, and a gin distillery looking to arrange an event, Lizzie was flat out over the next few days, though she managed to sort through her images from the festival and send off the best to everyone who'd requested them. She emailed her favourite three photos of Alec Sutherland to him, thrilled to receive a polite thank you in reply.

She wondered about letting him know she planned to be in Derbyshire on Sunday but decided not to. Whatever she wanted to say — and she still had no clear idea what those words would be — she felt they would be better coming in person rather than via an email. Telling Cal she couldn't see him on Sunday was harder and she hated making up a story about meeting potential clients who needed to speak in a hurry.

They were both full on with work and even when he was at Halesmere, he was busy with Simon's wedding present and Lizzie was slightly relieved they didn't have much time together, other than a quick shoot for his social media one afternoon. She was excited about what she'd learned of Alec yet nervous of telling Cal. But that day wasn't yet here and when it was, she would be ready, and she'd help him to be ready as well.

–

Lizzie drove to Derbyshire on Sunday morning and parked in good time. Alec was due to speak at eleven and she sipped at a coffee, waiting, wishing she could enjoy her surroundings more. The village was very pretty, the stone a more subtle golden shade to the one she was used to in Cumbria. She queued up and was in her seat early, hoping to remain anonymous in the crowd about halfway back so he wouldn't spot her before the end.

The talk about his latest book was excellent; engaging, funny, serious at times, and Lizzie tried to laugh along with everyone else while her nerves were in shreds. The crowd marvelled at the images he shared on a big screen: his favourite ascent, one of his toughest and in Alaska; and one in Nepal when he'd almost lost three fingers and the end of his nose to frostbite. He was clearly an adventurer as well as a farmer, and Lizzie saw the same drive in Alec as in Cal, to push and go further, to refuse to stand still.

She had already paid for a copy of his book and, adrenaline racing, she hung around for a place at the back of the queue for signings. He was happy to pose for selfies and chat to his fans, and it seemed an age until it was her turn at the desk where he sat. She saw the surprise register as he looked up, the memory of their meeting at the festival little more than a week ago, and the emails since.

'Hi.' Lizzie decided a pleasant smile and politeness coupled with confidence and honesty would be her best approach. She handed over the book and he opened it.

'Your talk was brilliant, thank you. I'm looking forward to reading this.'

'Thank you, Lizzie. This is a surprise. I didn't realise you were so interested in climbing.'

'I am, yes. I have a friend who climbs, and he's a qualified mountain leader too.' Pride for Cal rang clear in her voice.

'Excellent. Is this a present for him, then? Would you like me to dedicate it?'

Lizzie hadn't thought of that, and blood pounded into her face, leaving her scarlet. 'That would be nice, thanks.' She hesitated. 'His name is Cal.'

'Right. Cal.'

She was watching carefully to see how this registered with Alec, moisture gathering on her palms. Nothing. He wrote a few words, but she couldn't make them out upside down. His signature followed with a quick, blue scrawl.

'I appreciated your photographs, Lizzie, thank you for sending them on. You're very good, the composition was excellent.' Alec's gaze flickered over the few people behind her. 'Do you have any more for me?'

'I'm sorry, I don't.' She thanked him for the book he closed and returned, tucking it under her arm. Her heart was still thumping. 'But I do have another reason for being here today. I was hoping to speak with you. It is about my friend actually, the climber.'

'Oh?' An organiser to Alec's left was looking concerned and he nodded. 'I haven't got long, I'm afraid, and I'm leaving straight after the signing.'

'I won't keep you.' Lizzie swallowed, summoning all her courage. 'His name is Cal Ryan, and I'm helping him search for information about his family. I was hoping you might be able to help us.'

Alec pursed his lips, shaking his head. 'I'm sorry, I've never heard of the Ryan family or your friend Cal. Good luck with the search, I hope he finds what he's looking for.'

Oh hell. The organiser was looking as though she were about to intervene and send Lizzie away. She had seconds and she mustn't ruin Cal's chances of finding his father – she must speak carefully. 'It concerns his mother, Marianne. She used the surname Lindsay when she sang with a folk band about thirty years ago. Might you have heard of her?'

Lizzie had never seen the colour drain from a person's face quite as fast as it did from Alec's in that moment, and she knew the truth instantly. Now she must somehow find another opportunity to learn his and Marianne's story. He dropped the pen and it clattered to the floor as he gulped a mouthful of water.

'That was all a very long time ago and I barely knew her,' he said very quietly, those hazel eyes fixed on Lizzie. 'I'm sorry I can't be more helpful.' He glanced at the people waiting behind her. 'This is not the place, and you have to go.'

'I'm so sorry, I didn't mean to shock you. Please—'

'Go,' he repeated, and she saw the new tremble in his hand when he picked up the pen. 'I see no reason for us to speak again.'

Lizzie drove home in utter despair, convinced she'd ruined Cal's best chance of finding his father by blundering on ahead and tracking down Alec on her own. It wasn't her story, her history that he held, and now she might have alienated him from Cal forever.

Without knowing any different they'd always assumed his father knew about Cal and wanted no part in his life, but Lizzie understood all too well what shock looked like when it was staring straight at her. Alec had known nothing about Cal, of that she was convinced. She could still picture how quickly the blood had fled from Alec's face and left him pale and shaky.

She knew she'd made the situation worse and back in the flat, she opened her laptop before she changed her mind to compose an email she hadn't prepared, pouring her heart into the words she wrote:

Dear Alec,

Thank you for your time today and signing the book. I appreciated the opportunity to speak with you again. I'm so very sorry if I upset you, that was not my intention, and again, I'm sorry.

I've known Cal for twelve years and he has been searching for his father since we met. Marianne was his mother. He was born thirty-one years ago in Belfast after she returned home pregnant, and her family disowned her. I think it's only fair to be clear and say I believe you may be his father, one whose name he has never known as Marianne didn't provide it on his birth certificate. Again I apologise sincerely for the shock and any distress this may cause you.

Cal's only clue about his father is a copy of a photograph of Marianne at a festival in Cumbria with a man who we believe may hold the key to his past. Cal managed to speak with the founding member of the band she sang with and although he remembered seeing this man with her, he didn't have a name. I saw you at the festival last week, quite literally by chance, and I knew straightaway that I'd seen you somewhere before, and I realised it was from the photo.

With great respect, may I ask you to please reconsider speaking with Cal at some point? I do, of course, understand that this inform-ation is shocking, and I don't wish to cause any further hurt or upset.

Lizzie's eyes filled with tears splashing onto her laptop as she wrote the next lines:

Cal is a loving and kind man, and one who has achieved so much in his life despite diffi-cult and upsetting circumstances in his early years, finally losing his mother when he was seventeen. There's so much more I could tell you, but all of it should really come from him if you wish to hear it. I know that he simply wants to understand more about his family and who he is and has little expectation of finding out. He has always felt that half of his life is a blank page.

He doesn't know that I've met you or that I'm emailing now. I hope to hear back from you with a decision, and I will of course respect that decision. I must also share what I've learned with Cal. He deserves to know at least what I do, and it wouldn't be right for me to keep this from him.

Yours respectfully,
Lizzie Martin

Having done everything she could to make the situation better, she would have to take the information to Cal and try to help him understand. Over the next twenty-four hours she checked her inbox every few minutes, registering the disappointment whenever an email arrived that wasn't from Alec. The brand launch was on Thursday, and she decided that once the event was over, she would speak with Cal on Friday and share everything she had learned, whether she heard from Alec or not. She didn't want to distract Cal from the launch and fill his mind with something this shocking before then.

The buzz around the brand was growing daily and he was tagging her on nearly every shot he posted. Their followers, especially his, were jumping and Lizzie was receiving new enquiries about her services. The bouldering sessions he'd run at the festival had been a big success and she knew some of the participants had rebooked with him for smaller group instruction. He used the brand's rucksacks and kit everywhere, much to their delight, and it hadn't been long until he was linked to the company he'd set up in New Zealand.

Early on Thursday morning Lizzie was halfway through an online meeting with a potential new supplier when another email arrived. Casually checking her inbox, as she currently did about a hundred times a day, a leap of anticipation followed as she registered Alec's name. She ended the meeting as soon as she reasonably could and raced to open the email with a trembling hand.

Dear Lizzie,

Thank you for your thoughtful email and your concern, I am fine. I apologise for my brusqueness at the signing. You were quite right, your news did come as a tremendous shock, and I can't say that the few days since have given me much time to come to terms with it.

I did know Marianne – well, as it happens. I cared about her very much and I have reconsidered your request to meet. While I have no wish to expose anyone to further hurt, I believe it will be in all our future interests to explain the truth to Cal, given what you have told me of him.

I would also like to say that I had no knowledge of Marianne having had a son and I would have behaved very differently towards him in the intervening years had I been aware of this.

My home is in Cumbria, would you and Cal like to join my wife and I at our farm for lunch this coming Sunday? I apologise for the lack of notice, I am going away the following day and would like to meet before my trip if at all possible.

Yours,

Alec Sutherland

Lizzie screamed with joy, sending her phone flying from the table and fumbling to pick it up. She didn't have much time to prepare Cal for the shock and the meeting which would follow.

Chapter 19

Lizzie was flat out for the rest of the day setting up the launch. She tried to shelve all thoughts of Alec, but it wasn't easy, and as she welcomed the team installing the yurt and seating, she kept going over their brief conversations and emails. She was excited about telling Cal, even if part of her was worried about how he might react.

When Lily and Arlo returned from school they had to be nearly dragged from the yurt, begging to sleep inside with Prim, which Ella very firmly refused, much to their disappointment. Lizzie had brought in a lighting specialist recommended by the marquee hire company and the garden was all set for guests to find their way 'Into the Wild' in the woodland and enjoy some forest bathing.

Cal spent the day at Halesmere, most of it working on Simon's wedding present in the forge, and he posted a couple of behind-the-scenes shots for tonight. Gemma was desperate to see Simon's gift and Cal had arranged a viewing a couple of days before the wedding. He joined Lizzie in the flat to shower and change for the launch, and she laughingly dodged his request to try out the roll top bath as there simply wasn't time.

'I've never seen you dressed so formally.' She paused styling her hair, catching sight of him through the mirror on her dressing table. 'You look very different and utterly gorgeous.'

236

'Ach, thanks Lizzie.' He hands went to her shoulders and he dropped a kiss on one. His storm grey chinos with a turn up, a white T-shirt and navy blazer worn with black leather brogue trainers were a perfect blend of classic and informal for the evening ahead. 'You look wonderful. I think this night is going to be incredible, thanks to you.'

'That's very generous but Ella did most of the planning. I came to it late with some finishing touches.'

'It's not just the launch, it's everything.' The smile fell away as he stared into the mirror. 'The shots you've taken, giving us another chance, supporting me trying to find my father, all of it. I don't deserve it. Not after the way I left you.'

'That's over, Cal. You weren't the only one who made mistakes. We're different now,' she told him quietly. She turned her head to press a kiss onto his palm and a moment of uncertainty flickered into her mind. Was she ready to trust him with her life and let him hold her heart again, as he'd asked her to? And could she even make that choice when it seemed so far from her own control? Were they so very different now from who they'd been before? Almost all of their time together was spent alone. Her family was far away, and he assumed his own were non-existent. She knew better and anticipation was swirling in her stomach. Tomorrow she would tell him everything she knew about Alec.

'So tonight, we can be friends who are working together. Or,' he bent down, both hands sliding down her arms to find hers and cover them. 'I can support you, as your partner. Would you trust me with that?'

'What about me supporting you? It's your evening, not mine.'

'That too.' His smile was hopeful. 'Would you be my partner then? Look after me?'

'Are you asking about the launch, or something more?'

His head was beside hers and she saw only the confidence, the future in his gaze, reflected in the mirror. 'I'm here for more, Lizzie. It's not about putting something to bed and moving on. Not for me.'

'Nor me,' she said softly. 'And I'd love that. But if we don't get out of here soon then you're going to miss your own launch.' Cal's smile widened and he squeezed her hands before stepping back so she could finish getting ready.

Lizzie had chosen a high-necked, long-sleeved green dress and Chelsea boots with a low heel, drawing back the hair around her face in braids, leaving the rest loose and long to complete the informal look she also wanted. She didn't need Cal's compliment to let her know how good she looked, and she found his hand as they left the flat. All of the Halesmere artists, as well as Stan and Pearl, were invited and guests were soon arriving, their laughter and chatter floating on the summer evening air.

The garden looked magical as the sun slowly slipped away and Lizzie was in professional mode as she kept an eye on everything, including Cal. Everyone knew who he was and her images of him, enlarged, propped on easels around the garden and individually lit, were stunning and attracting lots of attention. He was shaking hands, smiling for selfies, and she saw how much easier he was in company now from the young man she'd known before.

The buffet was going down brilliantly, with a menu of fell-bred beef, roasted vegetable terrine, three different salads along with hot new potatoes and cheese from Luke and Marta's farm with a vegan choice, and sourdough produced by local baker Rowan, who supplied the community shop. Dessert was individual damson crème brûlées served with shortbread.

The forest bathing was a huge hit with groups of guests wandering into the woodland to take part in short sessions on breathing and appreciating the calm of the trees around them. Lizzie was on her way back from observing a session, and anxiety erupted in her stomach the second she spotted Alec Sutherland chatting in a small group on the lawn, drink in hand. She registered his surprise when his glance caught hers and he offered a quick nod, a brief smile. Her gaze left his to race around the garden, searching for Cal.

Aghast, she saw that he was making his way over to Alec's group and scarlet heat was burning on her face. She was half aware of words wafting on the evening air, the sound of laughter and vaguely registered Cal's smile as he was introduced to the group. She saw the handshake he and Alec shared, and she forced her feet to move, stumbling across the grass to join them.

She was staring at Cal, assessing his reaction. Did he know? Could he not tell? Surely the similarity between him and Alec was obvious? Lizzie's heart was thundering so fast she thought she might faint, but she knew from Cal's laughter that he hadn't detected his hazel eyes mirrored Alec's or the similar resonance of their voices.

'Lizzie, hi, let me introduce you.' Cal held out an arm to draw her into the small group before the other two people excused themselves. She fixed a frozen smile onto her face, felt the quick heat of his hand on her back. 'Alec Sutherland, my partner Lizzie Martin. Lizzie is the one responsible for these images, as well as most of my social media, and she organised the event. She's brilliant.'

'I must agree with you.' Alec's gaze was impassive and her own was imploring him not to reveal their secret. He offered the faintest of nods. He knew. He understood she had not yet shared with Cal what she had learned. This conversation would be a very different one were that the case. 'Actually Cal, Lizzie and I have already met, quite by chance.' His voice was a shade less confident than the one she heard from him before. 'We bumped into one another at the Ellthwaite festival a couple of weeks ago. She was kind enough to take some photos of me and send them on.'

'She's fantastic, isn't she? We were bouldering both days and the groups loved her shots. There was no one else I wanted to work with on my content.'

More praise from Cal and she didn't know what to do with it. She couldn't have described a single image in the garden right now or replied to a question about where she'd taken them. His hand found hers and he moved until he was against her side, keeping her close. She wanted to weep, to grip his hand tight and tell him what she knew. That all would be fine and she loved him, that they would find a way through this news together.

'I can see why.' Alec's gaze went to the nearest image of Cal. She'd photographed him scrambling between two crags in the rain, water pouring off his face as he aimed for an unseen summit smothered in mist, the ever-present rucksack on his back. 'I think she's very talented. It's not just the composition but as a viewer I can feel the sense of purpose you're conveying without even realising it. It's clear how much you love the landscape, how at home you are in it.'

'Ach, always have been, I suppose.' Cal's grin was self-conscious. 'I grew up in Belfast, but I ran off to the mountains whenever I could. My childhood was pretty lonely at times, and it helped to be out there. It was peaceful, you know?'

'I do.' Alec's voice was very low, and Lizzie saw the effort he was making to conceal a glimpse of pain as he stared at Cal. His hand went to Cal's shoulder, and he patted it, let it rest there for a second. Climber to climber, he understood. Only she knew how much more he was saying. His friendly gesture was surely also one from father to son, and she felt a rush of tears well up. They just needed to get safely through this night and then she could confess.

'Cal, I…'

Alec hesitated and the shake of her head was so minute she thought he might miss it. She felt for him, the importance of the knowledge he wanted to reveal, the similarities she was certain he'd seen, the note of tension in his voice now he had confirmed for himself the truth Lizzie had shared with him.

'I'd very much like to hear more about your time in New Zealand. Oliver mentioned you'd lived there and it's not a place I've climbed more than a couple of times. My trips tended to take me to the Alps or further east.'

'You would?' The grin of pure excitement Cal gave Alec almost took Lizzie's breath away. 'I'd love that. I think there's a lot I could learn from you.'

'Then why don't I leave you and Lizzie to talk about dates?' Alec smiled at her, and she nodded faintly. 'You should both come to lunch. Lizzie already has my email.'

Alec held out a hand to Cal and when he took it, Alec covered Cal's with both of his, shaking it warmly before doing the same with her. 'Would you excuse me? I can see my friend is ready to leave and we're car sharing. I look forward to hearing from you, Lizzie. Congratulations on the launch, it's been a wonderful evening. I wish you every success. Goodnight both.'

Lizzie watched Alec walk away, back straight, that same easy stride as Cal's. Couldn't he see it, wasn't it obvious? Those eyes, that ambition, the overwhelming need for the mountains and big skies.

'Wasn't Alec great?' Cal enthused, catching Lizzie around the waist. 'I really liked him. Do you think he's serious, about inviting us for lunch? He must meet loads of people, especially ones with way more experience than me. I think he's written a couple of books, I should get a copy.'

This was the moment. Telling Cal tomorrow what she had learned about Alec after meeting him now would be too late, she could hardly drop it into conversation over breakfast. The launch was drawing to a close and guests were wandering away. She took a deep breath, biting her lip.

'Let's escape for a minute.' She tried to smile but it was lost in the trepidation making her limbs tremble. She took Cal's hand, leading him to the terrace and through the open French doors into the drawing room.

'You read my mind. I can't wait to be alone with you.' His arms went around her as they entered the house and Lizzie wriggled free. She couldn't have the distraction of him touching her; her mind needed to be clear to deliver this news.

'Cal, I...' She hated that she might now be about to give him the shock of his life. Would there ever be a right moment to tell him about Alec, especially now they'd actually met.

'What's the matter? You seem upset, has something happened?'

'Not the way you think. I'm fine.'

'Lizzie, I know you and I know when something's not right. What's going on?'

'Let's sit down.'

'Okay, now I'm really worried.' Cal perched on the edge of a sofa, and she settled beside him.

'Don't be.' She took another deep breath, clinging onto his hand with both of hers. 'There's something you need to know and it's about your family. I'm so sorry, I hadn't planned to tell you tonight. I wanted the launch to be out of the way first.'

'Tell me what? Just say it, Lizzie, you're freaking me out.'

She was staring, imploring him to understand what she had done and why. To take in the news she was about to impart. 'Cal, I'm as sure as I can be that Alec Sutherland is your father.'

'You're not serious? That's funny.' Cal grinned but it slid away as he stared at Lizzie and the seconds passed. 'Shit. You are serious.'

'Very.' She was clutching his hand and he shook her off as he leapt to his feet. 'I promise you, I wouldn't joke about something like this.'

'How long have you known?' Already his voice had hardened, reminding Lizzie of the steel he sculpted. There was a flatness there too, and she flinched at the ice in it. 'Weeks? Days? When did you find out?'

'Cal, I'm so sorry, I've only—'

'How long?'

She was expecting shock and possibly disbelief, not this anger he was working hard to contain. A muscle was flickering in his cheek, the fingers she had just been holding tapping a furious, distracted beat on his thighs. She saw it again, the likeness between him and Alec. The shape of their faces, their eyes, there was so much they shared. She wondered Cal had not seen it too. But then he hadn't been looking at Alec like she had.

'A couple of weeks, since the festival. I met him literally just by chance. That time I had to go back for batteries, I saw him at the campsite and knew I'd seen him before. It was the photograph, the one of your mum. I was sure he was the man with her. I made some excuse about my camera, he let me take his photo and gave me his email address so I could send them on.'

'And what makes you think he is my father?' Cal's quick laugh was full of scorn, incredulity. 'He could be anyone, nothing to do with me.' An agitated breath escaped as he paced the room, reminding Lizzie of the wolf again. He tore off his blazer and threw it to a chair, running his hands over his face and into his hair. She stood, too, aching to go to him and help. She took a few steps and tried to put her arms around him. He shrugged her off, anger glittering in his face. 'Just tell me.'

'Because I've been in touch with him. I went to see him last weekend and we've emailed. He confirmed he knew Marianne and that they were close. I was going to tell you tomorrow, once the launch was over. I didn't want to upset you.'

'Upset me,' Cal shouted, staggering backwards. She went to grab him, and he shook her off a second time. 'What the hell, Lizzie? You knew all this, and you didn't think to tell me before? Did you ever stop with your assumptions to realise it's not your story to decide who gets to hear it? It's not your life you're playing with. You're doing it again, assuming you can make decisions for me and tell me how my life should be.'

'I'm not, I promise.' Tears were trailing down her face and she swiped them away. 'I just wanted to be clear before I told you. I didn't want to get your hopes up and you be disappointed if it turned out to be nothing. You said you'd decided to stop looking, that you were giving up searching for something you weren't going to find.'

Cal grabbed his blazer and snatched keys from his pocket. Lizzie nearly buckled at his fury and hurt when he paused the frantic pacing to glare at her. 'You had no right. I'm not still your plaything, your summer of fun. It's so much more than that.'

He stormed through the French doors, and she stared after him, wishing the last five minutes had never happened and trying to understand how it had gone so spectacularly wrong. The party was almost over and only a few guests remained in the garden. She couldn't think about that now. She couldn't think of anything other than Cal and his appalled and hurt reaction. She ran back into the garden, found Ella, and quickly explained that she had to leave.

Lizzie leapt into her car and tore down the lanes after Cal, her worry and sorrow for him bound up with anger. It was almost dark, and the roads were mercifully quiet as she flew along, letting out a gasp of relief when she saw his van outside the boathouse. She hadn't been certain where he might go after the news he'd just received. He could have taken off into the fells and she might not have seen him for days. She jumped from the car and hammered on the front door.

'You're not doing this again.' She was sobbing through the words pouring from her soul. 'I won't let you run off and leave me, not again. You can't just take off every time you get hurt. I know you're there, Cal, let me in, please. Let me in. You don't have to do this alone. I'll help you, I promise. I'll be there with you. And you're right and I'm sorry. I should have told you straightaway. I thought I was looking after you.' She slumped against the door, her voice falling. 'You've never been just my summer of fun, you're my everything.'

'It's not locked.'

Lizzie almost fell through the door when Cal opened it. He dropped to lift her into his arms and hold her tightly. 'I'm so sorry. I shouldn't have reacted like that. I know it's not your fault. I was stunned and I couldn't think straight. I still can't believe it. It feels too unreal to be true.'

'I know. I felt that way too, at first.' She tipped her head back and he wiped away the tracks of her sorrow with a finger still shaking. 'I never wanted to hurt you, Cal. I was just trying to help.'

'I know, Lizzie. Ach, I do. I'm sorry. I just didn't see it coming, any of it. After all these years, he's here? It's really him?'

'I think so, and Alec does too.' She took a breath, a shred of relief settling into her mind. 'We should talk, properly. I'll tell you everything I know.' She found Cal's hand and he followed her into the sitting room to settle together on the sofa.

She explained about the festival and learning Alec's name so she could google him and driving to Derbyshire to speak with him at the book signing. She told Cal about the conversation she had there with Alec and how shocked he'd been when he'd heard Marianne's name, and Lizzie had known the truth straightaway. She showed Cal her email and Alec's reply a few days later, confirming her suspicions and inviting them to lunch. Throughout, Cal listened in silence and she saw the shock slowly receding as a glimmer of curiosity began to replace it.

She cupped a hand around his face. 'Alec and I haven't talked much but I think he was in love with Marianne. He had no idea about you, Cal. None whatsoever. He was stunned she'd had a child.' Lizzie hesitated. 'There's something else you need to know. Your mum did leave you a clue. Alec's middle name is Hamish.'

Cal's eyes widened in new shock, and she caught him as his shoulders slumped, his head falling to her neck. She felt the graze of his beard, the wetness of his tears through her dress as he cried. She held him tightly as he shuddered in her arms.

'It's okay, you're not alone. You don't have to this by yourself. I'm here, I'll help. I love you.'

One hand went to his back to stroke it as she murmured her promise again and again, Cal clinging to her, holding on as though he'd never let her go. He lifted his head when he was all cried out, trying to smile through the wetness on his face. 'Sorry.'

'Don't be.' Lizzie kissed his forehead, smoothing the dampness from his skin. 'It'll probably help.'

She rearranged them until his head was on her shoulder, stroking his hair, his body still trembling in her arms. 'When you feel ready, you need to decide what to do about lunch on Sunday. You might want more time to think about it.'

'I'm going.' Some of the strength returned to his voice. 'I don't want to waste any more time.'

'I'm so glad.'

'Will you come with me, Lizzie? Please? I know I have no right to ask, not after the way I reacted.'

'Of course I will.' She felt a rush a pleasure that he wanted her to support him. 'As long as you're sure you want me there?'

'I don't want to do any of this without you, not anymore. I've always been a lone wolf. Always felt I had to do everything myself, on my own. I don't feel like that since you came back into my life. You're a part of it. Part of me.'

'Are you saying we're a pack of two now?' She felt him smile, his chin resting lightly on her chest.

'I am. And I heard what you said before. I love you, too.'

Chapter 20

The farm was as isolated as Alec had warned in his emailed instructions: deep in a valley surrounded by high fells, the lane narrowing between trees as it climbed, a river splashing below. Lizzie was nearly as nervous as Cal, who had one hand on her thigh as she drove, his other tapping a light beat against his leg. The past couple of days since the launch had stirred up so many memories for him, both good and bad, and Lizzie had offered him all the support she could as he'd turned to her.

'Okay?' She gave him a quick glance. This road was notorious in Cumbria, leading to a high and less travelled pass, and she had to concentrate. Drivers often got caught out and she didn't want to nudge a wheel over the edge.

'Yeah. I think so. As I'll ever be.' The smile Cal offered was an anxious one. Never had he been closer to understanding who he really was. 'I still can't believe we're going to meet him properly. And his wife.'

'Me neither.'

They rattled over a cattle grid, mobile signal lost miles back, and dropped down into another valley, the ground falling steeply on one side of the car. Eventually they reached a crossroads and Lizzie pulled up to check the sign. They'd met little traffic out here, though sheep and lambs were everywhere, and she'd had to dodge them more than once.

'This must be it. It does say it's unsuitable for vehicles and Alec said to watch out for it, and that we'd be fine in the car.'

'Good for keeping coaches away, I suppose. Turn right and the farm should be another mile or so further on.'

They carried on and Lizzie spotted the entrance first, a five-barred gate opening onto a track. Alec's farm was the last one in the valley before moorland met fell and the road ran out. 'It's beautiful. Looks like his kind of place, somehow.'

'Yeah.'

If strength and love could be imparted through a grip, then she was offering every scrap she possessed in her hand clinging to Cal's as they approached the house. It was hewn from grey stone and slate, a barn and small byre to the right, and despite the day's warmth, the breeze was still cool. A stone wall surrounding a garden was topped by railings, and Lizzie saw Cal's gaze fix on a swing and the children's toys scattered across the grass. Before they reached it, the front door swung open and Alec was there, striding down a path separating the two halves of the lawn. An attractive woman of a similar age was beside him, her grey hair stylish and short.

'Lizzie, Cal, welcome. We're so glad you came.' Alec halted in front of them, apprehensive and uncertain as he held out a hand to Lizzie, then Cal. 'How do you do? I'm Alec Sutherland.' The smile became a little less cautious. 'I thought it was perhaps best to begin again.'

'Callum Ryan.' He took Alec's hand, and they shook firmly. 'Thank you for offering to meet me. I appreciate it.'

'Well, Lizzie was very persistent.' Alec glanced at her, and she returned his smile. She liked this man. 'It's clear she cares a great deal about you. Do you prefer Callum or Cal?'

'Cal's fine, I haven't used Callum for years.' His quick laugh was self-conscious as he ran a hand over his cropped hair. 'I don't even know why I said it. I suppose I'm nervous.'

'That makes two of us, then.' Alec cleared his throat as he held out an arm to draw the woman beside him into their conversation. 'Cal, Lizzie, this is my wife, Evelyn.'

More handshakes were offered, and Lizzie liked Evelyn's welcoming and friendly manner at once. If she was fazed by meeting someone who was quite probably her husband's grown-up child, it didn't show.

Evelyn led them into the house and through to a lovely kitchen, large, messy and homely. Beef roasting in the AGA smelled amazing and Alec cleared a pile of newspapers, a box of Lego and outdoor magazines from the table. Chairs were pulled out and drinks offered as everyone attempted to make conversation around the strangeness of the situation they were in.

Lizzie presented the tin of homemade shortbread she'd brought, and Evelyn thanked her as she continued prepping the meal, accepting Lizzie's help to hand out the drinks Alec poured. He and Cal moved to the huge window and the spectacular view it offered, their shared love of the landscape apparent as Alec pointed out some of his sheep, hefted to the land every bit as firmly as he was, and some boulders in the distance he thought Cal might find interesting.

As it was just the four of them, Evelyn suggested they stay in the kitchen to eat, and Lizzie was glad to have something to do as she set the table. Once everyone was settled and almost finished with the most gorgeous lunch, Alec looked at Cal.

'Well, I think we both have some questions.' Alec's smile was nervous again as he pushed away an empty plate. 'How old are you, Cal?'

'Thirty-one. My birthday's in April.'

'I see.' Alec let out a very long breath and the hand around his glass of red wine was unsteady as he looked at Evelyn before Cal again. 'Then I think it's safe to accept that you are my son. Marianne loved a good time, but I doubt there was anyone else for her that summer, given the similarities between you and me. We spent every spare moment together and she was still very innocent in some ways.'

Cal's hands went to his face as his shoulders slumped and Lizzie was off her seat. 'It's okay,' she murmured, her hands smoothing his back. 'Just breathe.'

'All this time,' he muttered. He dropped his hands to the table. Alec's arm reached out and he touched Cal's hand, just once. 'All these years I've wondered and never known, and then you just walk into my life.'

'Would you like to hear my story?'

'Very much.'

'May I see the photograph you have, Cal, the one you believe is me with your mother?'

Cal unlocked his phone and slid it across the table. Alec put on a pair of dark-framed glasses and Lizzie was holding her breath as Evelyn's hand went to his arm, offering her own support. The seconds ran away as he stared at it. Finally he raised his head to Cal, a sad reflection in his few words. 'You have Marianne's smile. She loved to laugh.'

A single tear slipped from Cal's eye, and he tried to smile as he it brushed it away. 'No one's ever said that to me before.'

'Until now.' Alec cleared his throat.

'Until now,' Cal repeated and his eyes briefly landed on Lizzie's, full of wonder and surprise.

'We never would have met if the climbing trip I was supposed to be going on hadn't been cancelled at the last minute.' Alec picked up his wine, then put it down again. 'I was living in Edinburgh and staying with a friend in Cumbria. When our climb was abandoned, we decided to go to a festival instead. I saw Marianne's set with her band and introduced myself afterwards. I thought she was mesmerising.' Alec paused, looking at Evelyn and then Cal, Lizzie's hand tight in his.

'We just hit it off from the start and talked for ages. She was funny, beautiful and interesting, this wild Irish girl who'd run away from everything she knew to sing. I was supposed to be going home with my friend, but it was one of those days that you never want to end. Marianne and I stayed up talking until morning and I think we both knew something special was going on. Neither of us ever quite put it into words but I believe we both fell in love that night.

'Nothing happened beyond talking, that first night, you understand. We had one more day before the festival ended and we were together every moment she wasn't on stage. We kissed goodbye and I went back to Edinburgh, telling myself I wouldn't do anything about what I felt for Marianne, even though I desperately wanted to. I was ten years older than her and already engaged to someone whom I'd known for a long time. There was definitely a fond feeling between my fiancée and I, but it wasn't a grand passion for either of us. I do realise that's a very poor excuse for what happened next.'

Alec gulped a mouthful wine, his gaze clear on Cal. 'I didn't expect to see Marianne again and I was determined to do the right thing by my fiancée, which faltered as the days went by. I knew where Marianne's band would be playing next, and I went. We met up and it was clear we both still felt the same. We'd fallen madly in love in the space of a couple of days.' He smiled wryly. 'If you'd asked me beforehand, I would have said it wasn't possible and didn't ever happen.'

Lizzie glanced at Cal, and she saw the memory of their own meeting in his quick smile for her. Alec was continuing, becoming wistful as he summoned his memories, more than thirty years old.

'I took ten days off work, which was all I could manage, and that was it. I borrowed a cottage from a friend and Marianne joined me there so we could spend every moment of that time together. It was perfect and I was dreading having to leave her. I knew I had a decision to make. She was thinking of moving to London for session work and I was a barrister in chambers in Edinburgh. It was going to be difficult, but I was sure we could find a way, if we wanted it enough.

'But of course I had to be honest and tell her about my relationship, which I hadn't yet done. We couldn't continue as we were and have a future together.' Alec's eyes were shining, and Evelyn's hand was firm on his arm. 'Marianne was crushed, absolutely devastated that I hadn't told her before. There was an awful row and I stormed out into the hills, thinking we both needed to calm down. When I returned a few hours later she'd gone, and I never saw her again.'

Alec's head dropped and his voice was very low. 'They say you should only regret the things you haven't done, don't they? Not the things you've done. I've always regretted not being truthful with her from the start. If I had, our lives might have been very different and I'm so terribly sorry for how hers turned out. I went back to Edinburgh, told my fiancée about Marianne, and we ended our engagement. Falling in love with a woman who left me for being dishonest was no way to begin a marriage to someone else.'

Lizzie had the sense he wasn't prepared to shy away from what he'd done or put a clever spin on it as he faced Cal again. 'I did try to find Marianne, of course I did. I moved to chambers in London and trawled all the session studios, went to gigs, turned up at festivals the following summer. All to no avail. She was adamant when we were together that she wouldn't go home to Ireland.'

'She did go back to her family.' Cal's voice was flat. 'They didn't want anything to do with her. After I was born, we lived in a bedsit in Belfast, before I went to a foster family when she got really ill.'

'I'm so desperately sorry.' Alec's hand went to Cal's arm and Lizzie saw him staring at it, as though deciding whether he dared accept the sympathy being offered. 'I had absolutely no idea about you, Cal. I promise you I would have married Marianne if she'd come back to me. I loved her.' Alec's voice caught. 'But she left me the gift of a son and I'm so thankful to have found you.'

'She always told me you wouldn't want us.' Cal withdrew his arm and Lizzie knew he wasn't ready yet, not comfortable with allowing himself to hope for more after living with the dream of a father for so long. 'Your name isn't even on my birth certificate. She said you were called Jim.'

Alec attempted a smile. 'That was our little joke; she used to tease me about my ancestry. My father was a Scottish baronet and eventually I inherited his title, not that it matters to anyone, and I've never used it. Marianne called me Jim because it's a nickname for Hamish and in her words, much less posh. We used to laugh about it. I never dreamed it would ever matter.

'After two years in London the mountains were calling me back and I had this crazy notion that if ever I was going to find her, it would be in Cumbria because that's where we'd first met. Those ten days together, we'd had this dream about living in the wild off the land, in some place really remote where the world couldn't find us. I left my chambers in London and bought this place nearly thirty years ago.'

Alec offered Evelyn a bruised smile full of love. 'I was blessed to meet Evelyn when I did and I'm very grateful for the life we share here.'

'And a family?' Cal was staring at the Lego, the child's coat on the back of a chair. He swallowed and Lizzie squeezed his hand. There was more to this story. 'Do you have children? Other children, I mean?'

'Yes.' Alec stood and collected a phone from the window ledge. He swiped the screen, pushing it across the table to Lizzie and Cal. 'You have a sister, Cal. A half-sister,' Alec corrected, and his voice was full of pride and love.

'This is our daughter Rebecca, who is twenty-five, a teacher and the mother of two very lively little boys called Noah and George. They are your nephews, and I think they would be impressed by you. And that's her partner,

Justin, with them. He's a research scientist and they live about an hour away, near the coast further north. They know about you and would like to meet when the time is right.'

'A sister? Nephews?' Cal's voice caught on the words, and he lifted a hand to cover his sob as he stared at the screen. Lizzie stood to slide her arms around his shoulders, and she too, was looking at the lovely, tawny-haired young woman and her partner, each holding a little boy and laughing into the camera, the farmhouse behind them.

'Cal?'

He raised his head to stare at Alec, whose hand came across the table to grip his. 'Lizzie told me you always dreamed of understanding where you came from. You came from love and, even though it wasn't meant to be, and even though I'll always have my regrets and sorrows about how things ended for Marianne and me, Evelyn and I want to welcome you into our family and help you find your place in it. You're part of us, as we are part of you.'

It was a very different Cal when they left Alec and Evelyn as the afternoon was edging into evening. Cal's wariness had gradually diminished as he and Alec talked, and it was very clear to everyone that the two men had some things in common, not least a passion for outdoor life. Alec had taken them around the farm and in his study he'd shown Cal images of his climbing trips, shutting themselves away as Evelyn and Lizzie chatted.

Lizzie knew this was more than he'd ever dared hope for, and it was going to take each of them time to get used to one another and find a path forward into the future as a new family.

Driving them back to the boathouse, she and Cal sat up half the night, googling Alec and still trying to take in how much of Cal's father's life was now at their fingertips. Cal was very pensive when they made love and he fell asleep in her arms, exhausted.

In the morning there was a lovely email from Alec, thanking them for coming to lunch and Lizzie for being the means of bringing him and Cal together. Had her keen photographer's eye not spotted him at the festival, Alec wrote, then he and Cal might never have met, and he was grateful for her persistence. Lizzie sent her own heartfelt reply in return, so delighted they had discovered one another and had the beginnings of a future together.

She and Cal had both taken the morning off work and after breakfast they sailed the yacht on the lake, happy to have an hour on the water and a swim while they still had the use of it. Back at the boathouse, Lizzie was gathering their things as Cal sorted out the yacht. Ready to leave for Halesmere, she picked up their phones. Her pulse jumped as she saw the beginning of a text on his from a name she recognised.

> Hey, so happy for you it went well! And we're out there now, first post together, yay! It's incredibly good of you, if you're absolutely sure. I can't wait to see you, it's all

Lizzie couldn't read any more of Tash's message without unlocking the screen, and she wouldn't do that even if she'd known how to. Her heart began to clatter as she stared down the garden to the lake, and Cal. How, why was he still involved with his ex-girlfriend, the beautiful woman Lizzie had seen in those old posts time and again? No matter if Tash was in New Zealand or California or anywhere else in the world, apparently she was in his life, on his phone, still a part of him in ways Lizzie simply hadn't seen coming. And when exactly was he planning to see Tash?

Lizzie dropped his phone and opened her own. She went straight to his Instagram, full of likes and comments still coming in after the launch and all the images they'd created together. Hands clammy, fingers clumsy, she trawled through his followers until she found Tash and clicked on her latest image posted an hour ago.

It was of a surf shop in Cornwall, painted pale blue and close to a harbour full of fishing boats and a few yachts. Tash was outside, holding a surfboard with two other women, all beautiful like her and laughing into the camera. The post went on to say how excited they were to be launching the new shop this weekend and Cal was tagged, apparently joining them to take part. The post had already drummed up loads of comments and hundreds of likes, and suddenly Lizzie felt light-headed. Gemma and Simon's wedding was this Saturday, the same day, and Cal wasn't going to be there. He was choosing Tash over her. Over them.

Lizzie sank onto the sofa where she'd held Cal as he'd cried in her arms after hearing about Alec. Her breakfast was churning and tears filled her eyes. This was all her own fault. She'd launched herself straight back into his life and Gemma had warned her not to fall right back in love with the man who had disappeared without a word twelve years ago. How could Lizzie trust him now, as he'd asked her to do, after this?

'You ready? I didn't think we needed that much stuff.' Cal was at the bi-fold doors. 'I've got a couple of things to finish on Simon's present before Gemma sees it... What's up?'

Lizzie stared at him, white-faced and still. 'I saw your phone.' She reached for it, voice flat. 'Are you going to Cornwall this weekend to see Tash?'

'Lizzie.' He took a step inside. 'It's not what you think.'

'You have no idea what I'm thinking! But let me tell you.' She jabbed the phone towards him. 'She's tagged you in a post because you're apparently going to be at this new shop she's opening on Saturday. It's my best friend's wedding on Saturday! You were supposed to be going to the wedding with me.'

'Was I?' Cal slid hands into his pockets to stare. 'Because I don't recall you ever inviting me.'

'I was going to! I know Simon already did and you told him you'd think about it.' Lizzie couldn't seem to contain the anger and bitterness layered in her words.

'Ach, there you go again, Lizzie. Making assumptions about me. So you wanted me at the wedding, but you never actually said the words. Never invited me and gave me a chance to reply. You wanted it to happen, so therefore it must.'

'I do want you there, with me. I thought you'd want that, too.' Her voice had fallen to a shocked whisper after he'd delivered the hard truth with complete calm. 'My parents are coming for the rehearsal on Friday night and we're all having dinner afterwards.'

'And when were you going to ask me to that? Or was it another assumption, that I'd just turn up? It was the same with Alec. You went after him without me because you didn't think I could cope with the truth about my own father or should help you search.'

'You know why I did that. I was trying to protect you.'

'The night of the launch, Lizzie, I asked you to trust me. There's some stuff I had to work out before I told you about Cornwall and I'm sorry I didn't do that sooner. But it's not what you think.'

He crossed the room in three strides to sit on the sofa. She leapt up and dropped his phone, she couldn't be close to him while she levelled out the thoughts and hurt racing in her mind.

'Lizzie, we need to sort this out if we're ever going to move on. Yesterday you trusted me.'

'Yesterday I didn't know about Tash,' she said brokenly. 'I can't do this, Cal. I can't live with wondering when you're next going to disappear or what you're not telling me. I can't build a life on worry and wishes, hoping we're different. We hurt each other before and we're hurting now. Let's not keep doing it.'

'So, what, you're telling me it's over?' His voice was sharp, and shock was hovering in his eyes. 'Yesterday you loved me and stood by my side to meet my father. And now you don't?'

'I'll make myself get over it.' Lizzie was moving like a robot, trying to collect her belongings, forcing herself to step away from the pain in his face. 'I've done that before. We both have.'

One unsteady foot followed the other to the front door. She halted as Cal's voice reached her, the past and their history flashing into her mind.

'I know how you felt when your parents lost your home and why you find it hard to trust someone else with your future. I let you down when I took off twelve years ago and you know how sorry I am for doing that. Cornwall isn't what you think but as you don't want to hear it, then there's nothing I can do. I hope you feel happy up there on your pedestal, Lizzie, looking down on everyone else. Good for you that you can assume you've barely made a mistake in your life while you're busy holding everyone else accountable for theirs.'

The bitterness was unpleasant and new in the soft, lilting voice she'd always loved, and tears were pouring down her face.

'Gemma was right. She said I'd have to watch my step because one strike and I'd be out. I just didn't see it coming.'

Chapter 21

Lizzie was on autopilot ahead of Gemma and Simon's wedding as she moved through the week. They'd finished work and Simon was staying with Will, his best man, while Gemma was at her mum and dad's. A chill had settled around Lizzie's heart, and she was having to dredge up every ounce of enthusiasm and excitement to match her best friend's own. She stayed in the flat as much as possible and did her best to avoid any sightings of Cal as he worked in the forge to complete Simon's wedding present.

Her life was unravelling again. She thought of the future, one without Cal, and where she would live, how she would start again when her time at Halesmere was over. She couldn't stay in the flat forever, Max had already invited a friend of his up from London, a tree surgeon who would be working with him for a while. Lizzie went online to view some flats in gorgeous Georgian properties in the coastal towns further north, but they didn't look like home. She couldn't pin home to a place now because home felt like Cal, and she knew she'd hurt him, too.

She'd unfollowed him on Instagram and offered the merest of replies to the comments still coming in after the brand launch last week. Both of their followers were still growing, and she couldn't seem to stop herself checking some of Tash's surf shop posts, feeling sick when she found a throwback picture Tash had shared of her and Cal on the beach in New Zealand, and their mutual followers adored it. Why would she do that, if they were actually over? There was only one answer Lizzie could find, and it was surely that Tash was hoping they would get back together, and this weekend would be her opportunity.

Two days before the wedding Lizzie was curled up in the flat, trying to summon the creativity to plan a mood board for an event next spring. Her client had requested a secret garden theme but her imagination had fled to a place she couldn't find. She put the plans aside to pour a small glass of wine instead. Stan had known without explanation that something was wrong when she'd bumped into him yesterday. He'd given her a knowing look and informed her he'd be in his workshop if she needed him. When she'd opened her door to go for a walk early this morning with her camera, she'd found a homemade apple pie and a note from Pearl on her doorstep. The simplicity of their kindness made Lizzie cry, and she was dreading leaving Halesmere and the friends she had made here.

She hoped the wine would help with her inspiration and she settled down with her laptop again, sighing. A knock at the door had her glancing up and she heard Gemma's voice through it.

'Lizzie, can I come in please?'

She put everything down and jumped up to let her in. Gemma gave her a look and pulled her straight into a hug, one which had Lizzie sniffing when she eventually wriggled away.

'Don't worry about the pianist for the service, I've sorted it,' Lizzie said on her way to the kitchen to fetch another glass. 'I asked Max and he was happy to step in. Ella said he's wonderful, she loves listening to him play.'

'That's lovely, thank you.' Gemma curled up in an armchair. 'And yes please to the wine, I've walked down. I'm ready for it, I can't quite shake the feeling something's going to go wrong again.'

'It won't, I promise.' Lizzie passed the glass across and settled on the opposite chair. 'Everything's in place and I've gone over the timeline twice already. It's going to be wonderful.'

'Not quite.'

Her head jerked up. 'Have I missed something? I'm sure I haven't, I've checked...'

'Lizzie, I never thought I'd say this but...' Gemma hesitated. 'Have you spoken to Cal since, you know?'

'No, of course not.' Lizzie had called Gemma and Bea soon after she'd raced home from the boathouse. They'd done their best to comfort and support her from a distance and offered some wise advice she was still trying to digest. 'I'm doing my best not to even see him, much less speak.'

But he was in her every thought, and she felt as though a part of her had been crushed so flat it would never flourish again. She'd allowed herself to believe she'd known what they were going to share this time. Trust, security, family and friends. And an enduring, endless love.

'I just came from the forge; he's finished the sculpture. It's incredible, Lizzie, I can't even tell you. Simon's going to be ecstatic, how Cal's caught the way she raises her head, it's as though she's about to bark. It's perfect.'

'I'm so pleased. I felt the same when I first saw the wolf, how I could almost hear it howl. He is a brilliant sculptor.'

'He really is.'

'How is he?' Lizzie's question was a whisper, another moment of concern. She hated that they were both hurting. Was it all her fault?

'He's in bits if you really want to know. All that bravado stuff when you walked out was his way of looking after himself if you ask me. Do you actually know why he's going to Cornwall?'

'To see Tash.' There was only one reason stuck in Lizzie's mind. 'Why else?'

'Sometimes you're just too bloody hasty, Lizzie Martin. And stubborn, and occasionally stupid as well.' Gemma reached for her hand to grip it. 'I know you think you're protecting yourself by walking away, but did it ever occur to you that Cal might have had his reasons for doing what he did about Cornwall? Just like you with Alec?'

'That's not fair, Gem. I was trying to look after Cal the whole time.'

'And we know that's true. But if you're ever going to move on, with him, you're going to have to let him in. Really in, mistakes and all. What happened before was once, Lizzie, and everything he's done since he came back has been to try and put it right. For one very simple reason. Because he loves the bones of you, just like you do him.'

'But if I can't trust him not to run, Gem…' Lizzie's words were dulled as she recalled her running out on him, flying into the car, sobbing all the way back from the boathouse.

'He's not running. And it's not my story to tell but the very short version is that he's going to support Tash because he stepped in when she desperately needed some help. There's more to it than that and you're going to have to ask him if you want to hear it.'

'But I saw Tash's post, the old one in New Zealand. What if she wants them to get back together?'

'Oh come on, Lizzie, think about it! She's launching a business and has a friend who's going to attract attention. Anyone would do the same. You know that, it's literally part of your job.'

'Ex. Gemma. She's his ex.' Lizzie couldn't get it out of her mind. The years he and Tash had been a couple, the time she and Cal had shared so much less.

'Okay, ex. And she posted it this week, right after…'

'Exactly.' Lizzie was bitter. 'He and I broke up, and he's probably already given her the news.'

'I admit it looks a bit suspicious.' Gemma hesitated. 'But you need to ask Cal about that post and get his take on it.'

'I ran out, Gem,' Lizzie said brokenly. 'I left him. Why would he give me another chance, after I told him we were over?'

'Like, duh.' Gemma shook her head very slowly. 'Because every time he looks at his own arm and that waterfall he sees you, Lizzie. I don't think either of you should spend the rest of your lives living with broken hearts. You have to forgive him for not telling you about Tash and find a way to accept his reasons. He did the same for you. And quite frankly, being totally selfish, I don't want your face looking that like in my wedding photos.'

'I wouldn't do that to you.'

'I know.' Gemma smiled, letting go of Lizzie's hand as she stood up. 'But I'm serious. Go fix it before it's too late. He's leaving for Cornwall tomorrow. Look at what happened to Alec and Marianne.'

'That was totally different,' Lizzie said sharply. She'd thought it herself, but was this really so dissimilar? Alec made his mistakes and Marianne left him for it, making a choice that had affected every day of Cal's life until this point. Was Lizzie going to do the same and live with the regret, the loss of their love, because she was afraid of Cal having the ability to hurt her again? Because she refused to listen and to trust him?

'It doesn't look a lot different from where I'm sitting. But they didn't get a happy ending and you, my glorious, brilliant and beautiful friend, still have a chance to put this right. Where would you both be if he hadn't accepted you keeping Alec from him the way you did?'

'How can I go back, Gem?' Lizzie's voice was a frightened whisper. 'Why would he still want to explain after I ran out like that?'

'Because you did that for him and he knows it. The night you told him about Alec and went after him when he ran away. He let you in and listened, and if you love him as much as I think you do, you have to do the same,' Gemma said simply. 'He's changed, Lizzie. He's not the same boy who ran all those years ago, I realise that now. And you need to change, too. You need to trust him because if you'll let him, I think he very much wants to take care of your heart, not smash it up again.'

–

Lizzie knocked tentatively on the oak door of the boathouse. She hadn't seen Cal for three days and she'd missed him every single second. The last time they'd spoken she'd run away from him, replaying it as she stood trembling and waiting for a reply. It was late and maybe he was already asleep. She hadn't finished the wine earlier and as soon as Gemma left, Lizzie had gone for a walk to think over all Gemma had said before driving out here. She didn't have long, and she couldn't wait for morning when he would be leaving.

'This is a surprise.' He looked exhausted when he pulled the door back and Lizzie wanted to go to him, hope she could make him understand. But first she had to confess.

'Can I come in please?'

He moved aside and she went through to the sitting room, reminded of that first day here when she'd desperately needed a solution for the proposal she'd planned, and he'd stepped straight in. He'd had his own reasons for doing it, just like she had with the search for Alec.

'Drink?' Cal was in the kitchen, and she shook her head, her back to the view.

'Cal, I came to tell you I'm sorry for running out on you the way I did.' She took a deep breath. 'And for making assumptions without talking to you first. The wedding, and then Tash, even Alec. I'm so sorry and you were right. My parents have always supported me emotionally, especially when they couldn't financially. Since they moved, I've always felt I have to look after myself and back then you were the only person apart from Gemma I let come close to me. Gemma and I talked, and she helped me understand I've always been running, in a way. Not wanting to settle with someone or stand still long enough to lose them and have my world flip over again.' Lizzie tried to smile, but it was lost in a rush of tears. 'After you left, I locked up my heart and didn't really open it again, not properly, until you came back.'

'Lizzie, I—'

'It's okay, you don't have to say it again. I know you're sorry and that part of us is over. But I'm hoping *this* part isn't. That you'll give me another chance to trust you, please? And if you say yes, you don't have to tell me about Tash.' Lizzie forced the old image of Tash and Cal from her mind and swallowed. They couldn't do this if she didn't trust him. 'Go, do what you need to, and I'll be here when you come home. If that's what you want.'

'I can't do that.' Cal left the kitchen and halted in front of her, his eyes blazing with certainty. 'I can't come home to you unless you understand why I went in the first place. You need to know everything.' He took her hands, holding them gently. 'But yes, I hope you can learn to trust me with your heart. Mine belongs to you, it always has. No more running, for either of us. We have to learn to work stuff out together.

'Tash and I are business partners in the shop, and I promised her ages ago I'd be there to support the launch, long before you and I were back together.' He paused, a glint of sorrow darting across his face. 'We didn't plan to be partners. We broke up when the clothing company was sold because she wanted to compete again, and I didn't want to live out of a hotel. I wanted a home, and she wasn't ready, we both knew we weren't going to make one together, not forever.

'She decided to base herself in Cornwall when she wasn't travelling and the shop came up for sale, with a flat. She knew it would be a good investment but then her dad died suddenly and there were debts. Tash used her share from the sale of my company to clear everything and there wasn't much left. She wasn't a partner in the business, but we made sure she was okay. I heard she was going to lose the shop and I offered to help. She didn't want to accept

270

at first and we agreed it would be a loan and she'd pay me back.

'Lizzie, I made a lot of money when we sold the company and most of it went to a charity supporting young people coming out of care, but I kept some. I didn't tell you about Tash because I wanted everything between me and her to be clear and done first. I was going to let you know once I'd signed over my share of the shop, so that we could move on without my being involved. It was all agreed this week; I don't need her to return the money, I work for what I need. I was happy to help because if it hadn't been for her back then our brand might not have taken off in the way that it did and attracted the US interest. I realise now not telling you straightaway looks more awkward than if I'd just come out with it. I was afraid of giving you a reason not to trust me until I wasn't a partner in the shop any longer but clearly it backfired. I'm sorry I got it wrong.'

'I think we both did.' Lizzie hesitated, tipping her head back to find his eyes, heavy with regret. 'I saw some of the posts, of the shop. And that one of both of you.'

'I asked Tash not to tag me in anything until our launch was done, I didn't want to muddy the waters.' His hands went to Lizzie's shoulders, gripping them. 'Cornwall fell out of my head once I knew about Alec, it didn't even feature until Tash did that first post and got back in touch. I should have explained it to you sooner so that you didn't have to jump to the wrong conclusion. That post means nothing, Lizzie, it's literally history. Just two people with boards on a beach, it was taken before we were even a couple. Tash knew she could share whatever she wanted after our launch because none of it mattered to me as long as you knew the truth.'

Lizzie's heart was thudding, full of longing for Cal and the way he was staring at her, imploring her to understand this time.

'Tash knows exactly how I feel about you, Lizzie. What she doesn't know is that I hadn't told you about Cornwall or that you'd left me because of it. She won't have seen any harm in that post.'

'It was me who did that.' Lizzie's voice was very small. 'I made myself see what wasn't there because I wanted to.'

'We all do that sometimes.' Cal squeezed her shoulders. 'Tash has moved on too, neither of us were looking to get back together. I'll be there to see her get started and then I'm done. We're signing the papers tomorrow and I'll be home as soon as I can. I'm sorry I can't be at the wedding. I wanted to be, but I've made a promise and I won't let her down.'

'It doesn't matter,' Lizzie said truthfully. It wasn't difficult to recall those first frightening days when her own home and life had changed so swiftly, and she felt a rush of sympathy for Tash. 'It's much more important that you do what you and Tash need and honour your word. I'll miss you, more than you know.'

'I do, actually. Because it'll be the same for me. If it wasn't your best friend's wedding, I'd be asking you to come with me to Cornwall.' Cal gave her a wry smile. 'And can you please follow me again on Instagram? I can't stand not tagging you in my posts.'

–

Gemma and Simon's rehearsal went well the following night, and it was a merry party who took a table for twelve in the pub and sat down for dinner. Lizzie's mum and dad had arrived, and much to her amusement, they'd bought a tent and were camping with some of the other guests down at Marta and Luke's farm. There must be something in it, her mum said with a grin, because her dad was sleeping like a top, had taken up forest bathing and was thinking of having a go at wild swimming. Bea was delighted to have a friendly face sharing her misery at camping and she'd already moved her belongings into Halesmere as she, Gemma and Lizzie were spending this final night before the wedding in the house.

Lizzie missed Cal acutely, and Gemma and Bea stuck close, understanding the space she felt at her side. He'd messaged to let her know he'd arrived and had sent a few images of a stunning Cornish coast and beach. She was following him again on Instagram, liking his posts of the surf shop and commenting on a couple. She'd checked out the shop's Instagram account and was following them, too. There was a lot of excitement about having a pro surfer opening up in town and her ex-model, ex-boyfriend launching the shop with her. Cal was laughing and relaxed in the shots that were shared, presenting his more professional face. Lizzie couldn't wait for him to come home on Sunday. The wedding would be over, Simon's present on its way to his and Gemma's house, and Lizzie and Cal could take a bit of time for themselves.

–

The morning of the wedding dawned typically Cumbrian, with clouds drifting across a grey sky, but Gemma didn't care. This very special day had finally arrived and all that mattered was she and Simon finally having the wedding they'd waited so long for. Bea had bought matching pyjamas for her, Gemma, and Lizzie to get ready in and they were merry with glasses of champagne as they had their make-up done.

All three were wearing their hair loose and long to suit the festival theme, Lizzie's drawn from her face in thick waves. She and Bea both had pretty, white gypsophila flowers pinned throughout, and Gemma was planning to swap her elegant tiara for a flower crown after the service. The photographer was brilliant as he made them laugh and captured shots Lizzie knew would be natural and fun, especially when he disappeared to take some urgent images of Prim, who was trying to make herself at home in the yurt with Lily while Stan did his best to chase them out.

A horse-drawn carriage drove Bea and Lizzie to the church, and she heard the murmur of excitement as they stepped down and the carriage set back off to collect Gemma and her dad. Their outfits were a departure from normal bridesmaid dresses and they both adored their chiffon jumpsuits in vibrant lemon with high heeled sandals. Wide-legged, one shoulder bare, with a ruffle front and back, the jumpsuits were fun, elegant, and perfect for the festival reception later. Lizzie's mum and dad gave her tight hugs, her mum sniffing through her smiles.

The promised sun had broken through, throwing dappled shade onto the churchyard as they made their way into the building. Matteo, gorgeous in his suit, despite Bea's fear he would wash in a stream beforehand, was acting as usher and there to greet Bea as Lizzie made herself quash the longing she felt for Cal to be at her side, too. Sandy welcomed them and Lizzie shared a grin with a nervous-looking Simon, waiting at the other end of the aisle. Simon, Will and the groomsmen were all in burgundy tweed suits and she knew the pop of colour would be stunning against the fresh green and pastel colours in the garden back at the house.

Gemma's ivory, A-line backless gown was simple and stunning, with beaded lace over the bodice and embroidered flowers flowing into the satin skirt. Her bouquet was gorgeous: pink roses, white peonies and pale astrantias with accents of eucalyptus and lavender larkspur.

Sandy conducted a brilliant service with her usual cheer and warmth, bringing together serious words about marriage and the life Gemma and Simon were setting out on together, and the commitment they had made in front of their guests. Never had Lizzie been happier to have pockets in an outfit, pulling out tissues to wipe away tears that fell for her friends, sharing a grin with Bea when she saw her doing the same. Max, Ella, and the children were among the guests, and during the signing of the register Max's playing of 'Chasing Cars' on the piano, chosen by Gemma and Simon for this moment, was exquisite.

Everyone was ready for some festival fun when they arrived back at Halesmere, where the garden had been transformed. A wooden sign at the entrance pointed the way to the yurt, the children's chillout and the craft zones, branches adorned with brightly coloured ribbons to make mini tepees. The florist had filled old wellies and wheelbarrows with flowers matching Gemma's bouquet all along the drive and guests were given themed wristbands with the date, and Gemma and Simon's married name. Gemma immediately swapped her tiara for the flower crown and her heels for her white and floral bridal wellies. The tables set up inside the yurt were laid with bud vases and wildflowers below bunting strung with tiny bouquets of lavender and sweet peas, and the Prosecco stand was already a hit.

Straw bales were set up in a circle around a firepit which would be lit later, and an old camper van converted into a photo booth was already busy, with guests rushing to take images and suspend them on string in nearby trees. Lizzie had got Stan to repurpose some old pallets and they were filled with blankets in case the evening turned cool. He'd also painted one white and Pearl had put her calligraphy skills to brilliant use and created an itinerary for the day. Stan was in a suit, no matter how often Lizzie had told him he didn't need to be quite so formal if he didn't want to be. He'd given her a broad grin and said how often did she think his cherub tie got a run out these days when he never got the chance to dress up anymore.

Fairy lights were strung from trees and more wheelbarrows were filled with ice and an array of drinks. Wedding favours were plantable paper hearts studded with wildflower seeds and the first band was playing the romantic acoustic set. Simon had already been persuaded to borrow a bass guitar and join in, much to Gemma and the photographer's delight.

Lizzie was in semi-professional mode, her phone left with her mum for now, and thrilled with the tiny details she had planned so carefully with Ella. She was keeping an experienced eye on everything, although there was little formality here to worry about. The speeches would come later around the fire pit and the children had already taken off to their tepees around the edge of the garden. She missed Cal and couldn't check to see how the shop launch had gone with him at Tash's side for today. She'd have to rely on Bea to her keep her informed; she was bound to have her phone somewhere close at hand.

Ella's menu was fabulous, and guests loved being able to help themselves to a street food style buffet, with paella, vegan curry, Thai fish cakes, and fish finger butties. Desserts were a choice between salted caramel brownies, summer berry pavlova, lemon tart and Stan's personal favourite, sticky toffee pudding.

The whole day was a triumph and Gemma ended up crying through her laughter during her speech, hugging Lizzie and Bea tightly for all they'd done to make this day so special in such a hurry, and looking after her in the process. Afterwards the three of them were on the dancefloor most of the evening, determined to make the best of every minute of the festival. Lizzie's mum and dad had gone back to the campsite, having promised to see her again tomorrow before they left.

'Lizzie, there's someone here you need to see. I totally think you should check him out.' Gemma took her arm to turn her round.

Lizzie's heart somersaulted as she saw Cal walking between the bales, smiling at people he knew and dodging the firepit in the centre. Exhausted eyes fixed on hers, then she was running to meet him. He caught her, lifting her up as she kissed him.

'You're nearly as tall as me in those heels.'

'You're not here, you're in Cornwall,' she rushed out, arms tight around his neck and nearly dizzy with delight. 'I love your suit. You really didn't have to.'

'Yeah, I did, and I'm very much here. Stan just saw me without a tie and offered to lend me his. I think he's been at the sticky toffee pudding.'

'Have you really just driven straight back from Cornwall or am I dreaming?'

'You're not dreaming, and I have just driven straight back from Cornwall.'

'Why?' She drew her head back to stare and Cal put her down to grip her hands. She knew, but she very much wanted to hear him say it.

'Because I wanted to be here with you. For you.' He had to raise his voice over the din of the band and merry guests dancing behind them. 'I hope you'll forgive me for assuming you wanted me here, too. You never did officially invite me.'

'Cal, will you please be my guest for what's left of my best friend's wedding?' She had eyes only for him. The wedding was a huge success and brilliant fun, and she could finally relax and just enjoy it. 'There's your invitation, no more assumptions. I'm so, so happy you're here. I'm also sorry you did that horribly long drive straight after the launch. How did you manage to keep the van charged for so long?'

'I didn't, I hired a car. I wasn't going to be stopping to charge it every hundred and fifty miles. I needed to get back in a hurry to the woman I love. That is the sexiest bridesmaid's outfit I've ever seen, just so you know.'

'Thank you. I'm so glad you got to see me wearing it.' Lizzie was still processing the thrill of having him here and she kissed him again. She didn't think she'd ever want to stop. 'How was everything in Cornwall?'

'Grand, I'll tell you later. All done and sorted. Tash will be okay, we're good.'

'I'm so pleased.'

Someone staggered into Cal, apologising with a raised hand. 'We can't talk here, it's crazy. Come with me? There's something I want to do.'

'Me too.' She was laughing as she held his hand, running through the garden to the gate.

Chapter 22

It was rough in the meadow and Cal carried Lizzie to save her shoes. He didn't put her down until they were at the tarn, his quick laugh nervous as he took her hands.

'Twelve years ago I left you something here and I want you to have it back. Actually, it was two things.' He slipped a hand into his pocket and Lizzie's breath stilled as she saw the silver Claddagh ring in his palm. 'One of them was this. I've carried it with me every single day since you dropped it. I'd very much like you to wear it and for that I think I'm going to have to put it on your finger myself. May I?'

'Yes please.' Lizzie's eyes were sparkling, joy brightening her face.

Cal took her right hand. 'Third finger, heart pointing in. Do you know what that means?'

'I'm sorry, I think you're going to have to tell me.'

'It means you're in a relationship, that someone has captured your heart.' He slid the ring onto her finger, raising it to kiss the metal against her skin. 'To me this ring doesn't represent the past and what we did. It is part of my history and I want to carry it into our future. A heart for love, a crown for loyalty and hands for friendship. You have all of those in me, Lizzie, always. I hope you know that. I left my heart here with you that day.'

His eyes were shining with the same love she felt, and something more: hope, a new promise for the future, permanence this time around. A life to be built, a home to make.

'You took mine with you that day.' She tried to laugh, and it got caught on a sob as she glanced at the ring on her finger, binding them, holding them together.

'I loved the girl I knew back then, and I adore the woman you are now. I love how strong you are, how you always fight your corner and stand up for what you believe in. I love how you made a business from nothing and work for what you want, like me. I love your eyes and how you look at me, how we fit together. How you feel in my arms, and I wake every morning hoping to find you there.'

'Same,' she whispered. 'I loved you from the moment I first saw you. I didn't want you to leave and I'm sorry I didn't fight hard enough for you then. I love that you've found your family and have a place with them. I love how you look at me, and how you make me feel, and I especially love your tattoos and that they remind me of us. I love you, and I won't ever stop. I never have.'

Lizzie knew she'd never forget this moment, the music and laughter from the wedding behind them, fairy lights glittering in the distance. They wandered back, not wanting to miss what was left of the festival. Gemma and Bea came over to hug Cal, offering an unofficial welcome into Lizzie's circle of friends.

Bea was enjoying herself so much, she informed them, she didn't even mind the prospect of a tent for the night. The hug Lizzie and Gemma shared was a tight and loving one when she and Simon finally said goodbye. She thanked Lizzie for all she'd done, wanting to know with a grin when they might have another wedding to look forward to. Everyone else stayed on to dance until the very last song and finally the festival was over.

'Are you ready to go? Would you like to come home with me?' Lizzie was still glowing, but Cal's drive was catching him up and he looked shattered. Midnight was upon them, and darkness and another day had arrived.

'I'd love to but there's something I've got to do first.'

'Really? Now? Wouldn't you rather go to bed?'

'I very much would.' He slung an arm over her shoulders, pulling her in for a kiss as they left the garden, strolling towards the courtyard.

'To sleep, obviously. You need it.'

'It'll keep for a bit longer. Close your eyes. I won't let you fall.'

She knew from the cobbles beneath her feet they were approaching the flat and he halted, the midsummer breeze gentle and warm on Lizzie's face.

'You can open them now as it's after midnight.' His hands were on her shoulders, excitement, a suggestion of nerves lingering in his voice. 'Happy birthday. And anniversary.'

Lizzie's eyes flew open to see Cal's steel wolf poised outside the forge, a spotlight illuminating the powerful body and head tipped back in its familiar silent howl, just like the tattoo on his arm. It was utterly at one in its surroundings; breathtaking, elegant and timeless, and she almost believed she could hear it howl on the night air, calling its pack home.

'Is it mine? I thought you said you'd always keep it.'

'I said I'd never sell it, that I made it for me.' His arms were holding her from behind, his chin light on her shoulder. 'I didn't say anything about not giving it to the woman I love, because there's something she needs to know, and her wolf will always remind her.'

'Tell me,' she whispered, still staring, taking in the metal his hands had crafted into such a stunning life form that he was entrusting to her safekeeping.

'Do you remember that wolves mate for life, Lizzie? I didn't think of it until I saw you again and then I knew. They're like me. I'm like them.'

'Oh Cal,' She spun free of his arms so she could kiss him. 'Thank you. It's perfect and I love it, if you're sure?'

'I am, more than ever before. If you keep it, then you know what it means, right? Wherever I've been, whatever I've done, I want to live the rest of my life with you. You're my pack and I'm yours. If finding Alec and hearing his story has taught me anything, it's not to waste any more time. My heart and my wolf are yours, Lizzie. Mistakes and all.'

She wrapped her arms around Cal, whispering into his ear. 'I love you too. It's always been the same for me.' She was giggling as she led him to the sculpture, placing her hand on her present and feeling its solidity and strength. 'There's only one problem. You'll be leaving the boathouse soon and I don't think there's room for me and my wolf in that flat. At least not this one, and I can't keep the flat forever.'

'I'm not worried, there's always my tent if we get desperate. The wolf can sleep outside.'

—

Most of the wedding guests who were camping had made plans to return to Halesmere in the morning for a brunch Ella had arranged, with students from the catering college stepping in to cook. Lizzie and Cal slept in and when they woke, he casually suggested that they join the fun. Her mum and dad had been a bit vague on when they were setting off for home, and she needed to see them before they left. The garden looked remarkably tidy after the festival reception and Lizzie made a mental note to thank Stan; she wouldn't be surprised to discover he'd been out early and had restored a bit of order.

'Sounds like there's some good craic.' Cal was holding her hand as they crossed the garden. 'Do you think Bea dodged the tent and spent the night in the yurt under a blanket instead?'

'Probably. I love how well you're getting to know my friends.'

At the entrance it looked like half the wedding party was still inside and Lizzie had a second to take in the new balloons before a cheer went up.

'Surprise! Happy birthday, Lizzie!'

She was laughing, trying to process the astonishment and that Bea, who was making her way over and adored parties, had managed not to give the game away. So much had happened in just a few days and Lizzie turned to Cal. 'Did you know about this?'

'I might have.'

'Oh, Cal knew all about it, Lizzie.' Bea looked decidedly put together and fresh for someone who had apparently just spent her first night in a tent. She threw her arms around Lizzie. 'He planned it. With a little help from your friends, of course.'

'I hope you don't mind,' he said softly. 'We all thought your thirtieth needed something special and everyone would already be at the wedding.'

'Mind?' Lizzie's eyes were shimmering as Bea let her go. 'My mum and dad are here. My friends, and Stan and Pearl, and all the artists. And Lily and Arlo, and Ella and Max. Even Prim. This is wonderful, Cal, truly. I love it.'

'At last, the secret's out!' Lizzie's mum had found them and reached up to embrace Cal. Her dad was right behind, and the two men shook hands warmly as she turned to Lizzie, and they wrapped arms tightly around one another. 'Your brothers are sorry they couldn't make it on the last minute, but we'll see them soon. Cal rang us, Lizzie, and we had a long chat. Put some things to rights, especially those that should never have been said in the first place.' She sniffed, fishing for a tissue in her bag. 'He's a lovely man. He and your dad both apologised for what happened that night and your dad knows he was wrong about him. Not because Cal went on to have all that success, but because your dad thought he didn't really love you and we were worried. It's blindingly obvious we were dead wrong about that, too. He was wonderful on what it meant to have found you again and the life he wants to make with you. Happy birthday, my darling.'

Silent tears were sliding down Lizzie's face as she hugged her dad too, and he was nodding fiercely as he patted her back. They'd come through so much down the years and she was grateful her parents had managed to cling on to their marriage and the deep, abiding love they shared.

Someone thrust a glass of champagne in Lizzie's hand as Stan rushed past, apparently on his way to light the firepit and rearrange the straw bales. Two people were approaching Lizzie and she gripped Cal's hand.

'Oh, Cal. I am so, so happy you invited Alec and Evelyn.'

'You're sure?'. There was a moment of doubt in Cal's voice. 'You don't think it's too soon? It just seemed right, somehow.'

'It's totally right, they belong here.' Lizzie swiped at a tear. Her mum and dad had spotted them too and paused for a word. 'They're your family, Cal. Part of you.'

'Part of us, you mean.' His gaze was full of love, and he lifted her hand to kiss it. 'Alec and I have been in touch, and he was very keen to come when I mentioned it. He likes you a lot.'

'Maybe, but he loves you.'

'Ach, you think?' Cal's voice caught and he tried to smile. 'It's a bit early for that. But I hope we'll get there.'

'I know you will. I can't wait to get to know them better.' Lizzie took a mouthful of champagne, absolutely buzzing. 'This is just the best birthday ever, thank you. I'd practically forgotten it was even happening, what with the wedding, you and me, and Alec.'

'My pleasure. If you're up for it, I thought we could ask him, Evelyn, and your parents to go out on the yacht with us later. We're not going to have it for much longer and your dad's already said he'd love to see it. Could be a while before we're all in the same place again.'

'Both our families, together, with you and me? I can't think of anything more perfect for the rest of my birthday.'

'I love how that sounds even if I'm not used to it yet.' Cal swallowed. 'I'm meeting Rebecca, Justin, and the boys on Tuesday. Are you up for it with me?'

'Yes. I am. Anywhere with you.'

'Anywhere?' Cal raised a brow. 'Because Alec's invited me to join him on his next climbing trip and it's in—'

'Okay, not quite everywhere.' Lizzie's laughter fell away as she stared at the man she adored. 'That's something I think you need to do together, just the two of you.'

'It is. I'm so grateful to have found him and my family. Thanks to you.' Cal slid an arm around her. 'But I'll be coming home, Lizzie. Back here, to you.'

Epilogue

Three months later

'You look ridiculously gorgeous. I mean, properly, how–am–I–supposed to–concentrate, stunning? Whose idea was this? Actually, I've changed my mind. I'm not putting you on my social media looking like that. Instagram will melt.'

Cal shook his head with a wry smile and Lizzie laughed. It had taken a while but they'd finally arranged the styled photo shoot for her social media that he'd promised back in the summer. She'd had the idea that they could occasionally combine their businesses and plan romantic proposals out on the fells. Cal would take care of the practical details and Lizzie would look after the romance, and this shoot was to create content and generate some interest in what they had to offer.

Today she was going to photograph him in a location he'd found. It wasn't the rough fell, remote tarn or ruin she had been expecting but an overgrown meadow in a valley with a beck tumbling through the middle. They'd had to walk a little way along a track to get here and when she saw the old packhorse bridge crossing the water, she'd understood why he wanted to bring her. It was charming, beautiful and wild.

Cal had just changed into the outfit he'd picked out, not his climbing or walking gear this time, but more formal clothes they wanted to contrast against the natural landscape. A royal blue velvet blazer and white shirt were striking with his short tawny hair, worn with dark grey trousers and black leather Oxfords.

The colours of autumn were everywhere as green leaves made way for burnished coppers, reds and ambers. The light was perfect, clouds dipping from the sky and allowing in patches of sun to fall on the surrounding fells to create the perfect backdrop. A bottle of champagne was cooling in the stream, two glasses and a picnic on a blanket nestled among the wildflowers nearby. She and Cal worked so well together, and she loved his cheeky grin as she took a few warm-up shots.

Both of their businesses were taking off and they were busier than ever as he led clients across the fells and taught them how to stay safe, find their way and challenge themselves. He had accepted a couple more sculpture commissions, one of them from the hotel for whom Max was designing a garden. Lizzie couldn't wait to see the life-sized stag and its mate installed once they were ready next spring.

She and Cal worked out of his office above the forge at Halesmere and she had more enquiries for events than she now had time to plan them. Cal was still connected to the luggage brand with Lizzie taking shots for his social media, and they loved finding wild new locations to represent both the brand and her photography in her images. Lizzie was busy too, with the retreats at Halesmere. Forest bathing was a firm favourite and one which always booked up quickly. She'd even managed to get Stan to try it. He'd puffed his way through the woods, telling her with a wink he couldn't see what the fuss was about, they were only trees after all and they'd be here long after him and he could breathe in and out in his workshop with a brew and a butty, thanks very much.

Cal had given up the yacht and boathouse and he'd moved into the flat at Halesmere, Lizzie's steel wolf back in the forge for now as they looked for somewhere more permanent. Stan liked to remind them that they'd better not flood the fancy new studio underneath the flat with bathwater as he'd worked his fingers to the bone to make it look good enough for her photographs. She'd sold some prints and had photographed a remote bed and breakfast when the couple who ran it got in touch.

Cal had been on a couple of climbing trips with Alec, and he and Lizzie were enjoying getting to know his new family. His half-sister Rebecca and her partner had been very welcoming, and their two little boys adored Cal, especially when they'd all gone out on the yacht and he'd let the boys have a go at the helm and given them a tour of his workshop. Lizzie knew he loved them too, and it wasn't hard to imagine the family they might share one day. He and Alec were close, they spoke regularly and met up to go bouldering or climbing, when one would belay for the other. Sunday lunch with the family at the farm was becoming a firm favourite with everybody and they'd made plans for a first Christmas there.

'Good to go?' Lizzie was focussing on Cal through her lens as he positioned himself on the packhorse bridge, and he nodded. 'Okay. Look over the water, like you're watching for someone. Then over your shoulder, towards me. Perfect.' She lowered the camera a few minutes later, checking the screen. 'They're great. I think we'll give it a bit longer on the bridge. The light's going to change, and I'd like that cloud off the fell. It's moving quickly.'

'Lizzie?'

'What? Do you want to see?' She nearly dropped the camera as she noticed Cal on one knee on the bridge, holding a velvet ring box.

'No, I want you to come here and see.'

She swallowed. 'Okay.' She secured her camera around her neck, and slowly walked towards him, excitement already bubbling. She halted right in front of him. 'Is this part of the shoot?'

'It is not.' His grin was as gorgeous as it was nervous. The ring he took from the box was exquisite, a ruby surrounded by diamonds in a floral setting. 'I'm asking you to marry me, Lizzie. Our story began in Cumbria, and I want to keep on writing it here, if you'll have me? I hope you know how much I love you and the life we have together.'

'Cal, this is… Your romantic proposal planning skills are off the charts! We've even got champagne and a picnic. I don't know what to say!'

'Just say yes.'

'Yes, of course. I love you, too. You're amazing.'

He was on his feet and took a gentle hold of her left hand. His Claddagh ring was on her right; it never came off. He slid the ruby onto her third finger and followed it up with a kiss that had her clutching hold of him for balance.

'I'm in the wrong job,' she murmured, head tilted back to stare at him. 'You should be doing the planning, not me. This is the most romantic thing ever.'

'So if I said I wasn't done with the romance yet…?' He was smiling as he took her shoulders and gently turned her on the bridge. 'There's something else you need to see.'

'Seriously?' She was laughing with him, loving him. 'It can't be another yacht, that beck isn't deep enough. Or a sculpture, I don't think you've had time to make one. It's not my birthday or our anniversary. Or your birthday.'

'What can you see?'

'A lot of overgrown trees and long grass. Maybe something that used to be a garden. A path. Is there a building through there? It looks like a cottage. Cal, are we trespassing? Is this someone's garden?'

'Not exactly. Come on.'

The curving path was smothered in weeds between old shrubs mostly past their best. The setting remind Lizzie of a glade as they pushed their way through, and she saw that the busy little beck and the bridge divided an old garden from the orchard they'd just left. A cottage lay ahead, its stone walls rough between neat windows tucked into the eaves on the first floor.

'Is it yours?' Shocked, incredulous words. A flare of hope, a blast of excitement.

'No.' Cal grinned as he took a key from his pocket and passed it to Lizzie. 'But it could be ours. It's just gone up for sale and the agent is a client. I told him we were looking for something and he let me have a key for today. It's a mess from what he said, Lizzie, there's a lot to do. It's been in the same family for fifty years.'

'But there's a rose flowering around the door and a beck in the garden. And that bridge.'

'Yep. And a small barn we could probably convert into two working spaces.'

The walls were thick and quite probably damp and Lizzie was certain the cottage had once been a much-loved and cheerful home. No one who hadn't treasured it would plant a pink rose around the door and she was already deeply in love for a second time.

'What do you think, Mrs Sutherland-to-be?'

Lizzie whirled around. 'You're changing your name?'

'Yeah. I set out to find my dad, I never expected to have a home with him the way we do. It was his idea and we both thought it was right.' Cal was gripping her hand. 'Maybe if we ever have a son of our own, we could include Ryan in the name? I don't want to forget my mum and her family but I'm looking ahead, not back. What do you think? I am hoping it'll be your name too. We're a team, you and me.'

'I think you mean a pack.' Lizzie kissed him quickly, and Cal grinned.

'Yeah, I do. So are you okay with that, the name?'

'I love it, I think it's a wonderful idea.'

'Dead on, Lizzie. Shall we go and see inside Rose Cottage, then? To celebrate our engagement?'

She stepped forward, giving him a grin over her shoulder. 'We shall. I think this place might just be our happy ending. There's even room in the garden for my wolf.'

Acknowledgements

Returning to Cumbria with Lizzie and Cal was a joy, and I understand how they feel about the landscape there, even though I don't have all their skills! I drew on a shared love of the more remote and wild places for their story, and I felt every bit as connected to them whilst writing the book as they are. *Lakes Fest* in Seathwaite was brilliant to experience (from the ground), and I loved hearing from the legendary local climbers who spoke about their passion during that weekend. The Duddon Valley is glorious, and I always picture Lizzie and Cal there, maybe sharing a meal with other climbers at the Newfield Inn. Any mistakes in climbing or bouldering techniques are my own.

Sailing on Windermere is a wonderful experience and my trips with *Sail N Dine* helped to write those scenes. Thanks to John for making it so much fun and providing totally delicious lunches. There are around eighteen islands on the lake, and I used a little artistic license to devise the one Cal chose for Lizzie's clients to land on.

Walking with wolves at Predator Experience in Cumbria was a huge thrill, and thanks to the handlers and the two wolves we met for making it so memorable. The animals were exceptional, and I only touched on quite how much in this book. Their howls were unforgettable, and Cal makes use of some wolf characteristics for his own inspiration. Thank you to Sarah for sharing her event planning experience and helping to inspire Lizzie's.

Many thanks to Doug and Christy Barnes from the USA for naming two characters in this book. They were the winning bidders of my lot in the Book Aid for Ukraine Auction in 2022 and I loved creating two people who played their own part in Lizzie and Cal's story. Thank you, I hope you enjoy my fictional Doug and Christy's own love story!

Thank you to Susan Yearwood, Emily Bedford, all at Canelo, including the fantastic cover designers, and Katrina Power, for continuing to support my writing and helping me to reach readers. I appreciate all you do and being able to write about places I love.

To my fabulous family for everything we share; thank you. Love is at the heart of my writing and our home, and I couldn't do all of this without your support and encouragement. To my sister Deb, thank you for always being there and championing my books.

Thank you to readers and bloggers who love romance and sharing it with others. It's such a wonderful genre, and many people are so generous with their time and support for authors. To the RNA and all who work to keep it going, thank you. As a graduate of the outstanding NWS, I benefited much from the organisation, and I'm grateful for all it does.

There are many brilliant artists, producers, and craftspeople in Cumbria, and I love discovering more whenever I visit. Halesmere is a place of community and it's a pleasure to write about characters who feel at home there, creating something gorgeous for others to enjoy. Cumbria is a very special county and I hope I've brought a sense of its beauty and many wonders to the book.